Prai

One More Chance

"This was an amazing book by Vali…complex and multi-layered (both characters and plot)."—*Danielle Kimerer, Librarian (Nevins Memorial Library, Massachusetts)*

Face the Music

"This is a typical Ali Vali romance with strong characters, a beautiful setting (Nashville, Tennessee), and an enemies-to-lovers style tale. The two main characters are beautiful, strong-willed, and easy to fall in love with. The romance between them is steamy, and so are the sex scenes."—*Rainbow Reflections*

The Inheritance

"I love a good story that makes me laugh and cry, and this one did that a lot for me. I would step back into this world any time."—*Kat Adams, Bookseller (QBD Books, Australia)*

Double-Crossed

"[T]here aren't too many lesfic books like *Double-Crossed* and it is refreshing to see an author like Vali continue to churn out books like these. Excellent crime thriller."—*Colleen Corgel, Librarian, Queens Borough Public Library*

"For all of us die-hard Ali Vali/Cain Casey fans, this is the beginning of a great new series…There is violence in this book, and lots of killing, but there is also romance, love, and the beginning of a great new reading adventure. I can't wait to read more of this intriguing story."
—*Rainbow Reflections*

Stormy Seas

Stormy Seas "is one book that adventure lovers must read."—*Rainbow Reflections*

Answering the Call

Answering the Call "is a brilliant cop-and-killer story…The crime story is tight and the love story is fantastic."—*Best Lesbian Erotica*

Lammy Finalist *Calling the Dead*

"So many writers set stories in New Orleans, but Ali Vali's mystery novels have the authenticity that only a real Big Easy resident could bring. Set six months after Hurricane Katrina has devastated the city, a lesbian detective is still battling demons when a body turns up behind one of the city's famous eateries. What follows makes for a classic lesbian murder yarn."—*Curve Magazine*

Beauty and the Boss

"The story gripped me from the first page…Vali's writing style is lovely—it's clean, sharp, no wasted words, and it flows beautifully as a result. Highly recommended!"—*Rainbow Book Reviews*

Balance of Forces: Toujours Ici

"A stunning addition to the vampire legend, *Balance of Forces: Toujour Ici* is one that stands apart from the rest."—*Bibliophilic Book Blog*

Beneath the Waves

"The premise…was brilliantly constructed…skillfully written and the imagination that went into it was fantastic…A wonderful passionate love story with a great mystery."—*Inked Rainbow Reads*

Second Season

"The issues are realistic and center around the universal factors of love, jealousy, betrayal, and doing the right thing and are constantly woven into the fabric of the story. We rated this well written social commentary through the use of fiction our max five hearts."—*Heartland Reviews*

Carly's Sound

"*Carly's Sound* is a great romance, with some wonderfully hot sex, but it is more than that. It is also the tale of a woman rising from the ashes of grief and finding new love and a new life. Vali has surrounded Julia and Poppy with a cast of great supporting characters, making this an extremely satisfying read."—*Just About Write*

Praise for the Cain Casey Saga

The Devil's Due

"A Night Owl Reviews Top Pick: Cain Casey is the kind of person you aspire to be even though some consider her a criminal. She's loyal, very protective of those she loves, honorable, big on preserving her family legacy and loves her family greatly. *The Devil's Due* is a book I highly recommend and well worth the wait we all suffered through. I cannot wait for the next book in the series to come out."
—*Night Owl Reviews*

The Devil Be Damned

"Ali Vali excels at creating strong, romantic characters along with her fast-paced, sophisticated plots. Her setting, New Orleans, provides just the right blend of immigrants from Mexico, South America, and Cuba, along with a city steeped in traditions."—*Just About Write*

Deal with the Devil

"Ali Vali has given her fans another thick, rich thriller...*Deal With the Devil* has wonderful love stories, great sex, and an ample supply of humor. It is an exciting, page-turning read that leaves her readers eagerly awaiting the next book in the series."—*Just About Write*

The Devil Unleashed

"Fast-paced action scenes, intriguing character revelations, and a refreshing approach to the romance thriller genre all make for an enjoyable reading experience in the Big Easy...*The Devil Unleashed* is an engrossing reading experience."—*Midwest Book Review*

The Devil Inside

"*The Devil Inside* is the first of what promises to be a very exciting series...While telling an exciting story that grips the reader, Vali has also fully fleshed out her heroes and villains. *The Devil Inside* is that rarity: a fascinating crime novel which includes a tender love story and leaves the reader with a cliffhanger ending."—*MegaScene*

By the Author

Carly's Sound

Second Season

Love Match

The Dragon Tree Legacy

The Romance Vote

Hell Fire Club in Girls with Guns

Beneath the Waves

Beauty and the Boss

Blue Skies

Stormy Seas

The Inheritance

Face the Music

On the Rocks in Still Not Over You

One More Chance

A Woman to Treasure

Calumet

Call Series

Calling the Dead

Answering the Call

Forces Series

Balance of Forces: Toujours Ici

Battle of Forces: Sera Toujours

Force of Fire: Toujours a Vous

Vegas Nights

Double-Crossed

The Cain Casey Saga

The Devil Inside

The Devil Unleashed

Deal with the Devil

The Devil Be Damned

The Devil's Orchard

The Devil's Due

Heart of the Devil

The Devil Incarnate

Visit us at www.boldstrokesbooks.com

CALUMET

by
Ali Vali

2021

This Trade Paperback Original Is Published By
Bold Strokes Books, Inc.
P.O. Box 249
Valley Falls, NY 12185

First Edition: August 2021

CREDITS
EDITORS: VICTORIA VILLASEÑOR AND RUTH STERNGLANTZ
PRODUCTION DESIGN: STACIA SEAMAN
COVER DESIGN: TAMMY SEIDICK

Acknowledgments

Who remembers their last high school class reunion? My class decided our senior year ours had to happen every five years. They're always interesting in that you get to see in those increments of time what your fellow classmates have done with themselves. Some of them really surprise you.

Thank you, Radclyffe, for the opportunity to create my own version of whatever topic pops into my head. Thank you, Sandy, for keeping me on track and for all you do. The BSB family is an awesome group to be a part of, so thank you to the whole team for your support and hard work. I appreciate every one of you.

Thank you to my awesome editors Victoria Villaseñor and Ruth Sternglantz. Vic, thank you for all those lessons. I have to admit emotions are a good thing. You and Ruth have taught me so much and I appreciate both of you. Tammy Seidick, thank you for another awesome cover—I love it.

Thank you to my first readers, Lenore Beniot, Cris Perez-Soria, and Kim Rieff. Your comments, questions, and commentary really are always awesome.

A huge thank you to every reader. There's no way I would've ever gotten to thirty without you. You guys send the best emails, so every word is written with you in mind.

Hopefully, we're one step closer to finally seeing each other at different events and catching up. A worldwide pandemic was not on my bucket list, but hopefully everyone was in good company when the world went quiet. Thanks to C, who kept me laughing and sane throughout. There's a whole world out there yet to be explored and I can't wait to get to it. Verdad!

For C
and
all my English teachers through the years

CHAPTER ONE

Eager. Gung ho. Voracious. Zealous. Dr. Jaxon Lavigne glanced back at her class and saw none of that. They were a week into the semester, and most of the students in here would be free not only for the coming spring but for the rest of their lives once they graduated. The key phrase was *if* they graduated. For a few of the overly unmotivated, reality meant putting off graduation until the end of May or facing her again in the summer.

"Remember, people." She put her chalk down and turned after writing out the instructions on the board. "There will be weekly assignments, and no, they are not worth eighty percent of your grade. Your midterm and final will count for enough to pull you out of the hole some of you have already started diligently digging, so might I suggest you moderate your drinking and read."

They were awake enough to laugh and lift their heads from their various electronics so they could ask questions. As seniors they'd lost that shyness most college freshman had at the very beginning, which made for a better experience as a teacher. This was the reason she'd become an educator. It was a bug she'd caught in high school when she sat in Miss Landry's class, enraptured in the new world she'd introduced her to. All those books she'd read and found escape in were stories she wanted to share with her students, and she hoped they'd be as passionate about them.

"Time's up," she said when she looked at the clock by the door. "Don't forget the assignment and my office hours. Hopefully there'll be a vast improvement from last semester when I saw no one. If you follow that path, I'll have no choice but to believe you know all this stuff and don't need a grading curve on exams. If you need anything, stop by, but that doesn't mean I'm willing to listen to you beg if you haven't done the work. We should get that out there right off."

"Still a hard-ass." Dr. Robert Butler was waiting outside her classroom and shook his head as she shouldered her bag. "If anyone needs to find all the beautiful people on campus, someone should send them here. The sexy teachers attract all the sexy students."

"Have you always been this hilarious?" She lifted her hand to flick Bert in the head, but he moved too fast for her to make contact.

They'd been friends since the third grade when the new kid with the whitest sneakers she'd ever seen had come up and introduced himself. Bert was her best friend and had followed her from that small town in Louisiana to LSU when she got a scholarship to play softball, then on to UCLA where she'd gotten her master's and doctorate. That felt like a lifetime ago, and they were still at UCLA, only now they were faculty. Bert had received his doctorate in math a year before she'd finished, and she loved that she saw him every day.

"You know you're a superstar. Most of those girls sit in there and talk about Billy Shakespeare only so they can undress you with their eyes." Bert pushed his glasses up more out of habit than their needing adjustment.

"Billy Shakespeare?" She laughed and stepped outside. It was sunny and warm, but nothing like summers back home where the humidity alone would make you contemplate moving to Antarctica. "Thank God you understand calculus, buddy."

"What are your big plans for tonight?" Bert was successful in his career, but that luck hadn't translated into his dating life, so he often turned to her for company. "There's a showing of *Pride and Prejudice* at that place close to my house."

"Let me check with Margot, but that sounds good." They walked three buildings over and she let him enter first. Her office was on the second floor, and the department head was on the first. Dr. Ian Hadley was in his late sixties but still loved being in the classroom, and he loved the staff he'd put together. Jaxon was just glad to be part of his team.

"Please promise Margot's not going to try to set me up again. I love your girlfriend to death, but she has horrible taste in men. Not that

I mind going out with good-looking actors, but all that last guy wanted to do was comb my chest hair."

"Do you have chest hair?" she teased him, and it earned her a slap to her arm. "And of course Margot has terrible taste in men. That's a big duh."

"Well, I need her to start refining her talent. You found someone wonderful, and I have a magnet for weirdos."

"Come on, if I had chest hair, I'd like someone to comb it."

"You don't have chest hair? I find that shocking, Dr. Lavigne."

"Shut up and keep Viola company in case some of my students show up." Her assistant, Viola Morehouse, blew her a kiss when she walked in and followed up with one for Bert. "I'm sure there'll be a few sick grandmothers who need their attention, so they can't be blamed for their apparent laziness at the end of the semester."

"I fell for that shit the first year I was here." Bert shook his head and dropped into the chair across from her desk.

"The imagination of the young. It's entertaining but also annoying." She flipped on the coffee maker Margot had gotten her and set up two cups. "Are you getting your car back soon?" Her mornings this week had started earlier than usual since she'd had to make time to pick Bert up. "Buying a new car isn't a sin, you know."

"But I love my car."

"It is a step up from the purple Gremlin you had in high school, but not by much. I can go with you if the salespeople scare you. If you got rid of the rust bucket and the pocket protector, you might find someone without a strange hang-up."

"Why are we friends again?" Bert asked.

"Because you love me, and I don't ever want to comb your nonexistent chest hair." They laughed together as she collected all the papers she needed before she went home. It was nice to have Bert to talk to, and the next hour went by in a blink. "Do you need to change?"

"I want to take a quick shower—then I'll Uber to your place." He fooled with his glasses again, and she put her arm around his shoulders.

"How about we rent the movie and cook something for Margot? We can have a romantic evening of grading papers and watching the brilliance that is Jane Austen." She kissed the side of his head and pushed him out the door.

ALI VALI

"That sounds even better. You have all the good booze."

"Fantastic. Viola, anything else this afternoon?"

"No, but you have seven appointments in the morning, and I already told them you're not in the market for a girlfriend, boyfriend, or anyone to have your baby in exchange for an A."

"I'm sure none of them are interested in that, so stop threatening people."

"Honey, wake up. Margot wrote out a script for me, and I'm not sure I'll like what'll happen to me if I don't follow it."

"If you're done, I'll see you in the morning. Try to behave, so I don't have to bail you out of jail." She pushed Bert gently to get him walking and thought about letting Margot set him up again. There had to be one sane man out there who could appreciate Bert for who he was, pocket protector and all. "Have a nice evening, boss," she said to Viola.

She thanked the universe for her life as they headed for her truck. It didn't get any better than what she'd built, no matter what her family thought of her. Their disapproval of her *lifestyle*, a word her mother always said with the prerequisite air quotes, was plain. It was why she hadn't gone home after high school, and why she'd built her own family to share her life with. Happiness made it easy to forget all the things that brought pain.

"Get all that shit out of your head before you get in a funk." She spoke softly to herself as she unlocked her door and got in. There were some things that just were. They couldn't be changed, and trying was like hitting yourself in the head with a brick. Nothing good came of that.

❖

Iris Long Gravois clapped her hands to get everyone's attention. The reunion wasn't that far off, and they had a lot of planning to do if they were going to have another successful class event. Their class president had left for bigger and better things and had never looked back, so it fell to her and the others who'd served on student council to organize everything. This wasn't her favorite set of tasks, but her job at the high school meant she was one of the coordinators by default. The others reasoned she had all the information at her fingertips.

"Do we have a complete list of everyone from the last time?" she asked her good friend, Nancy Lyons.

"Everyone, including the spouses of the three people who passed away. Can y'all believe we've lost that many in only sixteen years?" Nancy shook her head as she handed Iris the list. "Adeline and I went ahead and got the invitations ready to mail," Nancy said, mentioning her daughter. "If everyone agrees there are no changes to be made, we'll mail them out today."

"Thanks for doing that, you two," Iris said. She placed a check next to invitations, so they could move on. "We've gotten permission from the school board to use the gym at the high school again. I spoke to the superintendent myself. It'll be like reliving prom."

"Let's hope not," Molly Speller said, making them all laugh. "I have no desire to go back to high school. That was a brutal time—brutal. The booze was horrible, and my bad hip means I have no desire to have sex in the back of a car ever again. The fact that I ever drank Boone's Farm pains me to admit."

"Not all of it was bad," Iris said softly. High school was a time most people chose not to think about afterward unless they were the captain of the football team, or a cheerleader, but she'd been happy all those years. After graduation she'd lost something vital to her, and she'd never gotten it back—not really. She wasn't unsatisfied with her life, but *What if?* was the question she asked more often than she'd like.

"Iris, girl, you have to stop romanticizing what was basically a hot mess of a time. None of us could drink legally, drive, or buy a vibrator," Molly said. "I'd never go back, and after kids and marriage if they outlawed wine tomorrow, I'd become a bootlegger. There are certain things I can't live without. The other thing we stupidly did was wish to be treated like adults and have children of our own. Remember how we said we'd raise them so differently?"

Tori Hopkins laughed the hardest and nodded. "God, yes, but then you have them, and you wonder how you can survive it without social services showing up at your house on a daily basis. If I'd actually cut a switch every time I threatened to do it, my trees would be bare. And now that they're teenagers, I have to keep myself from committing murder daily."

"I'd give anything to come home and go to my room and eat pizza rolls," Claire Guidry said. "I miss the days when my only responsibility was doing my homework and picking my dirty clothes off the floor. You were the one who started early on those kids, so you know what I mean, Iris."

Iris smiled, thinking of her after-school activities, then lost it when the gossip that never really died down was brought up again. "I wanted a family, but I didn't start that early." She'd actually been pregnant at graduation but had hidden it well. "If y'all don't mind, let's get back to what we need to get through. You can all reminisce about your childless selves later."

"But the gym, yet again? Is there anywhere else we can go?" Claire asked.

"It's the only place we could get with our small budget, and the decorations from the last reunion are in the attic of the high school." Iris swore these women did this every single time to be obstinate. "People act like they're destitute when we plan this thing, so it can't ever be elaborate. You'd swear they're still on an allowance from their parents and are saving for something special."

"Do you think our fearless leader will ever come back and help us with any of this?" Molly asked. "This was one of the things you had to promise to do when you ran for class president, plan reunions. Besides, I'm sure you'd love to see her again, Iris."

"Did anyone call her?" Tori asked.

The false sincerity in their voices was hard to take, and Iris knew there was no way any of them had the guts to call Jaxon and ask her to come back. Their graduation was the last day they'd all been together, and she missed those times most of all. If there was a way to go back to those years, she'd do it, if only to spend another afternoon with Jaxon Lavigne. She hadn't had any contact after Jax had left, and she'd never expected any. Not after how it had ended between them. For that, she was to blame.

"Did you?" Tori asked her. "You two were tight back then. Surely you've kept in touch."

Tori was always the instigator in the group, and not one of her favorite people. The town of Chackbay, Louisiana, wasn't that big, and pretty much everyone knew everyone. You were born here, you grew up, had your own family, and then you eventually died and were buried with all your relatives going back a few hundred years. That's the way things were done, and trying to change it was futile.

Some found it comforting that everyone was aware of their neighbors' business, but it was hard keeping secrets when you lived in a fishbowl. She'd tried her best to keep that part of herself she treasured hidden from everyone she knew, to avoid uninvited attention. Some secrets, though, were hard to hide in plain sight.

"I haven't talked to Jaxon since she left for college. Her mother gave me her address, and we've sent an invitation every five years, but she's never responded." That was all she could say without getting upset.

"Jaxon should be ashamed of herself for staying away for so long." Claire shook her head again and voiced what they were all probably thinking. "Her dad had those health problems, and her mom didn't deserve being cast aside like that."

They all saw Gene and Eve Lavigne at church every Sunday, and they never appeared happy. Gene still had that straight posture he'd perfected in the army, and Eve had that disapproving snarl that didn't exactly make her approachable. Iris said, "You don't know what goes on in families, so I try not to judge. It's not like any of us have given Jaxon any reason to come back." That part was true. There'd been nothing to do but figure out the next stage of their lives those last days before Jaxon left for LSU. It had quickly gone wrong, and it'd been brutal for her old friend.

"Come on, Iris, don't be so nice. That's one fucked-up family dynamic, and you know it. Jaxon's older brother, Roy, is the only one who turned out halfway normal, and that's me being generous," Tori said. "And along those lines, have y'all done any reading in the checkout lane at the grocery? I doubt any of it is true, but the *National Enquirer* reported *our* Jaxon is dating Margot Drake."

"Are you kidding?" Molly asked.

"They didn't mention her name, but the woman in the picture with Margot has to be Jaxon. I guess all those rumors about her in high school weren't bullshit after all."

Nancy glanced her way and gave her a slight smile. "Ladies, let's finish this and we can get some lunch. What are we going to do about music?"

Iris was grateful to Nancy for trying to get them back on track. She wasn't sure which of them decided on planning these every five years, but the avalanche of memories always hit her just the same. Not that she didn't think about Jaxon at least momentarily nearly every day, but she tried her best to submerge the thoughts beneath her daily responsibilities and her family.

"We ran into that poor Foret girl who got pregnant in our senior year," Molly said pointing between her and Tori.

"Y'all remember her," Tori said. "She eventually married the crackhead in our class long before we knew what a crackhead was. He left her high and dry with another three kids somewhere in Texas." Tori always seemed to know every bit of gossip, especially when it painted someone else in a bad light. "Her poor parents had to go and get her, so she's been back about a year now."

"I thought we were talking about music," Nancy said.

"We are, if you'd let us finish." Molly waved her off. "No sooner than she got back, she started up a pen pal type situation."

Iris nodded and sat back in her chair. When the committee got like this, they got very little done. "I'm almost afraid to ask, but with who?"

"Remember that weird little kid who went away for life when we were juniors?" Molly asked.

"Timmy Chapelle?" Iris still couldn't believe one of their classmates had beaten a man to death in Devil's Swamp. He'd been one of three attackers, and two of them had been in their year.

"That's him, and I would've voted him most likely to go to jail," Molly said almost too gleefully. "Tori and I were having lunch this weekend and ran into Donna. She told us she had an in to getting the Angola State Penitentiary Band to play at our reunion. Can you imagine?"

"And you said…?" Nancy asked.

"No, of course," Tori said as if Nancy was crazy for thinking otherwise. "Can you imagine the press we'd get if we agreed to that? Donna said Timmy's in the band, and if we agreed he could attend the reunion under guard. It's too crazy to think about."

"We'll hire a DJ like we always do, then," Iris said. She'd tried to convince herself this was going to be a good idea, but this meeting was a reminder of the landmines the past threw in her path. She'd never had any luck and usually stepped on every single one. "If that's all, I need to get back to work."

"So you'll take the job of calling Jaxon?" Molly asked, staring right at her.

"Let's send out the invitations and see how it goes." It would be as always, with Jax ignoring it, and in a way maybe that wasn't all bad. There'd be nowhere to hide her mistakes if Jaxon came back.

❖

Margot Drake flipped her hair and walked off the main set of the sitcom she was a regular on and entered what was supposed to be her bedroom as far as the viewing audience was concerned. The writers, she was convinced, hated her since the new season brought in a romance between her and one of her costars. Never mind that Mr. Grabby Hands was someone she couldn't stand. On-air chemistry was important, but in this case the only way the storyline would work was if it revolved around her planning his murder.

"What the hell?" she whispered as she shook her hands to relieve the tension she felt.

"You okay?" Judith Bradford asked. Judith was one of the producers and had gone to bat to get her this job. They were now at the start of their third season, and the show was a huge success, and it was Judith's job to keep their cast of seven happy.

"The writers hate me," she said, then sighed. "Did it have to be Britt Anderson, of all people? If I have to kiss him, I might be sick."

"The writers don't hate you, but the fans wanted you and Britt in a romantic relationship. You can't stand him, but on camera you two pop. According to the guys upstairs, the chemistry is undeniable, so you can see why they want that."

"Seriously?" She headed to the coffee stand, wishing they had a station that served vodka. "I would've thought Britney would be a better choice. There's no accounting for taste, but she really loves Britt almost as much as he loves himself. We all know no one will rise to that level of adoration, but Britney comes close. That would leave Shauna free for me," she said, batting her eyelashes at Judith.

"The show anchors our Thursday nights, and the ratings are

gold. There's no way the network is going to gamble with that. You're America's sweetheart, and they want to keep you on that pedestal. You don't hide your sexuality, but you were smart and fell in love with someone who's not famous."

"It depends who you ask on campus when it comes to Jaxon's star power." She laughed and poured two cups and handed Judith one. "It's been my experience that no one will put you on a pedestal more than a woman who loves you. Jaxon was a little slow out of the gate, but she finally came through, and now she's the biggest romantic in the world."

"I'm not disagreeing with you, but you know better than anyone that the networks are run by old white men who collectively are assholes." Judith followed her to the break area and sat next to her. "How is Jaxon these days?"

"Just when I think it can't get any better, it does. There are still parts of her I know she keeps hidden from me, but she's a wonderful person to go home to." Her phone rang as she smiled at Judith. "Hi, baby."

"Hey, are you having a good day?" The noise from wherever Jaxon was sounded like people having a good time outside.

"I am now. Are you done for the day?" She didn't mind that Judith stuck around for the conversation, but she did lower her voice.

"Just finished my office hours and talking to Bert and Viola. I missed you today."

"That's good to hear. We might run late, so can you find something to keep you busy?" She laughed and tapped her nail on the phone. "Just make sure it's not one of those needy coeds."

"I already have the coed I want, so no worries. Bert invited us to go to that art house theater by his house. They're playing *Pride and Prejudice*, but I thought we'd stay home and cook you something."

"I'd love to see that. Thanks for putting it off until tomorrow night, Mr. Darcy. Tell him we'll take him out to dinner somewhere fancy for his sacrifice. And I think I met someone he might love."

"He'll have to tell you the story of the last guy, so don't pout if he turns you down." The rumble of Jaxon's truck made Margot smile again. "How's your TV love life going?"

"Not as well as my true love life. I couldn't convince Judith that kissing Britt on set would make me look like someone is gagging me, but the higher-ups have confused that with chemistry."

"If he tries anything other than what's in the script, remind him that I'll be happy to rip his balls off." Jaxon sounded serious. "Your father taught me how."

"You'll have to beat me to it, honey, and I don't want to talk about that anymore. Make sure if you're grilling you save me some. With any luck I'll be home by…" Judith held her fingers up. "Nine."

"Call me when you're on your way, and I'll throw yours on the grill. Do you want me to come pick you up?"

"You don't mind?" She was sure how Jaxon felt about her, but she wasn't above being reminded.

"I'll tell Bert we'll make up tonight as well, and I'll come now. They're not going to strip-search me at the gate, are they?"

"No, but that might be a possibility when I get you in my dressing room."

CHAPTER TWO

Jaxon came home a week later and flipped through the mail as she made her way to her office. She knew Margot would be home in an hour, and they'd finally have a quiet night in. She'd been looking forward to it. Their few minutes at night before sleep, and another few minutes before they went to work, weren't enough.

This life they'd made together surprised her on a daily basis. Margot was the type of woman who kept her enthralled. It was the best way she could describe it, and what they had wasn't something she'd ever trade for anything. Love wasn't something that had worked out for her until now, but Margot had been patient with her and had spent plenty of time convincing her to believe their love would work.

The view from the back of the house was spectacular, and she took a minute to enjoy the pink and orange sky that made for a gorgeous sunset. This place was way out of her price range and a perk of Margot's salary. Moving in had taken a lot of convincing as well, but Margot hadn't given up there either.

She loved the house, though, and the office Margot had decorated for her was perfect. She looked at the envelope in her hand and sighed. Another class reunion. Why were her high school classmates so dedicated to seeing each other so often? Add to that you had to pay for that privilege, and it made even less sense. Most of these people were assholes back then and hadn't improved with age. It was like an asshole convention, and the people involved competed for the top spot.

Not that she knew from experience, but Bert kept her up on the gossip from a place that hadn't been home in a long time. The majority of the people they'd graduated with had stayed close to where they'd been born and would be buried there once their predictable lives were over. It was their mundane circle of life. She didn't open the envelope and threw it in her bag. It would be like all the others she tossed out. Walking into her past was something she had no intention of doing. There was nothing there she wanted to visit or relive. Add to that it was actually their *sixteen*-year reunion, and it made even less sense. They'd missed the first year but were committed to sticking to the five-year increments. It was as if human evolution had missed a few links in her hometown. The fuckers she went to school with couldn't even handle simple math.

"Jax, where are you?" Margot called out as the front door shut. "Tell me you're naked."

"I can be for the right incentive." She sat on the corner of her desk and smiled when Margot walked in.

"That sounds like a challenge, professor." Margot peeled off the sweatshirt, and her hot pink bra made Jaxon inhale deeply. "You know how much I love a challenge." The skintight jeans shimmied down Margot's legs, and Jax was surprised to see white bikinis. "Lose the pout. You ripped the matching panties, baby, and I haven't had a chance to go shopping."

"I'm not complaining." She put her hands on the desk and waited. If there was another truth in the world besides the fact that she loved Margot, it was that she was incredibly beautiful and downright sexy. "And I promise to be gentler this time around."

"Who asked you to do that?" Margot stepped between her legs and kissed her. She tasted like chocolate, which she knew was one of Margot's weaknesses. "I love that wild, can't-control-yourself side, honey. It makes me hot." Margot ran her hands from her shoulders down her chest to the alligator belt that had been a gift from her brother, Roy. "This morning was too rushed, so no more of that."

There were certain mornings…well, pretty much every morning, when she opened her eyes to Margot naked next to her and it turned her on. They hadn't had time to prolong the enjoyment they took in each other that morning, but it didn't mean they hadn't reached the promised land, as Margot called it.

"I agree with you," she said as she sat up slightly so Margot could pull her pants down. She was now trapped in cowboy boots, with her jeans around her ankles. "It'll be better if we move over to the couch."

"And lose my advantage? Not on your life, lover." Margot yanked down the underwear she loved shopping for and smiled as she dropped to her knees. "Pay attention now."

She nodded like an idiot and tightened her hold on the desk when Margot put her mouth on her and flicked her clit with the tip of her tongue. It was hard not to come right away, but Margot had a way of stripping away all her control. She put her hand on the back of Margot's head and closed her eyes, trying to hang on, but it was impossible. "Fuck...fuck," she said, fisting Margot's hair and holding her tighter against her.

"You taste so good," Margot said, kissing the top of her sex after she'd come hard. "And I've been thinking about that all day long." Margot stood and started unbuttoning her shirt as she kissed her neck.

"I think about that on a daily basis too, ever since you stripped for me and blinded me to the world."

"You say the most romantic things." Margot helped her off with her boots and pants so she could walk without killing herself. When Margot was done she pressed their bodies together and tugged on Jaxon's bottom lip with her teeth. "That's one of the many things I love about you."

"That you like the romantic sap in me is one of the many things I love about you." She kissed Margot and ran her hands down her back until it was under her panties and on her ass. "This butt is also one of the things I love about you."

"That's when I knew I had a chance, Dr. Lavigne," Margot said, laughing. "I caught you looking more than once when I walked out of your classroom. Right now, you can look all you want. You're entitled."

"Really? You won't think I'm a pig for staring?"

Margot put her hands around her neck when Jax stood and pulled herself up, so she could wrap her legs around her waist. "It'd make me think there's something wrong if you didn't."

Jaxon sat on the couch and smiled when Margot lay across her lap with her butt facing her. "You are perfection, my love." She started at the back of Margot's knee and moved her hand upward until she caressed Margot's ass. "What were you thinking about all day?"

"You, touching me like this—" Margot stopped abruptly when Jaxon ran her fingers down and through her wetness. "Yeah...like that." Margot's ass came up as if wanting more. "But you went inside, tease."

Margot turned her head and watched Jaxon put her fingers in her mouth. "Patience," she said, putting her hand back where it'd been. "I had to check and make sure you taste as good as you look."

"There's going to be hell to pay if you make me beg." Margot wiggled on her lap and kept her head turned so she could see her.

"You think so, huh?" She slapped Margot gently on the ass and loved the moan it got her. Margot was wet, and she hadn't tortured her, so she slid two fingers in and waited to see what pace Margot wanted to set.

"Oh yes," Margot whispered. She pumped her hips slowly, but that didn't last very long. "Please, baby…fuck me."

She knew from the few classes Margot had taken with her that she had a brilliant mind, but she could be succinct when she needed to be. The day of Margot's graduation she'd walked up to Jaxon and handed her a note with her address and the time she'd be ready for their first date. Margot's reasoning had been she was no longer a student. Because she wasn't, they were free to do all the things she'd fantasized about in class, and they'd wasted enough time already.

"Harder, honey, harder," Margot said, moaning again. "Yes… yes…fuck yes."

She felt Margot tighten around her fingers when she stopped moving, but she kept her fingers still until Margot was ready to let her go. "You really were thinking about me."

Margot moved so she could sit up and put her arms around her neck. "Would you consider an acting gig? If you were my love interest on the show, those idiots could see what true chemistry is. Otherwise, you have to promise to make love to me every night so I can stay sane."

"Sorry, my love. You're the star in this relationship, and I still haven't figured out exactly what it is you see in me." She lay back and held Margot on top. "Making love to you every night is a promise that'll easy to keep, though."

"You're my person, babe. I knew that from the first time I saw you. My mom always preached, from the time it was important, to find the one who was real and didn't have any hidden agendas." Margot pressed her hands to her face and kissed her.

"Your father is another story," Jax said, making Margot laugh. "I doubt I was what he had in mind."

"Daddy loves you." Margot kissed her again. "He just hides it well."

"We can agree on that." Major General Wilber Drake had proudly served his country in the Marines until his retirement. He was the walking personification of rigid. "I think he's been not so secretly plotting to kill me from the minute you introduced us."

"That's not true." The way Margot sat up a little made it hard for Jaxon to take her eyes off her chest. "He knows how happy you make me, and that's important to him. And as much as I love my father, I don't want to talk about him while I have you naked."

"Are you hungry?" She ran her hands down Margot's back to her ass.

"We're not grilling anything, caveman. Let's order some sushi after a swim." Margot stood up and held her hand out to her. "Want to go out to dinner with me this week? I want to go somewhere with plenty of paparazzi."

"Did you hit your head on the way home?" She stood still as Margot stood on the sofa so she could climb on her back for a piggyback ride to the pool. "You never want to give those vultures the chance to make a penny off you."

"It was Judith's idea, and it's so brilliant I'm sorry I didn't think of it myself. She figured if the studio execs saw us out, they'd rethink the new storyline with Britt. The bonus is, any plan that includes a date with you is something I can get behind." Margot kissed the side of her neck and pressed her sex into her back. "And think. Once we get home, we can cut the pictures out of the national rags and put them in our scrapbook."

"We have a scrapbook?"

"We could, but let's talk about our date instead."

Jaxon turned off all the lights by the pool and got in with Margot still on her back. This was one of the main reasons Margot had fallen in love with the house. It had everything they'd both wanted in a home and they'd been happy here for two years. "I'd love to take you out but talk to them if this is really bothering you. Can they force you to do something you really don't want to?"

"It's no secret how I feel about Britt, but it's more than that. I feel disingenuous going along with this. Not to mention, it makes my skin crawl." Margot held on to her as she headed for the deeper end. "I want you to be proud of me."

"Honey, it's called acting. I love you, and while I'll admit seeing you kiss someone else makes me crazy, it doesn't mean anything." She kissed Margot's temple. "Don't waste any time thinking I'm not proud of you. We both know it's only a matter of time before you springboard into something much bigger. You're better than everyone on the show, and they know that."

"You're good for my ego, love." The water temperature was starting to cool, so it was time for a shower. After the sex, no other exercise was necessary. "Do you want me to cook? If you really aren't in the mood for sushi, I'll make something."

"No, I'll run out and pick up dinner. When I get back, we'll have a picnic in the den and then go to bed. The weekend is almost here, and I've got a date." She moved Margot in front of her and kissed her. "The rest will work itself out."

"I love your optimism, honey. You always say that, no matter what." Margot wrapped her legs around her waist again as she started for the shallow end. "How was your day?"

"The usual around this time of year. Most of my students are great and are ready to discuss the assignments, but a few think I've never heard of SparkNotes." She rested her forehead against Margot's. "I wonder sometimes how they made it this far, but like I said, it usually works itself out."

"I miss those times. You were the best part of my day. You still are."

"You're the sweetest person I've ever met." She put her foot on the first step and smiled when Margot laid her head on her shoulder. "I love you."

"I love you more." Margot kissed the side of her neck.

Everything they had together, this life, this relationship, was so much more than she'd ever thought she'd have when she left home all those years ago. Their night had let her forget the envelope she'd put away, but for some reason she remembered it now. Nothing was worth gambling all this, and going back home and exposing Margot to her family would certainly do that. Those thoughts made her stop moving. She wasn't often embarrassed, but thinking of how her family would treat Margot made her stomach churn.

"You okay?" Margot lifted her head and ran her fingers though Jaxon's hair.

"Perfect." There'd come a day when she'd have to sit Margot down and tell her the truth of where she'd come from. The most important part of that story was why she'd run and why she didn't want to go back. There was nothing left for her in Louisiana, but keeping things from Margot carried its own set of risks.

"That you are, my love."

❖

Iris waited in the office of the high school, finishing her paperwork for the day. The busywork helped her get her mind off what was coming. It had nothing to do with reunions or a marriage that was getting ready to take some hits as the reunion neared. No, her daughter was a junior who was counting the days until she graduated and gained her freedom. That bothered her, but nothing she did or said persuaded Sean from wanting to fly away and not come back. That wasn't a surprise, but it was why Sean wanted to go that made Iris feel shame.

Her son walked into the office. "Hey, Mom," Danny said, louder than necessary.

"Hey, you don't have to shout." She closed the image she'd been staring at on her computer. Margot Drake was hanging on to Jaxon like she'd fall off the spike heels she was wearing without the support, but even with that Jaxon was taller and still looked good. There was no way she'd ever call Jaxon, but peeking in on her life every so often was okay. At least, that's what she told herself.

"I've been calling you for, like, an hour," Danny said in his overexaggerated way. "What the heck are you doing? Is it the math test for that asshole I have this year?"

"What have we said about you cursing? I know you're going to do it, but I'd appreciate not listening to it all day long." She powered down her computer and opened the bottom drawer of her desk to get her purse. "The one thing I've noticed is that the teacher is only an asshole when you don't study and aren't doing well. We've talked about that too."

"Come on, Mom. That guy has it in for me, and if he keeps slamming me, he's going to tank my chances of staying on the team."

His voice was starting to rise again, and she pointed at him. "Okay, I'll study."

"Good." She kissed his cheek. "Where's your sister?"

"She was in the library the last time I passed by there. You should bring her to some head doctor and get her fixed. All she does is study and work out. That's not normal."

"I hate to break it to you, but there's nothing crazy about that. You should try to cut back on hanging with your friends and having a good time, so you can get to know math better." She put her hand up when he started to disagree. "Stop talking before I ground you, and math will be the least of your problems."

"It's not like I'm going to college. Going to the police academy here doesn't require that." He was tall, thick, and blond like his father. That physique made him the perfect football quarterback and catcher on the baseball team. Danny was also his father when it came to what his future should be.

"What if you get a scholarship to play somewhere? Would you blow that off?" It was like talking to a brick wall, but she had plenty of practice with his father. Daniel had been a star in high school, and he still talked about the glory days.

She'd married Daniel when he'd asked, and she'd paid the price for saying yes. He'd blamed her for a long time for everything he'd given up. Her pregnancy had forced him to pass on the scholarship he'd been expecting to a university in north Louisiana. That offer was a figment of his imagination, but that hadn't been important. His star power hadn't been enough to get him to the next level, and somehow that had been her fault.

He'd asked for her hand, and she'd agreed for her own reasons. She'd never asked him to give up a damn thing, and nothing she'd done since had made Daniel stop talking about his glory days. Her rational brain was convinced he'd married her to prove he'd won against the one person in high school he hated above all others. It wasn't the romance written about in books, but it wasn't bad enough to walk away from.

"You think I can?" Danny pushed his hair back with impatience, and she smiled. That move reminded her of Jaxon when she'd finished practice and wanted a shower. Her son had gone out for the JV football team, and his hard work had paid off when they'd put him in at quarterback. His season so far had been pretty good, and he had two wins as a starter.

"If you keep those grades up and don't get hurt, I'm sure you can. Instead of making fun of your sister, maybe you should ask her to help you with math. She had the teacher you don't like two years ago, so I'm sure she'll be happy to get you back on track." They walked down the deserted hallway and stopped at the library. Sean had her head down, and she was bouncing the eraser of her pencil on her notebook.

Iris knew it was her way of concentrating, and it never failed to bring her a level of happiness that was hard to describe. Sean was as different from Danny as two siblings could be, and while she loved them both, her daughter was a gift. "Hey, you ready?"

Sean glanced up but didn't smile. "Sorry, I was trying to finish my paper before the weekend." The books scattered on the table were jammed in the bag Sean had carried around for three years, and she stood. It never made Danny happy when his sister stood next to him and showed that she was three inches taller. They were like night and day in appearance, and over the years, that had triggered a lot of gossip.

"Do you guys want to go out to eat? Your dad is working tonight, and it's already after five." They walked out, and the guys playing outside yelled at Danny. It didn't take long for him to ask if he could go with his friends, and she handed him a twenty and waved, then turned to Sean. "What are you in the mood for?"

Sean didn't answer and got in the car. The silent treatment had started that summer and nothing she'd tried had broken through. She had to give it to Sean for her mental toughness. Taking a chance, she drove to the Italian place in the next town. They sat across from each other, and the only words Sean spoke were to order. Then she leaned back and crossed her arms over her chest.

"How was school today?"

"Fine," Sean said, and that was it. It wasn't exactly rude, but it wasn't a conversation.

"If there's something bothering you, there's no way I can help you if you don't tell me what it is." She put her hand on the table but didn't reach for Sean, not wanting to be rebuffed again.

Sean stared at her and shook her head. "Tell me about her?"

"Who?" Iris knew exactly who, but she didn't want to talk about it.

"Please," Sean said with absolute teenage sarcasm. "It's like you think I'm clueless. Not to mention deaf and dumb."

During the summer Sean had found a box of her old things and had gone through it. The pictures she'd stared at for hours made the questions start pouring out, but Iris didn't want to answer them.

"I don't think that at all, but just like you don't tell me everything about you, there are things I'd like to keep private. It's nothing sinister, but sometimes memories are best kept buried." She didn't raise her voice, and she tried not to show too much emotion.

"Whatever," Sean said, rolling her eyes.

Iris sighed and had an urge to go home and close her bedroom door. Purging all this crap out of her head was the best solution, and to avoid this in the future she'd have to commit to letting go. Her family and the life she'd built were more important than something that was never going to be anything other than what looped in her mind like an unwanted old movie.

"It's more than *whatever*, Sean, but I can't talk about it. I know you think I'm trying to put you off, but I really can't." The tears that were ready to fall seemed to move something in Sean to back off, and she finally lost her angry expression.

"Forget about it, and please don't cry." Sean reached across the table and touched her hand. It was the first time in weeks Sean had made a move like that.

"Thank you, and I promise we'll have the talk you want. Only not today." It was ridiculous, really, but her hometown was all she knew. There was a place for her there, both socially and figuratively. She'd made that place by keeping her head down and fitting in when all she really wanted to do was shout from the rooftops what was in her soul. Doing that would come at a cost, even now. It was a price she wasn't capable of paying.

Chapter Three

The invitation sat in Jaxon's office drawer for the next week, and the only one who wanted to talk about it was Bert. He'd been hounding her for days to get her to agree to join him. Why in the world he wanted to go back to a place that didn't hold many happy memories, especially for him, was a mystery, but he wanted to go. She had a short window of time before he told Margot about it, and then she'd have nowhere to hide.

Margot was curious about her childhood and asked about it all the time. It wasn't something she liked talking about. Her family was like every other Southern family, full of people others liked to call eccentric. Behavioral sciences had other names for it, and there was extensive research on each condition that stemmed from one form of mental instability or another. The last time her family had gotten together in Orange Beach, Alabama, for a reunion about twelve years ago, they'd spent the whole time whispering to one another. That stopped whenever she walked into any room, but she hadn't said anything, surprised she'd been invited at all.

Yep, there'd been some big secret they weren't sharing with her, and that was fine. She didn't need a crystal ball to guess what it was. It was no secret she was gay and was going to hell faster than adulterous Satan worshippers. That long weekend was enough to drive her to alcohol, and she'd still be drunk in a ditch right now if she hadn't possessed stronger willpower than the average bear. The most ridiculous thing was that she'd gone in the first place, but it'd been her family. In her heart they deserved another chance to get it right, and it wasn't a total shock they'd failed in spectacular fashion.

The only person she missed was her brother, Roy. Their late nights talking while sitting in the large oak in their yard helped her forget her mother's constant disapproval. Even he, though, had been quiet that last time they'd been together—not that he'd engaged in the whispered conversations, but something was different. Not even Bert had shed any light on why that could be when he went back for regular visits to see his parents.

"Dr. Lavigne?" The young woman standing in front of her appeared worried. "Are you okay?"

"Sorry, did you say something?" Great, that's all she needed. Blanking out at work because she was thinking of things not worth remembering was just fantastic.

"I was wondering if you knew the book we're reading next?"

I'm teaching the fucking class, so yes, I do. It was the way she wanted to answer sometimes, but the kids appeared so earnest she didn't have the heart. Asking questions like that was their way of breaking the ice with her, so she grinned and Ctrl+Alt+Deleted her brain to reboot it. Now wasn't the time to worry about what her family thought. "Stop by my office, and pick up the reading list. Ask my assistant for it, and she'll be happy to get you up to speed. The essay on that first book is due soon, so don't take too long."

"Want to grab a coffee and talk about it?" This young woman was something else. She was gorgeous and had the body to match.

"I only see students during office hours, sorry." Her phone rang, saving her from any more of this innocent flirting. She answered with, "Hey, gorgeous," waving as the student left, looking disappointed.

"And you wonder why I love you so much. You always make me smile when you answer the phone," Margot said. "Are you busy?"

"Not at the moment. I was walking to class, so I can sit and start writing up my tests." Her worries evaporated at the sound of Margot's voice. For once in her life she'd gotten it right by taking a chance. Margot was the real deal when it came to returning her love.

"Does that mean all the cute girls on campus who are suddenly in love with English are trying to trade certain favors for a good grade?" Margot was kidding, but there was that slight edge to her voice.

"You were the only one who offered that, darlin', but you should be proud—you got that grade all on your own." She laughed at the memory of Margot trying the same thing, only she'd been much more persistent. It was the only time in her teaching career that she'd gone home hard, wet, and extremely horny. Margot's office visits were an exercise in temptation.

"That's the only reason I don't handcuff myself to you every morning when you leave for work. Now that I know how to make you sweat, you can admit you were tempted."

She could imagine the smile on Margot's face. "Is there a person alive who wouldn't be tempted? You are, my love, the one woman who fuels my dreams, not to mention my desires. I thought that even when it was inappropriate for me to even contemplate it."

"Good comeback, baby. Listen, I'm due on set soon, but Mama called and invited us for dinner." She heard Margot snap her fingers. "Don't spend the rest of the day trying to think up reasons you can't go."

Margot's parents had a lot in common with her own, only they were accepting of what they had and who their daughter was. They were also completely crazy. "Would I do that?"

"Yes," Margot said with no hesitation. "I know you, Dr. Lavigne, and you have to realize Daddy doesn't really want to kill you." Margot laughed, and she had to join in.

"He has a funny way of showing that, and we'll talk about this later. There's a few students waiting for me." She waved to the group headed into the classroom.

"Oh no, we'll talk about it now. Repeat these words," Margot ordered. "I will be at dinner tonight."

"I will be at dinner tonight."

"That didn't sound very convincing, but I'll take it."

Still smiling, she sat with her students and talked about a slew of different topics that didn't all have to do with class. These guys had been in her classes from freshman year, and most of them were headed to law school after this. It was a pleasant afternoon until she glanced up and saw Bert waiting on her again.

"Unequivocally no."

"Unequivocally? That's harsh. You just have to sort out your feelings, and you'll be fine." Bert softened his voice, trying a new tactic. He cocked his head to the side and seemed to be trying to appear sympathetic.

She took a deep breath, not wanting to pop his bubble, and jammed her papers in her bag. "You think that's my hang-up? If I haven't been perfectly clear, I just don't want to go. Besides, it makes no sense. It's a fifteen-year reunion happening sixteen years after the fact."

"They actually had the first five-year reunion at year six, but they said buying decorations makes more sense in increments of five, so they went with it. As a man with a doctorate in math, it really doesn't make sense, but that whole town is full of idiots, so you have to learn to let it go."

She shook her head and he frowned. "I'm not going."

"But why? It's been years, Jax. It's time to go back and tell Margot all the stuff you haven't yet. She deserves to know before she starts popping out little Jaxons into the world. Your family isn't your fault, and she loves you. She's not your mother."

"That's the last thing I want to do. You know the hell my parents put me through, and as long as they're alive, they're not done. I'm not subjecting Margot to that kind of bigotry, much less an innocent child we haven't even talked about yet, though Margot's probably ready for one. How the world treats us is bad enough, but when it comes from people who are supposed to love you, it's doubly painful." She pointed at him as she spoke. "Nothing conjures up a single wonderful, warm, fuzzy memory, so I'm giving it a pass like I did the first two times they sent an invitation. It would be nothing but four days of forcing myself to be nice to people I didn't like, who didn't like me."

"I know, and you're probably going to punch me in the nose before all this is over, but I still think it'll be good for you to go back. It might get better, or it might not," he said softly. "Putting it to rest once and for all might be a relief."

"I put it to rest already, but there's one thing I don't understand. Why do you want to go? You're the last person in the world I need to be explaining this to. Your experience wasn't any better than mine. Why the sudden urge to fly back and face the abuse you know is coming?" She gripped the leather strap of her bag, wanting to be finished with this conversation. Her day had been good until now.

Bert could be more persistent than a tick when it came to something he wanted. They'd met when they both wanted ownership rights of a book in the library. Bert had been the class punching bag, but he hadn't backed down when she threatened to clock him. They'd been as close as siblings ever since.

In school they'd participated in different activities, but they'd always been there for each other, cheering their triumphs no matter what. At their high school graduation, they'd shared the valedictorian honors, but he had gladly let the writer in their friendship give the commencement speech. In college they'd been roommates once they moved off campus, and their plan had been to end up on the same faculty.

When he wasn't teaching he'd come by and sit in her class and listen. He often told her how much he envied her passion in the classroom, and nothing she said made him believe he was just as good. There was no way he'd be teaching at one of the most prestigious universities in the nation if he wasn't excellence personified, but his impostor syndrome refused to allow him to believe it.

Granted, his coeds didn't look at him like they looked at her, but Bert had his share of fans. They were usually more in awe of his grasp of numbers than his looks, but they loved him. She often teased him that it was because literature and poetry were way sexier than algorithms.

She finally smiled as he seemed to be thinking of his next best move.

"Come on, doesn't a part of you want to go back and show them up?" Trying to appear earnest, Bert put his hands out to his sides and tried his best pleading expression. "They all thought I'd shrivel up and die after graduation, but I didn't, and neither did you. We need to show them what we've achieved."

Pleading had never worked with her—he had a slow learning curve on that. "Bert, that's about the saddest thing you could've come up with." She started walking, and Bert skipped to keep up. "If you're dying to go, then go. I may not understand your reasoning, but I won't think any less of you for going back to that hellhole. Besides, it'll give you a chance to check on your parents. Regular phone calls can't take the place of seeing you. They're some of the few sane people in that town, and it's been months since they've seen you."

"But I don't want to go by myself."

Jaxon was waiting for him to stomp his foot and clench his shoulders to go with the whine as he lengthened the last word. "Does it really matter that much in the realm of all things what those cretins think of you? Right now, considering where you are and what you do, it means you won. I doubt anyone else has been as successful. Look around—this isn't Hicksville, USA."

Bert ran his hand through his hair, releasing a small cloud of chalk dust. It was one of the endearing things about him that went with the pocket protector. Why he couldn't purchase a pen case like everyone else was a mystery. There was no reason to shove them all under your nose like that. "Yeah, it matters just a little bit. Can't we just go and show them geeks can be really cool?" The pleading face was back, and this time it softened her a bit.

He had to stop and turn to face her when she stopped short. She smiled when he stared back at her with his hands up again. "Bert, buddy, you're my best friend, and I love you, but you, my man, are not cool."

He frowned as he looked her up and down. The minute Margot had gotten her to commit, she'd had to agree to stop seeing other women and stop shopping for her own clothes. The women were a given, but Margot really enjoyed shopping for her, so the white shirt, dark brown suede jacket, and comfortable jeans were all thanks to her loving partner.

The only thing she'd been allowed to keep was the pair of well-maintained cowboy boots. The footwear was commented on by her students when she'd sit on the desk at the front of the class and swing her legs. Margot had told her they pretty much cemented how cool they thought she was. Plus, Margot thought they were sexy.

"Doesn't this school have a dress code?" Bert followed her into the English department. He straightened his tie and smoothed down his own slightly wrinkled shirt, oblivious to the ink stain at the very corner of the front pocket. It clearly hadn't prevented him from putting it on that morning, though, because it didn't appear fresh. Yet one more reason for the pen case.

"No shorts," Viola said with authority as Jaxon dropped into her chair in her office. "Boy, don't you know they pay her to look like that? Dr. Jaxon's a star, and her looks keep those kids packing those classrooms. She's what they call a cash cow over in the business school. All the girls want her, and the boys are all praying that they'll get a glimpse of Margot."

"Viola, stop tormenting Bert." The stack of pink message slips Viola handed her made her sigh. She tried to put faces with some of the names, but for once most of them weren't from students. If they didn't leave a reason for calling, she threw them out.

"Thanks, Jaxon." Bert stuck his tongue out at Viola.

"That would be my job," Jaxon finished the joke. "Now, beautiful one, what's on my schedule for the rest of the day?" Today and Thursdays were her long days, and she'd been in class except for the hour she'd spent at the coffee shop.

Viola held up her appointment book and opened it like she was getting ready to read from some holy book. "You have office hours for the next hour, but don't worry, I've run off most of the ones who think they'll be the next Margot Drake. After that you're expected downstairs for a faculty meeting. Once that's done, Margot will be waiting for you out front. I'm sure you've conveniently forgotten that you're having dinner with her and her parents tonight."

"But..." Damn, she *had* conveniently forgotten that.

"But nothing, Dr. Jaxon, you're going, so don't even try your shenanigans. You don't go, and I'm going to get blamed." Viola put her hand up and shook her head. "Don't give me any bullshit. Every time you don't do something, you blame it on me, and the people you lie to believe you because of those dimples of yours. Margot Drake can be scary when she wants to be, and I'm not going to be the first person she runs over with her car."

"I don't blame you—I blame work. There's a difference."

"Uh-huh. Did you know she's got the most popular hair in America?" Viola cocked her head to the side and smiled.

She almost fell over when she leaned her chair back too far. "What? Is that some sort of trick question?" She dropped her feet and narrowed her eyes at Viola. "Wait, let me guess, the rag that pretends to be news strikes again?" Jaxon was convinced she was the only English professor in America who had an assistant hooked on tabloid news.

"Don't knock my favorite publication, Doc. At least they're giving her good press, unlike some of her costars. Did you know that one girl on the show's got a coke problem?"

"I didn't need help from the news toilet bowl to figure that one out. The fact the woman stumbles through her lines and is constantly sniffing gives it away. Now back to this dinner. There's no chance Margot's working late tonight, is there? I love her parents, but I'm not going over there alone."

Viola rolled her eyes at nearly the same time Bert rolled his. Neither of them understood the way Margot's father liked to torture her, and no one in their right mind lined up for torture. She was many things, but masochist wasn't on her list.

"If you knew Wilber, you wouldn't want to go over there either. That's who taught Margot all her scary ways, as you put it."

"What's it you people from the south call it? Scaredy-cat?" Viola laughed when she frowned. "She wrapped up for the day an hour ago and called. If you're worried the general is planning to beat you up, don't worry. You won't be going into the lion's den without backup. Margot made me promise to mention she'd be there to protect you as a way to keep you from running away from home."

"Why doesn't that make me feel any better? Send in the first victim, taskmaster," Jaxon said to Viola. "As for you, whiny boy, will it make you feel better if I said I'll think about it?"

"It's not no, and I'm not giving up." Bert slapped his hands together, stood, and wiggled his hips in some sort of happy dance. Either that or he was having some kind of fit.

"I'm so glad you're so optimistic. It'll make it easier to pop your balloon later when I say no."

"Will that be unequivocally no?" Bert asked and laughed.

"It'll be no punctuated by me kicking your ass."

❖

Margot spread cleanser on her face, more than ready to shed her television persona. The thought of a few days off was making her tingle. All she had to do now was talk Jaxon into having one of her grad assistants take over her classes, and she would have nirvana. It had been weeks since they'd had any significant time together. All she wanted was a long weekend somewhere where there was room service. They had plenty to talk about, starting with whatever was bothering Jax. She'd denied it repeatedly, but there was something rattling around that brilliant mind, and it wasn't a good thing.

"Big plans for tonight? If you do, change them." Britt Anderson sat in the chair next to hers and dipped his fingers into the jar she was using. "I have tickets to a new show in town and decided you're the lucky girl who gets to go with me." He snapped his fingers and winked at her in the mirror. How any man could pack so much obnoxiousness and so many clichés into such a short frame was a mystery.

With a disgusted look, she tossed the jar of cleanser in the trash. Judith sat next to her and put her hand on her forearm as a way to calm her down before she said something that'd require intervention from HR. Judith seemed unable to hold in her laugh at Britt's never-ending, always unsuccessful quest to get her to notice him. Maybe one day he'd come to accept that Jaxon wasn't just sleeping over because it was her job to clean the pool.

She'd told him on numerous occasions that she wasn't interested because she only dated women. Gossip on set spread faster than the plague, but there was one item Britt hadn't latched on to because he refused to believe it.

His biggest problem was that she'd been the pursuer in her relationship with Jaxon. Her lover was brilliant, but not too many people knew she was actually shy. Margot would've grown old waiting for Jaxon to make a move if she hadn't taken the initiative. All it had taken was patience and a slew of sexy underwear.

Jax had lasted about two weeks after her graduation before saying yes to their first date. She'd never wanted anyone as much as Jaxon, and she'd been a pest until she'd given in. At first she'd thought Jax was just appeasing her while she was busy changing her phone number and taking out a restraining order. Fortunately, that hadn't been the case.

Jaxon had finally agreed to go out, but she'd insisted on making the arrangements. The picnic on a private stretch of beach was one of her favorite memories, and the most romantic date she'd been on until then. Jaxon Lavigne was a Southern gentlewoman who'd swept her off her feet even if she had been the one who'd technically asked Jax out.

A year and three months had passed since then, and Jaxon hadn't had a chance to utter a no yet, and if Margot had her way, a negative response to the life she wanted with the professor wouldn't be coming until death robbed one of them of breath. She'd argued away every one of Jaxon's objections until she'd gotten her first real good night kiss, followed by more convincing so they could move in together.

"Britt, go back to your own trailer and leave Margot alone. You insisted in your contract you had to have one, so go there and lock yourself in." Judith crossed her arms to signal there'd be hell to pay if Britt didn't get up and move. He harumphed dramatically and flounced out. The click of the door closing made her and Judith laugh. If she was lucky, Britt heard them as he skulked away.

"Cretin."

"Honey, methinks you've been hanging around Jaxon too long." Judith plopped down in the seat Britt had been using.

"I think cretin's a perfectly acceptable term. It is, after all, used by someone who has a doctorate in English."

"Uh-huh, and you would explain the use of Jiminy Cricket as a curse, how?"

Margot laughed, thinking of Jaxon sitting in front of the television invoking the name of a beloved animated character to show displeasure at everything from sports scores to the news. The funniest part was, with Jaxon's inflection, it was almost as good as telling someone to fuck off. "There are two reasons for that."

"Yes?"

"She's a little nuts and a lot adorable."

"With the way she feels about you, I'd have thought you'd be sporting a big ring by now. Once you say yes, think how much easier it'll be to keep fools like Britt at bay." Judith laughed at her own joke but stopped when Margot didn't join in.

"If you think I'd say no if she offered, you're more delusional than Britt. I can never be sure, but I think she holds back a little because she's afraid. Of what I don't know for sure, and I try not to let it hurt my feelings. Jaxon can take all the time she wants to figure out what she wants, because in the end, I know whatever those decisions will be will include me." She finished wiping all her makeup off and put some light pink lipstick on.

Judith stared at her in the mirror and didn't comment for a beat. "Want me to kick her ass?"

"No," she said and laughed. "I don't ever doubt that Jaxon loves me—it's that she's skittish when it comes to thinking long-term." She leaned closer. "Between you and me, I think it has something to do with her family. Don't repeat that because she's never admitted it, and I feel funny talking about it." Judith shook her head. "Jax is cautious when it comes to everything in her life except her writing and telling me how she feels about me." She moved behind the screen in the corner to change into her sweater and jeans.

"What're you doing with the long weekend? I still can't believe we finished that episode in record time."

"All you need is your imagination for the answer to that, sweetheart." She dropped a kiss on Judith's head and winked at her reflection in the mirror. Judith just laughed when she grabbed her car keys and purse before heading out the door. "Now all *I* need is one sexy professor and a quiet night after dinner."

There were parts of Jax that were as unexplored and elusive as the ocean floor, and that bothered her on a deep level that left her insecure about what their future would be like if Jax didn't start opening up. It boiled down to trust, and Jax not trusting her squeezed her heart painfully, but she wasn't giving up. Jaxon was too important to her.

Chapter Four

D r. Lavigne." Jaxon accepted the phone on Ian Hadley's assistant's desk and smiled at the young woman with the pinched appearance. She'd worked for Ian for a few years and never seemed happy, and that demeanor really took a skid down perturbed mountain when she had to interrupt a department meeting to call someone to the phone.

"Whoever that is has called three times," she said. "You might want to warn them about that on staff meeting days. I think I recognized the voice, so she should know better."

"Jaxon?"

"Yes?" She nodded at the woman and smiled. The frown she got in return almost made her laugh.

"What're you wearing?"

Jaxon laughed harder and turned her back so she wouldn't see the assistant's head explode. "You do realize I was in a staff meeting? Ian's assistant wanted you to know you shouldn't call on these days."

"Uh-huh. That totally slipped my mind, and I wouldn't have had to call and bother her if you'd answered your phone." Margot sounded totally insincere. "Aren't you going to ask what I'm wearing?"

"Considering it sounds like you're driving, it better be something, I don't know, existent. And should you be talking to me if you're driving?" Jaxon moved as far as she could from the assistant's desk, but the cord only let her go so far.

"Why, Dr. Lavigne, you sound a little jealous, and if you saw the way some of the frat boys are looking at me right this second, it might make the unflappable professor draw blood."

Jaxon had to take a breath and close her eyes. If she had to admit it, she was the jealous type for the first time in her life, but there was also the factor that she hated how some guys objectified Margot. According to Margot, that was solely Jaxon's job, and that kind of objectification Margot didn't mind. "Where are you?"

"Outside waiting for you." Margot blew her horn again, and that couldn't be good if she was sitting still.

One of her colleagues stepped out of the conference room, holding her bag. "Don't get out of the car." She shouldered her bag and scribbled a note for Ian, giving him her apologies for skipping out a few minutes early. The last thing she heard before hanging up was Margot's chuckle.

Margot was smiling and sitting on the hood of her car when she made it outside. There were some guys standing close by, trying to engage Margot in conversation, but Margot wasn't looking at them. She waved when she saw Jax but didn't move from her spot. Jaxon took the steps as fast as she could without falling on her head.

"Sorry about the interruption, baby, but if I had to wait for some of those guys to stop talking, we'd be late for dinner. You know how my father is about promptness." Margot reached for her hand and pulled on her fingers. "Would it help if I told you I brought my favorite teacher an apple?" The Gala apple in Margot's other hand was the only kind Jaxon ate.

That she wasn't a big fan of fruits or vegetables was a constant war between them, and Margot won more battles than she lost on that front. Truthfully, any front. It wasn't that she was spineless but giving into Margot was a lot more fun than trying to prove a point. Her reward system was truly inspiring. "If I'm spending the evening in the company of your father, you should have brought me a big bottle of apple-flavored vodka." The statement would have sounded like a reprimand had it not been for her smile. "And Ian's assistant is eventually going to come out here and kick your butt. How many times did you call this time, really?"

"Only three, and I think she doesn't like me because I don't want my character to date Britt's on the show. She looks like the type who'd be a fan of the tabloids and of my asshole costar. For once, on this subject anyway, the assholes got it right. I'd rather join a convent than date Britt." Margot slid off the car and blew her a kiss while pointing to the passenger side. With all the cameras around they tried not to add to the pocketbook of every opportunist in the crowd, but Jaxon opened Margot's door for her. "And does it help to know that Wilber's daughter loves you more than anyone else on earth?" Margot blew her another kiss and backed out. All the guys standing close by waved as she glanced in their direction, and Margot waved back.

Jaxon kissed her once they were down the block, and Margot pulled over so she could get a proper greeting. "It's the most important thing, my love, and I missed you today." They kissed again, and Margot pulled the hair at the back of her head. "You do realize, though, if we ever have children, we're not naming any of them Wilber, right? I don't care how much you love your daddy."

Wilber Walker Drake was a Green Beret who had few loves in his life. The first of his passions was his family—his wife of twenty-seven years, Patty Sue, and their only child, Margot. The second was a profound love for the country he had served and fought for. The same country he had stopped understanding when he returned from the Iraq war as a battle-weary soldier.

Jaxon hadn't understood the reasoning for the war in Iraq either but was proud of Wilber's service. It was the one thing she'd learned from her father. You served because you wanted to, not because anyone forced you. No one made a career out of the military unless it was something they believed in and cared deeply for. It was her job as a civilian to thank and be grateful for all those who stood on the wall so she could sleep safely at night.

After her first dinner invitation to the Drake house because Margot wanted her to meet her parents, she'd become aware of a few obstacles she'd have to find a way over. Going around them would be admitting defeat, and that wouldn't go over well with Wilber. Only cowards took shortcuts. No, the man was like the apocalypse, and she had to find a way to survive him.

If there was a Drake rule book, Jaxon had broken quite a few of them, and eventually the punishment would be swift and painful. She called him Willy Walker, irritating him massively, and he'd made his feelings clear when they'd been together for over a year and she still hadn't offered Margot the future she deserved. The no-commitment topic had come up more than once, and the more often she didn't say what he wanted, the less he liked her. Taking advantage of his little girl was not on Wilber's list of acceptable behavior, and there'd be a stiff penalty if she fucked up.

"Oh, we'll be having children, Doc. You're not getting out of that, but I promise—no more little Wilbers." Margot tapped her finger against the tip of her nose and put the car back in gear.

They talked about their days and Margot's unexpected time off. If anything, Margot's job usually cut into the free time she was entitled to. For the time being, Jaxon kept silent on the subject of her reunion, knowing Margot would move the world to go, given how curious she was about Jaxon's past. There was no way Margot *wouldn't* side with Bert, and Margot's pout was much more difficult to say no to than Bert's. Margot's begging expression usually appeared when she was naked, and that alone was enough to turn her brain to mush.

Margot's purse started ringing when they were about five blocks from their destination, so she squeezed Jaxon's thigh. "Could you answer that for me, sweetie?"

Jaxon reached into the leather bag and answered the cell without looking to see who it was first. "Margot Drake's phone, can I help you?" She made Margot laugh and then sighed when she heard the gruff voice.

"So, you're joining Margot, then?" Wilber asked like he did every single time they came over for dinner, which was sometimes twice a week. He always acted surprised that she was in his house, sitting at his table. "I can't wait to see *her*."

"Yes, sir, I'm looking forward to dinner and spending time with Margot myself." She shot Margot a dirty look when a mirthful snort slipped out.

"Have you passed the grocery store close to us?" There was some kind of scraping noise from his end, and her first guess centered on him sharpening his bayonet. The day would come when he'd snap and drive it through her heart, then claim she'd made him insane. When he sat on the witness stand in his uniform with all the medals, like Jack Nicholson in *A Few Good Men*, no jury of his peers would find him guilty.

"No, sir, we're two blocks from there."

"Good…good. Stop and buy two gallons of milk, and when I say that, Jaxon, I mean *you* go in and buy it." Wilber always made her name sound like it should translate to *you fucking asshole who's touching my daughter and I don't like it*. "Think you can handle that, Jaxon? You're not going to forget, are you?"

"No, sir, I don't mind doing that at all. Is that all you need?" She glanced at Margot, wondering how she'd turned out so normal.

"Two gallons, that's what you're going for."

"Yes, sir, two of them, got it."

"What's up?" Margot squeezed Jaxon's thigh again as if trying to ease any tension caused by whatever her father had requested.

"The general wants us to stop and pick up two gallons of milk before we come over." She tapped the phone against her chin, trying to convince herself this wasn't some elaborate booby trap. If she ended up in the emergency room later because of some milk-related injury, she was not going to be amused.

"Two gallons? That's a bit excessive, unless Mom's baking something." Margot pulled into the grocery lot and stopped by the main door so Jaxon could get out. Going into public places had become a problem for Margot recently, and it was best avoided.

Trips to run quick errands often turned into ordeals lasting a couple of hours because of overexuberant fans, most of whom didn't know how to take no as an acceptable answer to bizarre requests or comments that made Jaxon want to start hitting people. Just because you were on television every week didn't give anyone the right to ask if your breasts were real.

A group of teenagers were pointing toward Margot's car when Jaxon walked out loaded down with dairy products. "Perfect timing, sweetie. My manager lives in fear of the day I mow down my adoring public. Though, when it's kids that age, I do think I should stop and at least say hi as I roll over them."

"Calm down, prima donna, they're just pointing, and without them, you wouldn't have the most popular hair in the country."

"Put your seatbelt on, smart-ass, before your purchase goes sour." Margot stopped and took a few selfies with fans through the window, leaving a shrieking group behind. They laughed for the final blocks remaining, hoping there wouldn't be a crowd surrounding the house before dessert was served.

Wilber was waiting outside so he could come around and open Margot's door. He wrapped her up in a bear hug before Margot had the chance to get her right foot out of the car. Jaxon waited in the passenger seat, enjoying the last moments of peace before Invasion Drake began. Wilber's usual operating procedure was to divide and conquer. Margot was sent off to talk to her mother while she spent time with Wilber in his torture chamber study.

"Thanks for having us, Daddy." Margot's feet were now out of the car. "Jaxon, honey, don't you want to get out here and tell Daddy hello?"

"I'd rather take what's behind door number two, Monty," Jaxon mumbled to the dashboard. She was holding her two gallons of milk, and the coldness against her hands meant she was indeed awake, and this wasn't a nightmare.

"Jaxon, get out of the car now." Margot had gotten away from her father and sounded menacing as she stuck her head through the window. "Remember, you have to go home with me later. God only knows what'll happen to you once you fall asleep."

"Yes, dear." She winked and hefted the two jugs. "General Drake, sir, how are you?" Wilber looked at the hand she was holding out before shaking it.

"Hello, Jaxon. Did you stop and get what I asked for?" It was a redundant question since he was looking right at the milk.

"Yes, sir." Jaxon fought the urge to snap to attention and salute, remembering how Margot had made her sleep in the guestroom for two days the last time she'd caved to the temptation.

"Bring it into my study, and I'll be right in." He put his arm around Margot and kissed her temple.

"Wouldn't it be better off in the kitchen, in the refrigerator maybe?" Jaxon held up the bag to remind the crazy son of a bitch he'd asked them to stop for milk.

"Set them both on my desk, and I'll be right there as soon as I deliver Margot to her mother. Think you can remember all that?" Jaxon walked toward the front door before the voice in her head that told her to start hitchhiking took over. The voice had come as a coping mechanism after meeting Wilber, though it often gave really bad advice.

She felt Margot's arms slide around her waist from behind, and she pressed her cheek to her back. "You know I love you, right?"

Jaxon led them into the small bathroom off the foyer and locked them in. "I do know you love me, and your father loves you. That's a good thing, honey."

"If you want, I can intervene on your behalf and save you another trip into the inner sanctum." Margot sat on the counter and put her legs around Jaxon. Kissing like this in the Drake house was a bad idea, but Margot was hard to say no to. The woman had the best hair in America, after all.

"Me refusing to go in there is like throwing blood into a tank with the biggest great white known to man. Believe me, it's safer being in the water and making no sudden movements. Show no fear is my motto." She kissed Margot again then took three very large steps back when someone banged on the door.

"Jaxon, are you in there with Margot? I'd think you're old enough to know what to do in the bathroom by now." Wilber's voice could be used in promotional videos to make you stop whatever bad behavior you were looking to cut out of your life.

"Sorry, sir, we were discussing a scheduling problem. We're done."

"Just don't let him scar you mentally. I've got plans for you later."

"I'll try my best, but I'm not making any promises."

❖

Iris glanced down her list of reunion RSVPs she'd just received from Nancy. There was only one name she always searched for, and it was never a surprise when there was nothing next to it. Jaxon never sent a response either way. She'd left them all behind and built a life somewhere else, and that obviously didn't include any communication of any kind. And why should it?

There were certain things she realized as she got older, and the one thing at the top of her list was that regret never eased no matter the number of days from your initial mistake. Regrets were real, and they had a way of getting heavier to carry as the days passed. The memories were crueler now, not because of anything Jaxon had done, but because of her own stupidity. They'd met in high school, and she'd fallen for Jaxon the minute she saw her walking down the hall talking to a group of girls.

It was a new experience for her. Young women from south Louisiana did *not* fall for tall, handsome, butch women. That went against everything she'd been taught by her parents, priests, and friends. Gay people lived in sinful places like New Orleans or California. Small towns were supposedly full of righteous people with Christian morals.

All those upstanding people had never gotten a look at Jaxon with her easy smile and fluid stride. She rested her head against the window pane and let the memories wash over her.

It was the first day of high school.

"Who is that?" she asked Tori as they walked down the hall to put their books away for lunch. The campus was a definite change from the school they'd attended from kindergarten until the eighth grade. They now were in the next town, and the high school was a magnet school for the surrounding area. All of a sudden there were a lot of new people in their lives. It would be a different experience for the next four years.

"You don't recognize Jaxon Lavigne?" Tori asked. "She lives a few miles from us but went to Catholic school until now. She switched to public school to up her chances at a scholarship in either softball or track. At least, that's what my brother told me."

"I don't think we've ever met." Iris did, though, recognize some of the girls from the cheerleading squad, and they acted like they were old friends with Jaxon.

"We live closer than you do, and she's freaking tall enough to play pickup games with my brothers. Total lesbo, though."

"I don't think that's a nice way of putting that." She lost her smile as she glanced at Tori, but her friend's depiction didn't surprise her. Her family wasn't the most tolerant of anything, and Tori had learned that way of thinking from birth. "I was just wondering."

"Stay away from that, or people will start talking about you." Tori waved as she headed to her locker, and Iris did the same. When she started twirling the lock dial to open her locker, she noticed that Jaxon was only ten lockers down.

The long fingers made quick work of the lock, and Jaxon dropped off her books and took something else out. Iris knew she was staring, but she couldn't help it. Jaxon smiled at her and tapped what appeared to be a leather-bound journal against her thigh and shut the metal door. She was staring as well.

"Hi," Jaxon said.

"Hey." Her voice was slow and didn't sound like it usually did. "I'm Iris."

"Jaxon. I saw you in homeroom this morning, but you were talking to someone."

Homeroom was new as well, and they'd told her she'd spend fifteen minutes of her mornings with kids bunched together by the letters of their last name. It'd be roll call, the Pledge, and announcements. Those would be read by that senior year's council president and the principal. She'd been talking to Ron Lyons, who she'd known since they were two, and hadn't really looked around the room. The day had been nerve-racking enough, and it was nice to see a friend right off.

"Yeah, my friend Ron. Are you from Chackbay?" She wasn't used to talking to people she didn't know, which meant Jaxon was probably going to wave and walk off if she got any more boring.

"We're right on the border with Thibodaux, but yeah." Jaxon pointed behind her. "Want to have lunch with me? I'm going to the cafeteria, then to the library. It's okay if you want to take a pass."

"No, I want to." She was supposed to meet her best friend Nancy and some other people to eat outside, but they'd have to understand. "Did you bring lunch?" The bag her mom had packed her was in her hand, but she'd gladly throw it out if Jaxon had something else in mind.

"I was going to grab something." Jaxon waved her along to the cafeteria. "You can find us a seat and you can have whatever's in the bag."

Their lunch that day was way too short, and she'd followed Jaxon to the library and read as she watched Jaxon write in a journal she explained she'd been keeping from the time she was ten. It had been her plan to spend that one day with Jaxon, but lunch and then watching Jaxon write as they spoke about every subject that came to mind made her crave more.

It wasn't much later that she was in Jaxon's bedroom one weekend, and she realized what she hadn't wanted to face. While all her friends were going crazy over the guys who were walking the campus, she'd fallen for a girl. Jaxon made her feel good about herself, and she made her want things she definitely shouldn't want in small-town Louisiana. Falling in love had been so easy, and Jaxon had agreed to keep their secret. *It was the same secret she was still carrying.*

"Hey," she said, startled from her reminiscing when Nancy entered the school office.

"Hi, I wanted to come by and check to make sure you got the list I put together." Nancy leaned against the counter that separated the staff from visitors.

"Got it, and we should start talking food and drinks. Do you think we should charge more and get something other than a keg?" She'd swear, at every one of these things, most of the people who attended wanted to relive every high school experience. They were happy with a beer keg and hot dogs.

"Why do you think I bring my own wine? I came by because my kid forgot his PE clothes, but do you want to go for a drink later?" Nancy smiled, and Iris was glad she was still a part of her life. "I know Daniel is working late this week, and so is Ron. If you want, we can take the kids out to dinner, and then you can come over."

"They're at the age where they'd rather not be seen with me in public. I'm sure they'll be fine. Whenever I ask them if they'll be okay on their own, they jump at the chance. Let's make it just the two of us." She needed someone to talk to about what she was going through with Sean. The story had to be told, but she was trying to put it off as long as she could. Saying it all out loud would be gambling on losing something she wasn't prepared to part with.

"Great," Nancy said. "If I have to cook another thing this week, I'm going to scream. Besides, I figure it's about time we talk about whatever's going on in your head. The last meeting was enough to aggravate anyone, and Tori really laid it on thick when it came to Jaxon. It's not like you control her and can drag her back here."

"Good, I do need to talk to someone, and Sean wants me to tell her why all these people are talking about her behind her back. I'm not sure what the hell I'm going to say," she said in a whisper. "These stupid reunions stir all that back up again, and it's like parents forget their kids are listening to every damn bit of gossip they share, so the next month should be fun."

"The truth is always the best thing, but maybe in this case you should wait. She's still young and might not understand what you were thinking." Nancy reached out and took her hand. "You also need to decide what that truth is before you open your mouth. I love you no matter what, and I've known you forever, but even I don't understand."

"Not now, okay?" The sensation of being trapped made her want to tear her hair out and run. She wasn't ready for all these questions about her past. If she'd waited this long to unburden her soul, what was another sixteen years? By then Sean would probably be lost to her, and whatever she had to say wouldn't matter, but that might be for the best.

"Let's head to Thibodaux tonight. We'll find a place where no one knows us, and we can talk. No matter what, it's going to be okay."

She nodded. "Somehow I don't believe you."

"Honey, no matter what people say or what rumors they spread, Sean is your daughter. She's a teenager, and right now, like my kid, she hates the world simply because it's spinning. Buried deep under all that angst, she loves you. She loves you and is going to understand you because she's not that much younger than you were when you had her." Nancy kept her voice in a whisper and squeezed her hand. "You know I'm right, so lose the frown."

"Thanks. I hope on all that's holy you're right."

When she thought about it rationally, it was ridiculous. Jaxon had been gone for sixteen years and had probably forgotten about her the second the town was in her rearview. That made her an unknown, so truthfully it wasn't even about that anymore. It was about her and what was in her heart.

The only time in her life she'd been free to be who she truly was had been with Jaxon, and that made her want to cry from sadness. She'd settled, denied, and buried herself in marriage and children, hoping it'd be enough. It was fine, mostly, except for that one part that had shriveled and died a hundred times because she couldn't ever be honest—not even with herself.

CHAPTER FIVE

Jaxon sat in Wilber's study looking at the dark paneling, the numerous bookcases full of commendations, and the family photos. There was plenty to look at, and while she was alone, waiting for Wilber to join her, she indulged in her favorite hobby.

The objective of her game was to find something new and somewhat bizarre in the room and wonder about its history and if it was real. That question of what was real always came to mind as she briefly stared at the shrunken head hanging from one of the shelves. The exercise usually relaxed her for whatever surreal conversation Wilber wanted to engage in. It took total concentration to follow his train of thought that usually centered on Margot.

The first time she'd sat in the chair across from the big desk and waited, the most prominent wall hanging had kicked off her hobby. She'd gotten up to get a better look after not being able to take her eyes off it. The M16 camouflaged weapon mounted on the wall above Wilber's chair looked at first like all the other army issued rifles she'd seen in the movies. It was the little lines carved into the stock that had piqued her curiosity.

The sound of the door closing as she'd leaned in for a better look had scared the hell out of her, and Wilber had only added to the feeling. He'd taken great pleasure in telling her about his time in the military and some of the things he'd done in the years before he sat in the command center and gave orders. He'd cradled the gun like a baby as he talked and stared at her. It was like a warning about what she had in store if she hurt Margot in any way. Her life would come down to a little carved line on that gun.

In hindsight, Margot had been smart. Jaxon had completely fallen for her *before* she'd met Wilber. That she was in love had kept her from heading directly for the exit after her first private visit to his study. It was hard to miss his finger close to the trigger as he gave his running commentary.

"I wonder if anyone in my life knows someone who has killed that many people?" Jaxon spoke to the rifle before turning her attention back to the two gallons of milk sitting next to two empty glasses. The door clicking closed behind her made her wish, as the sound always did, for some memory of the prayers her Nana Lavigne had faithfully taught her as a small child.

"Jaxon, how are things?" Wilber's big hands came to rest on her shoulders, and he squeezed just a little tighter than was comfortable.

"Just fine, sir." She maintained eye contact as a way to gauge any change in Wilber that would require evasive maneuvers. "Thank you for having us."

"And school. How's school going?" Wilber moved to the leather chair with the army seal on the headrest and took a seat. He tore off the seal on one of the gallons and filled the two glasses almost to the rim.

"Just fine, sir, thank you for asking. The beginning of any semester is always an exciting time." *Doesn't he realize milk leaves that disgusting film on your tongue, or that I only like it as a chaser for brownies?* Jax carried on a separate conversation in her head while Wilber finished pouring and pushed one of the glasses toward her.

"I'm glad to hear it. Tell me, Jaxon, are there a lot of pretty girls taking your classes these days?" He raised his glass and waited for her to tap the other one against it.

"This is California, Mr. Drake—there isn't a shortage of pretty girls." The first sip went down smooth.

The milk, which was still ice cold, reminded Jaxon of the hundreds of school lunches she'd consumed in her life and that first long sip out of the tiny short straw after she fought to get the carton open. The only reason she drank it back then was to avoid the barrage of guilt the nuns piled on—*Think of the starving children in the world!*—if you didn't finish the small carton.

The other reason she drank it back then was so she could use the empty carton to hide the disgusting vegetable medley that made an appearance twice a week. Taking the time to shove the little chopped carrots, peas, green beans, and corn into the carton always beat getting the evil eye from the old woman who collected the trays and dishes at the end of all those meals. In Jaxon's opinion, claiming to have grown up in the Depression only gave you so much leeway to terrorize children with stories of starvation because they didn't want to eat the vegetable medley.

"Pretty girls seem to flock to you, Professor. You want to tell me why that is?" Wilber sat back and took another sip and stared at her until she did the same. "Take me, for example. I sent my little girl off to get an education, and she came home with you. Don't tell me—let me guess." He waved his hands at her. "It's the boots."

Jaxon moved to put her glass down, but Wilber gave her the same skunk eye the old lady in the lunchroom used to, so she took another sip. "Sir, I didn't take Margot anywhere until after she graduated. I don't want you to get the impression I'm in the habit of dating my students. I'd like to think I attract people in general because I'm a good teacher. If you make learning fun, you'll be rewarded with kids who are enthusiastic. I love Margot more than I love teaching and anything or anyone in my life, but that doesn't mean I don't love to teach."

"Well put, Jaxon." The conversation continued with the annoying habit he had of repeating her name over and over again as a form of intimidation. Either that or it was to aggravate her into running out the door, so he'd never have to see her again. "But if you love Margot so much, why don't I see a ring or hear about promises you've made?" He took another long drink from the glass, looking at Jaxon over the rim.

She drank with him until they drained the first glass. Jaxon didn't think he'd find any humor if she requested a healthy spiking of whiskey in the second glass he was pouring. He didn't seem to appreciate her smacking her lips together as she finished the glass.

"As trite as this may sound, sir, Margot knows how I feel about her."

"Jaxon, real men do not use the word *trite*, so unless you want me to get my gun down and add another notch, refrain from doing so." He never looked up as he concentrated on pouring the second glass so he didn't spill any on the leather-topped desk.

"Sir—"

"I know you're not a man, bookworm, but you're as close as I'm going to get to a son-in-law, so I suggest you sit there and listen to what

I've got to say." He handed her the glass before picking his up and pointing at it. "Did you go in and buy this milk?"

Folks, we apologize for any inconvenience, but we've left the main highway and veered off to Crazyville. Please sit back and enjoy your nice cold milk, so the guy with the large weapon won't go postal on you. Jaxon tried to keep up with their talk. Why she was in the midst of Willy Walker's company hadn't made itself clear just yet.

"Yes, sir, I went in for the milk."

"Did the people at the store give you all this for free?" He held up his glass again, appearing serious about the line of questions as he tapped on it.

"No, sir, they were about four dollars each."

He put the glass down so he could drum his fingers on the desk with enough force to splinter the wood and gave her a hard look. "So they weren't free is what you're saying?"

She let the corners of her mouth curl slightly, finally understanding the purpose of her trip to the woodshed, Wilber style. A full smile would earn her a warning shot over her head. Though, if Margot heard him, it'd be Wilber who'd be running for his life. "No, sir, I had to pay."

Wilber jumped up and pointed his index finger at her. "Precisely, so what makes you think my daughter's giving it away for free? This bull didn't bring offspring into this world to be left hanging in the wind when you're ready to move on."

He thumped his chest with his fist before turning an accusing finger on her. "My suggestion to you would be to make up your mind as far as Margot's concerned. If your decision is to leave her for some other young coed, I'll be busy carving another notch in that baby." He pointed his thumb over his shoulder, so there would be no misunderstanding.

"General Drake, sir, I can understand where you're coming from. I also realize you don't especially like me, but I do love Margot. I can only hope you know how special she is to me, and it won't take getting me to some sort of altar at gunpoint."

"I don't think I'll have to force you, bonehead. I just want us to be of the same mind. Now finish that glass and get out of here before my little girl thinks I'm cutting your ears off."

"Yes, sir." Without Margot looking on, she couldn't help but salute him before turning for the door.

❖

Nancy picked a place close to the campus of their local university and asked the hostess for a booth in the corner. Iris was glad to not recognize anyone. They ordered a bottle of wine and sat back. The day had been long, and all Iris really wanted to do, craved really, was to put her pajamas on and sleep.

"Okay, spill it." Nancy ran her finger along the top of the wineglass and sounded resolute. "You've been down since that committee meeting, and that means something's not right. Is it you and Daniel?"

"We're fine. You know what the next month is going to be like. Only this time there's no way to protect Sean from all the gossiping our neighbors like to do. She's old enough to understand." She took a big gulp of the wine, but that wasn't the answer. "Hell, I don't like listening to those idiots either. It's not like I don't think about what I did and never considered the long-term consequences."

"You've never told even me what happened, and I haven't pushed because I know you don't ever want to talk about it. All I can tell you is that I'm here for you, and I will be no matter what you tell me. You, though, need to cut yourself some slack. You were young, and no one is a genius when they're young." Nancy smiled at her and refilled their glasses. "You know I'm not going to spread gossip like some other people we know."

"What I can admit is that I miss her. I thought it would've gotten better by now, but it hasn't. That might disgust you, but Jaxon is hard to forget."

Nancy laughed and Iris joined in. "I've never been interested in anything like that, but I could see what attracted you. She was such a...I can't think of a good word." They laughed some more. "I know a lot of people talked behind your back, but all I saw was that she made you happy."

"I was, and then I stupidly threw it all away." She took another sip of her wine and closed her eyes, trying not to face Nancy or the truth.

"Hey, she left. How can that be your fault?"

Iris wiped her face, surprised she was finally crying, something she'd rarely allowed herself to do over the years. "She asked me to go.

I could've gone to LSU with her, but I decided I didn't want to leave my family. Once Jaxon left, I knew she wouldn't be back. That part I was right about. There was nothing here for her, but I had some fantasy that she'd change her mind and come back because I was important to her. I was a moron for thinking that." She wiped again, hoping her mascara wasn't smearing across her face. "Besides, I was pregnant by then."

"She asked you to go?" Nancy seemed totally sympathetic. "Why didn't you?"

"Because I was scared. You know what people were already saying. I was terrified my family would turn their backs on me, and then there'd really be no coming back." She clenched her hands into fists and shook her head. "I never wanted to think about it, but a part of me always thought I wasn't enough for her. It was like I was the only girl back then who was willing..."

Nancy smiled at her and shook her head. "To sleep with her. Is that what you were going to say? I'm not that sheltered, my friend."

"Yes, I was very willing, but once we went somewhere else, there'd be more willing partners, and she'd leave me behind."

"I wish you'd told me this a million years ago. Jaxon was someone I thought had loyalty, and she cared about you." Nancy took her hand. "I doubt if she'd made you a promise, she would've broken it, even if you were just teenagers."

She nodded. "That's true, but would you want someone who only cares about you? I wanted someone wild about me, because that's how I felt."

"That's just it, sweetie. Jaxon *was* wild about you, and she hid that because you were terrified. She loved you. I'd bet anything on that."

"Thank you for not judging me," she said and smiled. "I was young and dumb. There might be something to what I believed, though, since she never called or tried to get in touch. The fact that she's now living with Margot Drake means she's changed dramatically from that rosy picture in my head, and there's no going back. How does anyone compete with that?"

"Give Jaxon a break. It's been years, and you're married with two children. Daniel can't be all bad."

"He isn't, and I complain about him, but I love him. Not as much when he's being an ass about things, but he's good with Sean and Danny, and he tries."

"You can't ask for more than that."

She could and often did, but her life wasn't horrible. It was just... basic. "No, and thanks for talking to me."

"It might take more of these dinners for you to tell me everything, but I'm here for you. Now that we have teenagers, we have to stick together."

"You're a good friend, and you're right. I have a feeling we'll be talking about Sean and Adeline for years to come for a whole bunch of reasons."

"They're cute together, and I hope that doesn't freak you out."

Nancy shook her head. "I couldn't give a shit what people think. All I want is for my kid to be happy."

If only life could be that easy and someone like Nancy could've been her mother. That was the thing about what-ifs, though—if they were quarters, she could power every machine in a Laundromat for a hundred years. Her chance at passion had passed, but damn if she was letting Sean's chance slip away from her even if it didn't work out. Her daughter at least deserved the chance.

CHAPTER SIX

G et in here, girl, and leave them to their talk." Margot's mother pointed to the stool at the island in the center of the kitchen. "What are you so worried about anyway?"

"I know you're married to him, but you have to see that Daddy's a little"—she put her hands up as if trying to find the right words—"intense, when he wants to be."

The mixer came on, and when her mother started pouring ingredients into the bowl, it stopped their conversation for a moment. "Sweetie, don't take this in a way that'll make you believe that I think your father's insane. I try real hard not to think about his intensity and why it exists. The world's a much happier place if you try not to dwell on that." Her mother ran a scraper along the side of the bowl.

"So, you don't think he's crazy?" Margot stared at her mother, trying to figure out if she was hiding something, and if she needed to run and save Jax from some life-altering visit.

"I could lie and say it's a law of the hills to think ill of your spouse in that way, but the truth of it is, your daddy's a wee bit of a wing nut." The blender came back on but only for a minute.

"So you *do* think he's crazy." She moved to stand up but didn't make it to her feet when her mother waved her back down.

"I didn't say that, and don't be putting words in my mouth. I've got enough with keeping up with what I come up with on my own." She tapped the side of her head and laughed.

"So you *don't* think he's crazy?" Margot scrunched her brows together in confusion. Hopefully Jaxon was having a better time of it.

Her mother paused to flour a couple of pans and turn on the oven.

"Oh no, he's crazier than a flock of loons in heat, but that ain't all bad. In fact, it can be downright useful at times."

"Useful in what way? Assuring that I'll have no love life at all?" Great, now she felt bad for pushing Jax into humoring her father.

"That's more of an unfortunate side effect. I was talking more along the lines that it's been years since one of those religious-type people pushing fire and damnation, or a Girl Scout peddling Thin Mints has darkened our door." They both had to laugh at that. No one ever wanted to interrupt her father in the middle of something he thought important by ringing the bell. If someone was peddling a religion he thought was crazy, they'd pray there really was a benevolent God waiting with open arms when he went for the assault rifle.

Margot accepted the empty bowl from her mother and ran her finger through the remnants of batter as her mom put the cake pans into the oven. "He won't hurt her, will he?" She turned back to the door and strained to hear something.

"Who, Jaxon?" Her mom set a timer shaped like a hand grenade her father had bought her on one of his many trips to the army surplus store. Instead of dinging, it made little explosion sounds. "The thing you should realize is if Wilber didn't know how important Jaxon is to you, she'd be sitting in here with us swapping recipes." Her mom pointed in the direction of the study. "But she's not. She's in there, so your father can bend her into someone worthy of his little girl. It's a duty he takes as seriously as he did his commission."

"As cute as that sounds in concept, I am more than capable and old enough to make my own decisions."

"In General Wilber Walker Drake's world, you'll always be that cute little five-year-old we sent off to kindergarten with her cute little Barbie lunch box, equally cute little pink backpack, and pigtails so that kid could pull your hair."

"Mom, I'm sure that girl is still in therapy over what happened with my pigtails. Though it was somewhat comforting to see the big bully scream and run out of the room whenever she saw anything remotely resembling a knife. But then again, the radical haircut Daddy gave her that morning with his chilling running commentary will do that to a person. How you two didn't get arrested is the true mystery."

"Your father's talent for persuasion is extraordinary. I gave him my underwear on our second date."

"Oh no." She put her fingers in her ears and closed her eyes. "Lalala."

"Oh, come on. The stork didn't deliver you in a cute pink blanket. Your father was sexy as hell in that uniform, and he made me hot." Her mother affectionately patted her hand before moving to fix them both a drink. "Is that what you're afraid of? That he'll hang a good chunk of Jaxon's hair on the wall with the rest of his trophies?"

She nodded and put her hands over her face. Thoughts of her parents having sex were warring with what was happening behind the closed oak door. "My biggest worry is Daddy will give her some sort of posttraumatic stress that'll cause her to react like I'm a big pile of hot coals when we're alone."

"Well, honey, I kinda hope she thinks you're hot." Her mother fanned herself. "I mean, if she doesn't, we need to be having a whole different conversation. Perhaps I could give you some pointers on where to buy lingerie."

"Oh my God. You don't have to be so understanding all the time, you know."

"Hell, I don't want Ellen DeGeneres's mom to get all the good press, but enough of that. What's new with the two of you? I'm guessing Jaxon should be enjoying the semester by now. You two have any plans?" Her mother gave Margot her full attention after she checked everything.

"We have another month to go before the breathy messages from coeds on the machine in her home office start." The baby carrot she'd picked from the salad bowl snapped in half at the confession. If she could get away with it, she'd put a No Trespassing sign around Jaxon's neck.

"Let's say a quick prayer she doesn't tell your father that while they're in the inner sanctum. It'd thrill him to be able to get in some sleeper hold practice, but I don't think Jaxon would appreciate the headache when she came to."

"Would it have killed you to fall in love with an accountant?"

"I could ask you the same thing. Now stop trying to change the subject. Breathy calls—what else?" Her mom snapped her fingers then twirled them. "You know you'll feel better once you tell me."

"It's the same every semester. She just makes a list, so Viola can tell them no free rides and to do their homework. It's the same message

I got from her when it was me calling." After playing with it for a few minutes, she finally put one of the carrot pieces in her mouth. Truth serum–infused carrots wouldn't have surprised her.

"If we're honest with ourselves, it was more like stalking," her mom said in a singsong voice that made Margot throw a dish towel at her. "But I'm your mother, and looking past your shortcomings is part of my job." Her mom poured ingredients into a shaker and laughed.

Margot rolled her eyes before taking a large drink from the glass her mother had given her. "Explain to me again why I like coming back here so much?"

"Lemon cake with cream cheese icing."

"Aside from that?"

"You're conditioned to react to the sound of my voice. It's rather Pavlovian, but I had to entertain myself somehow while waiting for your father to get home from the base." When Margot gave her a bored look, her mother laughed again and started fixing another batch of drinks. "Let me try another change of subject. How old is Jaxon now?"

"She's thirty-three. She graduated early from everything, so she's younger than you'd think." She smiled at how proud of Jaxon she was. After some of the people she had to deal with in the business, Jaxon was brilliant and real.

"Maybe we're going about this the wrong way." Her mother was talking more to the vodka bottle than to Margot.

The confusion of following any conversation with her mother came back at that statement. "I know I shouldn't ask, but what are you talking about?"

"We're not, any of us"—her mother made a circle with her finger as if to include everyone in the house—"getting any younger. I want to have grandchildren before it takes a bottle of 5-hour Energy to get me out of a chair, so we gotta get that girl moving in the right direction."

With her finger in the air Margot started shaking her head. "No, no, no!" She raised her hand in her mother's direction. "I know Jaxon better than anyone, and she does not react well to intimidation or pressure. I want her to make a commitment to me, but not while staring down the barrel of Daddy's assault rifle. Tell me this isn't what these dinners have been about the last couple of months. And if you decide to lie and tell me no, then promise me you won't continue to try your version of persuasion. I want kids, but waiting a few years isn't going to kill us."

"I promise a few things. One, there's always going to be lemon cake when you come over, and two, that your father's always going to be intense. If you're asking that the two of us stop ganging up on the world to make our little girl happy—no can do, baby. Besides, if she loves you like I know she does, Jaxon's going to grin and bear it like a champ because she knows Willy Walker's got your best interest at heart." She shook her finger back at Margot. "Didn't think I'd heard that little nickname, did you?"

"And if the sleeper hold comes into play?"

"Then there'll be some serious issues clouding your sexual horizon, but the silver lining will be that she won't be lying when she tells you, *Not tonight, dear, I have a horrible headache.*" Her mother laughed and refreshed their drinks.

"You two are as odd as they come, but I doubt I'd be as artistic as I turned out had you been an accountant and your average Girl Scout leader."

Her mother threw both her hands up and shook her head. "You're never going to forget that little incident, are you? It's time to let it go, pumpkin."

"Mom, I love you both, but you also gave me more than my share of memories growing up. The trip to the Grand Canyon with my troop is one I don't think I'll ever forget. Though it's one of Jaxon's favorites from my collection of childhood stories." She'd never seen Jaxon cry from laughing so hard as the night she'd shared that gem.

"Talk to me after you take a pack of prepubescent girls rafting down the Colorado for seven days without being able to pack a healthy supply of vodka." Her mother shivered as if the memory was too much for her.

Margot started laughing when her mom put another splash of vodka in the shaker. "That part was all right, with the exception of when you fell out of the boat."

"Come on, honey, that was my last pair of dry underwear." That made her mom pour just a little more liquor before adding the cranberry and orange juice.

"And the hike back up to the top? It's a shame there isn't a badge for cursing. We would've all gotten that one, no problem."

"Hey, no one told me when I volunteered I'd have to hike down there, carrying three times my weight in gear, ride a raft that smelled like someone died in it, then walk back to the top. And is it my fault every tourist on that trail wanted to have their picture taken by me to prove they could get their fat asses down there?" Her mom's hands rose along with her voice. They'd had to sell a hell of a lot of cookies to get to go on that trip. Once they were on the river, all the adults who'd come along looked as miserable as her mother.

"I'll give you that one."

"It was an awful lot to ask of a woman with damp drawers and no nerves left. The amazing thing, really, and what you should be asking yourself, is why a large number of those mules don't contemplate jumping into the canyon to end it all. After taking a look at that guy with the *Sex Machine* ball cap—in his dreams, by the way—I would've given it more than a little thought if put in BoBo's position." Her mom came around the island and sat next to her so she could put her arm around her.

Margot had to stop and wipe her eyes she was laughing so hard. "Who's BoBo?"

"The poor animal struggling to keep his four hooves on the steep incline while lugging the incredible beer gut Mr. Sex Machine was sporting. I swear I heard a pained *help me* as we strolled by."

She walked to the door again and looked down the hall as she continued to laugh. "Thanks for trying to keep my mind off whatever's going on in there, Mom, but what do you think is taking them so long?"

"Sit back down, Margot. I'm sure they're fine. There haven't been any gunshots, right?"

"No gunshots is your threshold of everything being all right? With expectations like that, it's no wonder life never gets you down." The kitchen was starting to smell great with the baking cake, and she inhaled deeply. "And I'm not letting our kids come over here alone. God only knows what you'd teach them."

"We know where you live, so that's a no-go. Grandkids are what me and your father have been waiting for, and when you have them, you might have to add on to the house. We may never go home once they arrive."

Hearing the door of the study open, Margot glanced over to see if Jaxon needed any help. "She looks like she remained conscious the whole time," she said in a whisper to her mom, who was glued to her back. "What the hell is happening to me if that's *my* threshold for success?"

Jaxon closed the door behind her and smacked her lips together a bunch of times for some strange reason. Hopefully her father hadn't challenged her to some hot-chili eating contest or something equally stupid. She smiled when she saw Margot heading her way and put her two gallon milk containers down to take her hand. One was half empty for some reason.

"Are you okay?" She ran her hands down Jax's chest and arms. "Do you need to lie down?"

"Keeping watch, huh?" Jaxon glanced back before kissing her. "I'm fine, and the rifle actually stayed on the wall for this little tête-à-tête," she said softly. "This time he only shoved bamboo under my fingernails." The way Jaxon laughed meant everything was fine. "Stop worrying. Your father just wanted to go over a few things with me."

She lifted Jax's hands to make sure she really was kidding. "You can't ask me not to worry. I fell in love with the whole package, and I'm vested in keeping it whole. So yes, I'm going to always look out for and worry about you. Are you sure everything's okay, honey?"

Jaxon led her back into the small bathroom and put her arms around her. "Your father's perfectly fine. He just has a way of making me take a look at life from an angle I hadn't thought of. This usually means me hanging by my toenails with my head cocked funny, but that's not all bad."

Margot smiled and put her fingers into Jaxon's belt loops. "Doc, you know my parents love me and just want the best for me, right?"

Jaxon nodded. "I do know that, and I'd have stayed home if this wasn't important to you. I also want the best for you if you're worried about that."

"Well, my parents know you're what's best for me. Dad will come around if we give him time. It'll just mean more opportunities for you to sit and talk to him." Margot came closer when Jax put her hands on her butt. "I love you for doing that, but I want you to tell me if he makes you uncomfortable. I want him to love you, but it won't hurt to keep you in one piece until Daddy comes to the same conclusion I did."

"What conclusion is that?"

"That you're the cutest thing alive, and you're all mine."

"Are you kidding? You don't think your father knows that already? Wilber's crazy about me. We took so long in there because he was trying to find the words to express his feelings for me, and the happiness bubbles inside him that I'm here."

"Uh-huh, are you sure everything's all right?"

"I'm from the South, sweetheart—eccentric people are as common as surfers are here. Everything's great, and to prove it to you, let's go talk to your mom and round out my Drake experience for today."

"She was asking about you." She stood on her tiptoes and kissed quickly.

"Is she making cake?"

"Are there happy cows in California? Of course she's making cake. That way I can look pregnant for the next episode, and the viewers can fantasize I'm having Britt's baby."

"I can help you out and lick that icing off you later. If I try that in this house, your father will chase me out of here with the shotgun I'm sure he has hidden in that study somewhere."

Margot laughed before kissing Jax with enough passion to hopefully clear her mind of whatever her father had put in her head. "I'll make sure Mom packs us a big piece to take home if you're promising things like that."

They sat and watched her mom bending down to check on it. Jaxon took a sip of her drink and coughed. She shrugged and kissed Jax again. After the alcohol and cake, she'd be sleeping all the way home.

"Hey, good looking, what you got for me?" Her mom gave Jaxon her usual warm reception but seemed confused when Jaxon put up her finger and walked away. She came back with the milk she'd purchased.

"Just a little something to go with the lemon cake I'm sure is in the oven." Jaxon kissed her mom's cheek and gave her a big hug.

"I'm not that predictable, am I?"

"Predictable is not a word that can be used to label anyone in the Drake family. That's so true that I sometimes regret wasting all that time learning Shakespeare and the like, and not getting a doctorate in psychology instead. Armed with some training in behavioral sciences, I'm sure I'd be so much more up to speed on these family traditions." Jaxon kissed her mother's cheek and hugged her again.

"Being such a smart-ass will take you far in this family, Professor."

She swatted Jaxon on the shoulder before going back to her room temperature blocks of cream cheese.

"Did you finish your homework?" Jaxon asked. She sat and put her arms around Margot's waist when she moved in front of her and leaned back. She handed her glass over so Jaxon could take another sip of her drink.

Margot turned and pinched Jax's cheek. "What homework? Are you holding out on me, Lavigne?"

"You know me, spreading learning wherever I go."

"You're spreading something all right, if you think that book you made me read is a classic," her mom said as she slapped Jaxon's hand when she broke off a piece of her cream cheese and popped it into her mouth.

"*Lord of the Flies* is a classic. It's a superbly written piece that displayed what could happen in a group dynamic. I thought it was a good depiction of how far people are willing to go in an environment that holds no promise of punishment because you make up the rules as you go along."

Margot smiled at how Jaxon's whole demeanor changed when she talked about books. The only other times she was this passionate couldn't be talked about in public, much less to her mother. Not that her mother wouldn't love hearing about their love life, but there were certain things your parents didn't need to know.

Her mom said, "I grew up with a mother who could put fear into the devil himself, whether he was in Knoxville or on some desert island. Had Dolores Johnson written that book, on the last page she'd have been on the dock with a switch in her hand, waiting to show that pack of hoodlums the error of their ways." She flipped her pans onto cooling racks and stared Jaxon down when she went for another piece of cream cheese. Jaxon retreated, empty-handed.

"Granny was pretty scary when she wanted to be." Margot shivered at the thought of some of the times she'd spent with Granny Dolores.

"She hit you with a stick?" Jaxon asked, embracing Margot from behind. Margot placed her hands over Jaxon's where they lay on Margot's abdomen. She pressed down when her father walked in, and Jaxon went to move away.

"Didn't have to. She had a look that just screamed sit down, shut up, and stop whatever the hell you're doing right now. I never wanted to see what the next level was. Even I wasn't that brave." Her mom dropped the cubes of cheese in the mixer with some sugar and lemon juice. "Not even Wilber messed with my mother, and he has plenty of medals for valor and bravery."

"Dolores was no joke," her father agreed.

Her mom started the blender again, and her father spent the time staring at Jaxon and where her hands were.

"Daddy, are you and Mom free this weekend? We were thinking of going somewhere and thought you might want to come." She ignored Jaxon's pinch to her stomach.

"I'm sure Jaxon would love that," he said. He narrowed his eyes.

Margot kicked Jaxon on the shin, and she took it as a sign to start talking. "No, sir. We thought a trip to Big Sur so we could do some hiking would be nice."

"Do you like to hike?" Her father stopped making a face when her mom whacked his butt with a spoon.

"I do, and Margot loves it, so that's good enough for me. There's a nice resort that you'll like, Patty Sue," Jaxon said, knowing Margot's mother wasn't a fan of hiking. "I hear their wine selection is supposed to be fantastic."

"I'm sold, and as a peace offering I'll be happy to take one small hike," her mom said as she stirred all the pots on the stove. "And if you're lying about the wine, I'll have Wilber find a snake and put it in your room."

Jaxon winked at Margot. "How you turned out so normal would make a great mystery novel."

"I heard that," her mother said over the mixer that was now whipping up icing. "Now make yourself useful and set the table. That'll give you a chance to talk about how crazy we are."

"Just remember that it's a good defense in court should something tragic happen to you, and I'm somehow blamed," her father said as he put his arm around her mom. "Not that anything tragic will happen to you." His words didn't match his expression.

"Yes, sir," Jaxon said, smiling.

Margot doubted her father would ever stop teasing Jaxon, but it was good that her lover took it in stride and was able to joke about the possibility of death. "Let's go, baby, and you two stay in here."

"Jaxon, don't think of fooling around in my house," her father said. "Keep your hands to yourself."

"Yes, sir." Jaxon's arm flexed, and Margot stared back at her in warning. "We're just setting the table. Fooling around is not on the menu."

"Speak for yourself," Margot whispered in her ear.

"Talking about how crazy we are isn't on the menu either," her mother said, holding her spoon like a sword.

"Setting the table won't give us enough time to delve into the first layer of that conversation," Jaxon said, and her mother laughed.

"Ain't that the truth, but you have five minutes before the squirrels in the pot will be done." Her mom pointed behind her to the stove, teasing about her Tennessee upbringing.

"I promise we'll figure out where all the forks go before you're finished." The gift of finding Margot was not only her beautiful soul, but her family. There was common ground between them since they were from the South as well, but they hadn't treated their daughter as a means of social climbing. They'd loved and nurtured her into the gorgeous woman Margot was in more than just her looks. That they'd accepted Jaxon gave her back a sliver of what she'd missed for so long. It was more than she thought she'd ever have.

❖

"Have you missed me?" Daniel Gravois asked when he came in and dropped his cap on the table. Iris had talked to him about that for years, but it was a habit he obviously didn't want to break.

He'd been working nights for two weeks, which meant he slept most of the day, and if she was honest, she didn't mind since it kept them from talking about the reunion. Admitting that to him was a sure way to get into another argument, and she wasn't in the mood. The kids were still upstairs getting ready for school, so she nodded and poured him a cup of coffee.

"Are you going to be on the night shift much longer?" She sat across from him and made an effort to smile. It wasn't him per se that accounted for her mood as much as it was how tired she was.

"One more week and it's back to my regular hours. After all the years I've put in, the sheriff should've picked someone else to cover for

Jones. If the idiot knew how to drive, he wouldn't have needed to take all this time off to recover from an accident." If Daniel had one talent left, it was complaining.

"I thought he was sitting on the side of the road watching for speeders." She tried to remember the details, but she was pretty sure the deputy had been parked, and someone had slammed into him.

"He was, but parking on that curve was asking for trouble. He's going to be out another month, but someone else is taking over for him." Daniel leaned forward and slid his hand along the table and turned it palm side up.

She put her hand in his and thought about the years they'd spent together. Overall, Daniel wasn't a bad person, but he wasn't the grand love affair she'd wanted in her life. Leaving him wasn't something she'd ever thought about, though, since he was a good husband and father. They'd had their troubles, but nothing that rose to divorce. That act of freedom would really get the rumors going, and he'd be the martyr in that scenario. She'd have nowhere to turn.

"Maybe this weekend we can go out to eat before I have to report for duty," he said.

"I'd love to," she said, liking that he was trying. "They opened a new Mexican place close to the post office."

"That sounds good. What have you been up to every night? I drove by last night, and your car was gone."

"I had dinner with Nancy while the kids were out with friends. We got roped into the reunion committee again. Make sure the sheriff gives you the night off." She got up to finish making breakfast. "Think that guy in dispatch would mind being our DJ for the night? There's no way we can afford a band."

"It's that time already?" Daniel didn't sound thrilled with the news.

Reunions had a way of reminding people of all the things that could've been, and all the things that had never become a reality. All those dreams and aspirations you had when you finished school served as a reminder that you weren't the success you thought you'd be. In Daniel's case, it was a reminder of his time on the field and being adored by everyone on campus. Now he was just a small-town cop among other small-town cops.

"Honey, I put it on your calendar. Maybe you should plan

something with all the guys before that night. I'm sure they'd love to get together." She put a plate of eggs in front of him, and he nodded as he flipped through the mail.

"What's this?" He held it up like it was some obscene thing their daughter had ordered.

The letter was for Sean, and Iris had forgotten to take it out of the stack and put it on Sean's desk. Because Sean's birthday fell after the registration cutoff, the school hadn't let her start until she turned six. Their daughter was gifted, though, and had skipped ahead a year, so she was now a junior, planning for college. Part of that plan was to go somewhere that was miles away from here.

"It's only her junior year, but the guidance counselor told her to start applying. The sooner she starts, the easier it is to figure out what scholarships she can qualify for." She stacked toast on a plate and put it in the center of the table.

"California? There are perfectly good schools here." He kept staring at the envelope like he needed to attack it. "Is this your idea? Don't I get a say?"

"Daniel, I'm trying to talk her into staying at least a year. She won't be quite seventeen when she graduates, and that's too young to be on your own, but I don't want to hold her back, either. She has a right to chase her dreams." She softened her voice, hoping he'd calm down.

"At that age we *can* force her to stay here." He tossed the letter away from him and scowled. "And California is out."

"Then I'll take out a loan and go. I'm not staying here," Sean said, coming in from outside.

"Where were you?" Iris glanced from the stairs to the door.

"I went for a walk around the block and tried to clear my head for my test today. I also don't want to fight about this for the next two years. There's no way I'm staying." Sean strung together more words than Iris had heard her say in months.

"I'm your father, and I don't want to fight about it either, but I'd also like to be involved in what you decide." Daniel's voice rose enough that Sean left the room. He stared at the door and then at her. "What?"

"Nothing, but you might want to start listening to her. Sean's having a hard time lately, and I've been trying to reach her. I've accepted that she'll tell me what's going on in her own time. Pushing her and demanding things of her isn't the way to go."

"I can't have an opinion in my own house?"

Danny came down the stairs like he was dragging bowling balls behind him and slapped hands with Daniel before kissing her cheek. "Hey, Dad, you're home early."

"I wanted to see you guys," Daniel said, his eyes still on her.

"To answer your question, yes, you can. Don't be shocked, though, that people are old enough to have their own opinions as well." She took her coffee cup and headed back to their room. The fact that Sean wanted out of here bothered her as well, but she was trying her best.

The main thing, baby, is not to be afraid, she thought, staring down at Sean sitting on the rope swing in the front yard. Sean deserved to have the life she wanted and never look back. She heard Daniel come in and step up behind her, staring out at Sean as well.

"What's her problem lately? She hardly says anything, and when she does, she sounds like one of the punks I have to deal with on the job. Is she into something I should know about?"

"Sean's a good kid, and she'll be fine. We gave her a good foundation, and she knows we'll both be there for her. Call it growing pains."

"Why does she want to leave so bad?" Daniel was three years older than her, but at times his immaturity reminded her of a six-year-old.

"Because of the mistakes of her mother. It's got nothing to do with you."

CHAPTER SEVEN

Jaxon didn't glance behind her, not wanting to give up her advantage as she raced down the trail. Wilber wasn't that far behind her and wasn't even breathing hard, which was aggravating. She was sweating as she ran down the incline to the beach, glad to see there weren't that many people out this early in the morning.

They'd decided on Half Moon Bay and had flown instead of taking the nine-hour drive down so they could enjoy all the time Margot had off. The Ritz-Carlton right on the coast was nice, and even Wilber had thanked her for making all the arrangements. They hadn't done a lot of hiking, but every morning Wilber challenged her to a race where the loser had to buy breakfast.

She was in good shape, but Wilber defied age in the way he could push himself. Their finish line was coming up, and she dug deeper to make it across before him. Once he lost, he rested his hands on his knees and whipped his head to clear the sweat from his eyes. She was walking in a circle trying to keep her muscles loose and plucked her soaked shirt away from her skin.

"You're getting soft, Professor." Wilber straightened out and kicked his shoes off. They were over a mile away from the resort, but the walk along the beach was nice. "You should've beat me by a mile."

"Maybe I was trying to make you feel better about yourself."

"Fuck that. Remember, not everyone gets a trophy, and the sooner you learn that, the happier you'll be." He started for the water and stopped when a wave came in and made his feet sink in the sand. "Now that you've done your sweating for the day, tell me what the hell is wrong with you?"

"Sir?" She stood next to him, enjoying the shock of cold that raced over her feet. "Wrong with me?"

"When my wife spends most of the night wondering what's on your mind because my little girl talked to her, it upsets me." He put his hand on her shoulder and squeezed hard enough for her to grit her teeth a little. "So…what the hell is wrong with you? I would think you're smart enough to know by now that I don't like my little girl upset."

"It's nothing to do with Margot, sir. There's something on my mind, and I've put off telling her, but I'll do that today."

He applied more pressure. "You're not fixing to really upset my baby, are you?"

"No, nothing like that. I promise it's nothing bad, but would you mind if I talked to Margot first? After that she can tell Patty Sue, then she'll tell you. We'll compare notes after and see how much the original story changes." She moved to start walking if only to save herself the bruise she was sure she'd have on her shoulder. He finally let go.

"If you need to practice, you can tell me over the breakfast you're buying me."

"I won, so you pay. That's the deal." She tied her laces together and threw her shoes over her shoulder.

"You held back because you think I'm an old man, and that makes you a loser. Losers pay for breakfast. I'll make sure to order two large milks. You haven't forgotten that talk, have you?" Wilber gave her his *I'll mess you up* expression.

"Not one word, not to worry."

"Did you share anything I said with Margot?" His hand came up again, but this time he pointed at her.

"I'd never do that." She hoped she sounded as indignant as she felt. "I gave you my word."

"Calm down, bookworm. I like to check on you every so often, but I don't doubt your integrity. I also want my kid to smile on her vacation and not be worrying about what's going on in your head."

"I promise, and if you'll take a rain check, I'll talk to Margot this morning." They started up the slope, and Wilber slapped her on the back. "And I promise you won't be hearing about it later from Patty Sue."

Wilber laughed, and she thought it was the first time she'd ever heard him let go like that. "I'm beginning to see you're a lot smarter than I gave you credit for."

Margot was still sleeping when she quietly opened the door, so she headed for the shower. Her morning runs usually weren't quite so intense, but she was enjoying the workouts that were probably tame compared to Wilber's old military days. She put her head under the rain shower and scrubbed the salt off her face.

"I thought you'd never get back," Margot said when she put her arms around her waist.

If there was one sight she'd never tire of, it was Margot naked and wet standing before her. "I was picking flowers with your father. You don't want me to cut those bonding times short, do you?" She dropped to her knees when Margot pushed down on her shoulders.

Margot smiled when she moved her hands up from the backs of her knees to her ass. "Thank you for humoring him, my love." Margot spread her legs when she brought her head forward and bit the skin right under her navel gently. "What are you up to?"

"If you need to guess, I've been doing something wrong," she said, chuckling. She moved so Margot could rest her back against the shower wall. The way Margot ran her hands through her hair was distracting but not enough to keep her from what she wanted. She spread Margot's sex open and smiled before she put her tongue on her clit.

"I might invite Daddy to run with you every morning if this is the result," Margot said, pulling her hair.

She changed tack and sucked Margot in, loving the taste of her. Margot responded by lifting her leg over her shoulder, and she sucked harder as she entered her fast and hard. If there was one thing she wanted to do well in this life, it was to please Margot. She'd been the one person in her life who'd kept her promises and had loved her with the kind of devotion that had healed the raw parts of her soul.

"Oh, baby, like that," Margot said when she curled her fingers. "Harder." She locked her body when Margot's weight came down on her shoulder, but she didn't stop. "Fuck me," Margot said loudly. "Yes, yes...*yes*," Margot said, lengthening the last word.

She kept up the fast, hard pace and felt Margot's moans through her chest. The way Margot was thrusting her hips was a sign she was close. "Give me what I want, baby," she said before putting her mouth back on her clit.

"Jesus," Margot said as her hips sped up. "Don't stop, don't stop… oh fuck," she said as she slowly stopped moving and pulled Jaxon's hair. "Get up here."

"I love you," she said when she stood and put her arms around Margot. The press of her skin made her close her eyes and concentrate on the moment. "And let me finish in here since I sweated enough to gross you out."

"I doubt that," Margot said, slapping her butt. "I love you however I can get you."

"How about a walk along the beach before it gets crowded?" She lathered up her hair and smiled when Margot ran soapy hands along her chest.

"Are you okay?" Margot asked as she rinsed off. "Is something wrong? Did Daddy do something?"

The questions were rushed, so she put a finger to Margot's lips after she'd rinsed her hair. "Everything's fine, I promise. Your dad will never stop being your dad. Do you know what I mean? He's always got something on his mind and finds unique ways to express his thoughts, but he does it in a sort of sweet way. Up to now I'm glad to report he's done that without poking any new holes in me."

"Are you sure Daddy didn't threaten you?" Margot put her hands on Jax's shoulders and gazed at her like she was studying her expression for any hint of what was going on.

"Is it so hard to believe I just wanted to take a walk with my favorite girl? I give your dad a hard time, but I put up with his interesting little pep talks because I know he loves you. Though, I hope you know I love you as well."

Margot wrapped her hand around Jax's bicep and smiled up at her as they stood under the water. "You know, all these romantic declarations are why I love you. That you deliver them in that slight sexy Southern drawl of yours make them even better."

"Wow, say that five times fast," she said as she started washing Margot's hair.

"I do love you, and I appreciate you humoring him, honey. There's part of his brain that'll always think I'm five and in need of a champion.

Daddy's having a hard time with the fact you've stepped into that role. I think he's feeling obsolete."

Jax laughed at the possibility that twenty years down the road she'd be the nut with some sort of weapon warning off some would-be suitor from one of their kids. With any luck Wilber would leave her the automatic weapon he was so fond of. "I don't blame him, baby. You're no wilting flower, but I love that you trust me to take care of you." Jax led them out of the shower and handed Margot a towel. "It's still cool outside, so put on a sweatshirt to go with the big sunglasses and ball cap."

They held hands as they took the path that would lead them to the beach. It was nice that they were alone for the moment, so she put Margot's glasses in the pocket of her hoodie. It wasn't often they were able to go out and not have someone point in Margot's direction. Those fans didn't bother her as much as the ones who thought nothing of walking up and starting a conversation only they were interested in having.

"What did you want to talk about?" Margot said as they stopped to listen to the surf. She pulled on Jax's fingers and led her to some rocks they could sit on.

"The passage of time." She sat with her back against a rock and stretched her legs out, so Margot could sit on her.

"What? Honey, just tell me already. You've been walking around with a worry line in the middle of your forehead, and it's only getting deeper." Margot moved some damp hair off her brow and smiled at her. "Whatever it is, I promise we'll be all right."

"I'm talking about time. You know, like Geoffrey Chaucer said, it's the one thing that waits for no man or woman."

Margot groaned. "I know you have more quotes in your head than there are grains of sand on this beach, Professor, but focus." Margot put her hands on her cheeks and gazed at her. "What the hell are you talking about?"

She sighed and tried not to think of the disaster this was going to turn into. "My high school class reunion's coming up, and I'm thinking about going. Wanna come with me?"

"This must be throwing you off balance if you're using words like *wanna*. What aren't you telling me?" Margot's eyes narrowed a tad, but she didn't seem mad yet.

"I didn't think I wanted to attend, but Bert's been dogging me for a week."

Margot closed her eyes and took a deep breath. Now she appeared a little peeved. "I'm going to do my best to try not to read anything into the fact that Bert has known for that long, and I'm just now hearing about it."

"That's what I want to talk to you about." She shut up again when Margot took another deep breath.

"I mean, I can see if you were someone who had nothing to show for the life you've made. People who are losers are the ones who usually don't want to reflect on what people are going to say. But for you?" Margot poked her in the chest. "You're going to show up and make anyone who passed on the chance to share in the experience that's been your journey sorry they missed out."

"I love you, but you're way prejudiced on the subject." Jax wasn't sure if she was glad for the reprieve provided by the tangent, or if she just wanted to get it done with. She let Margot talk.

"For someone I think is brilliant, you can be a brick at times." Margot threw her hands up and shook her head. "Have I ever told you about the first time I saw you?"

"In my class, you mean?" She loved Margot, but conversations with her were like wandering around a maze, and the answers you wanted were hidden—not in the middle, but along every turn. If you missed one clue, there was no way of following along.

"Wrong. I saw you in that coffee shop close to campus, and you were writing like a demon on your laptop. I didn't think anyone could type that fast." Margot lifted one of Jax's hands and bit her finger. "I thought to myself how good-looking you were. You're that classic butch who's comfortable in her own skin, and it shows. When I stepped into class a few hours later"—Margot fanned herself now—"I thanked all the deities I could think of because there you were."

"Ah…thank you, but I'm not sure why we're talking about this, and you're not lecturing me about keeping my class reunion from you."

"I'm not finished talking about that first day." Margot bit her finger again only this time with a bit more pressure. "I was sure of two things after that hour of listening to your lecture."

"What's that?" She held Margot, and the conversation made her relax. All that pent-up anxiety about going home disappeared under Margot's talent at telling a story.

"One, Poe was a brilliant writer I'd underestimated for thinking the only thing he had written was the raven thing, and two, that I'd spend the rest of my life happy if I spent it with you." Margot's voice got softer, and she closed her eyes again when she kissed her. "You're brilliant, you're successful, and you're the best partner I could have ever asked for. Why don't you sound excited about going home and showing up the people you graduated with?"

"It's a long story that's way overdue."

"Nothing you say is ever going to change what I feel for you, honey." Margot sighed as she put her hand over Jaxon's heart. "Let's start with an easier question. What changed your mind? About going, I mean."

"Your father and milk." She made Margot laugh and lean in closer as if to get warm.

"Is this one of those conversations where you have to kill me if you have to explain?" Margot's breath was against her neck, and she put her arms tighter around her, finding it easier to stare out at the water.

"It's not that I've tried to keep it from you because I didn't trust you, but because I didn't want to face the truth of my past." Jax rubbed Margot's back and kissed her temple. "I know how important communication is to you, and on that I agree."

"Tell me then, honey."

Jax took a deep breath. Now or never. "High school had its moments, but the day they handed me that diploma, I packed my bags and left for LSU with no intention of going back. I was so ready to get out of that small town and the people who'd given me shit from the time I could remember what shit was." All the taunts and vitriol played in a loop in her head at times, and it was hard to break the pattern.

"But why?" Margot asked, sitting up and facing her.

"Small towns in the Deep South aren't as evolved as California, and being the gay kid wasn't fun. I didn't advertise it, but I was a baby butch who wasn't at all comfortable in my skin back then."

Margot ran her fingers through her hair and kissed her cheek. "It's all right, sweetie. Take your time."

"I drove to Baton Rouge, buried myself in my books and in

softball, and tried my best to come to the realization that I was alone." Jax stopped and took another deep breath, trying to keep her voice from cracking.

"What are you talking about? You had your brother and your parents." Margot's voice faded away as if realizing what she'd been trying to say.

"I came out to my parents right before graduation. My mother flat-out asked, and I told the truth. She couldn't accept who I was and still can't. Her reaction was to throw me out and say I didn't have a family anymore. My father went along with what she wanted because it was either that or buck my mother. That he wasn't about to do and hasn't ever done. Considering all that, I haven't taken you home because I didn't want to subject you to that. The only way she'd accept me was if I changed. And obviously that wasn't going to happen."

"And you haven't been back in all these years?" Margot wiped her face, and it made her realize she was crying.

"Once. College revolved around hard work, so there wasn't a lot of partying for me. It was the only way to keep my scholarships—with the help of a few professors and my old high school English teacher, I was able to come here." She looked out at the water so she wouldn't see pity in Margot's eyes. "The last time was a family reunion, but nothing had changed, and my parents still weren't speaking to me, so there was never a need to go back again. I still don't know why they invited me in the first place. The only people I hear from are my grandmother Birdie, Eugenia my old English teacher, and my brother, Roy, who is a perfectly happy single lawyer one town over from where we grew up."

"I'm sorry you had to go through that, love, but I'm proud that you made it on your own, and you should be too. Your mother sounds like someone should explain a few things to her, but maybe she's seen reason now that you've given her what she thought she wanted."

It sounded so reasonable, but her mother was anything but reasonable. "I doubt that, honey. She stripped me of my family, at least some of them. And other than that weird reunion, neither she nor my father has ever tried to reach out."

"You have a family in me, and I happen to think you're perfect. So do my parents."

"I doubt your father would totally agree with that, but I love you for saying so." She stopped and kissed Margot, needing the connection they shared. "Don't think I didn't tell you because I'm missing something. I love my life with you."

"Why go back, then? You don't sound like it's something you really want to do."

"It's not to prove anything to anyone I grew up with. I don't really want to, so I ignored the invitation. The truth is, I didn't like most of the people I went to high school with, and sixteen years ain't going to make them more enlightened. To them I'm not someone you invite over for dinner." She tried to ignore the twinge of irritation the thought brought with it.

Margot pressed her lips to the side of Jax's neck before kissing her with every bit of passion she possessed. "Why, because you're kissing a girl on the beach?" she finally asked when she leaned back.

Jax smiled at how easily Margot made the residual bad feelings go away. "Correction, because I'm kissing a *beautiful* girl on the beach." The compliment got her another kiss.

"How did drinking milk with Daddy convince you to go to your reunion?"

"It made me think of how I handled bad situations involving mixed vegetable medley." She winced when Margot pinched the top of her hand. "Okay, forget the mixed vegetables. What really made up my mind was waiting for the general to come in, so we could have our talk."

Margot's brows came together. "Explain, please?"

"All that stuff in his study made me think that Wilber may not have always wanted to be in every dangerous situation the army put him in, but I don't think it's in his makeup to ever think of running away. He may have been ridiculed for thinking like that, but I admire and respect that about him. I figure I want him to think about me like that, even though it's something as trivial as a fifteen-year reunion and the possibility of running into my family."

"Fifteen years?" Margot had to laugh. "Who the hell has a fifteen-year reunion?"

"My class. They made a pact to meet every five years, since they'd never be able to live without the friends they made in high school. I begged to differ, but I was outvoted. The strangest thing of the whole scenario is that I actually graduated sixteen years ago, but the people in my class organizing this can't count, apparently."

"This sounds fascinating already." Margot smiled and threaded their fingers together. "How about this—you put on your best suit, Dr. Jaxon, polish the boots, and take your girl to a party. We'll drink, jitterbug, and give them something to talk about at their crawfish boils for years to come."

"Baby, I'm older than you, it's true, but the jitterbug was a little before my time."

"Do you know how to jitterbug?" Margot leaned in and bit her earlobe, laughing at the shiver it caused.

"Yes."

"Then me and you have a date, Professor."

Chapter Eight

Nancy stood outside the high school office and waved Iris outside. The way she was moving her hands made Iris think she was trying to swat away an invasion of pissed-off bumblebees. She nodded and pointed in the direction of the teachers' lounge. At this time of morning there'd be no one in there.

"Are you okay?" She moved to the chairs in the corner, thinking Nancy would want the privacy. "Is it one of the kids?"

"No, those little bastards will kill me from stress and exhaustion before anything happens to them. I picked up the mail today, and I thought you'd want to open this one." Nancy held up an envelope.

She felt the breath leave her lungs in one quick whoosh. The handwriting had gotten messier through the years, but she recognized it as Jaxon's. "What do you think it says?"

"There's only one way to find out." Nancy placed her hand on Iris's forearm and shook it gently. "It's been a long time, so maybe it's time for her to come home. Don't get your hopes up, but I doubt she'd have sent anything if she was giving this thing a pass."

"She waited until the last minute if that's what she had in mind." She stared at the letters, scrawled as if Jax was in a hurry to get somewhere and didn't have time to be neat. The paper sounded loud as she tore it. She ripped the card out and closed her eyes at the check mark next to *yes*. Also enclosed was a check for the registration fee, and it was weird to see Margot Drake's name after Jaxon's on the check. "The gossip columns got it right for once."

Nancy plucked the check out of her hands when she said that, and her eyes widened. "Damn, she paid for three people. Do you think

Margot Drake is coming? If she is, everyone including anyone who didn't graduate with us will want to come."

Iris looked at the plus-one section. "She put down Margot's name, and Bert's. I haven't talked to him in years, but I know he comes home to see his parents a few times a year." The committee would have a field day over this.

"Once Tori and the others find out, you're not going to get any peace. Are you sure you're going to be okay?" Nancy touched her again before glancing down at her watch. "I have a house showing in thirty minutes, but call me later if you need to talk."

"Thanks, but this isn't going to change anything. The only thing I'm going to have to do is talk to Sean, and as soon as I find a way to do that, I'll let you know."

"That kid is brilliant and, more importantly, compassionate. The only thing that's bothered her all these years is your silence. I understood why you never said anything, but Sean needs to hear all this from you. If you don't believe me, ask Adeline." Nancy kissed her cheek and waved over her shoulder as she ran out.

She sat for a little while longer and didn't acknowledge whoever came in, hoping they'd leave her alone. It startled her when someone was suddenly in her personal space and kissing her cheek. "Hey, I called you, but you were in a daze," Daniel said, cramming in next to her. "What are you doing in here by yourself?"

"Nancy came by for a minute about some reunion stuff. What are you doing awake? And here?" She put the card down on her lap and turned to look at him.

"I'm going back on days starting tomorrow, so I'm trying to change my sleep pattern back to normal. Think they'd miss you if you left for lunch?"

"Why don't you pick something up and bring it back? I'm sure the kids would love to see you."

"This time I want my wife to love to see me. I'm not sure what the hell I've done, or what's the matter, but something's off. I can tell. Just spit it out already."

Daniel was starting to get upset, and she didn't want that at her job. "Not now, okay? I don't think you'd appreciate it if I came to your job and raised my voice, so either calm down or go home, and I'll see you later." She started to stand up, and he held her back, making the card drop to the floor.

He reached for it and held it away from her when she lunged to grab it. "Never mind," Daniel said sarcastically when he read the name on it. "I know exactly what's wrong, and it sure as hell doesn't have anything to do with me. How long, Iris? How the hell long are you going to mope around, thinking how much better your life would be if only you'd followed her instead of marrying me? Son of a bitch, it's more than I should have to put up with."

"What are *you* talking about? I'm on the committee, Daniel, and I get all the responses. That's all there is to it." She stood and grabbed the card back from him. "We're married, and I love you. I sit around thinking about how I can make our lives better, so don't start with me. Sean and Danny barely talking to me is enough to deal with."

"Your problem is that not even you believe that. The other thing is you think I'm a complete idiot."

She put her hand on his cheek and shook her head. Her touch made him close his mouth. "My life is here with you and the kids. That's all you need to know."

"I'm not your first choice, though, am I?" Daniel spoke much more softly but didn't move away from her.

"Does that really matter? If you'd be honest for once, you'd admit I'm not exactly what you had planned either. What matters is we've made a life together that we can be proud of." It was time to take her head out of the clouds and start paying attention to what was right in front of her. Daniel wasn't her first choice, but he'd been a stand-up guy.

"You're right. This isn't the place to talk about it, but I'm not going to sit back and watch you fall all over that asshole at the reunion. Don't expect that."

"I'm not, and don't worry. If you want, go and get lunch. We'll find a place outside to talk."

"Forget it—I've lost my appetite." He walked out.

The next week was going to be delightful if he had that in his head. Between that and the committee, it was going to be a hellish week, leading up to the big day. And did Jaxon have any idea what she was in for?

❖

"Bad news, Margot." Judith was the last person Margot wanted to hear from only a day after they had gone on a temporary unexpected hiatus.

The unexpected time off had cleared her to leave with Jaxon the next day for her reunion. The week since their getaway had been filled with planning for their trip to Louisiana to see old friends as well as going to the reunion. It was almost like the universe wanted her to go when a pipe broke in the studio. The rupture had happened after-hours, and by the time they'd discovered it, all the furniture on their set was drenched. The studio had to shut them down for five days while it dried and they sanitized the space.

"Please tell me we didn't luck out and get the one honest plumber left in the world?" Jaxon had started her time off today, so they could have breakfast together before they headed to her parents' place again for one more dinner before they left. With their schedules, it was a treat when they could squeeze in a whole day together that wasn't on the weekend.

"There's that, and the furniture had the nerve to dry without so much as a waterline." Judith didn't sound excited either. "I'm not sure what they did, but the studio is back to normal, which blows my chance to try that resort you and Jaxon went to last week."

"When do we go back?" She tapped her fist against her forehead.

"This afternoon. Sorry, kid, but before you go cursing out the messenger, just remember all those starving actors out there waiting tables hoping for their big break on a hit series." The snort Judith let out meant this was the speech she was giving everyone.

"They told you to say that, didn't they."

"Yes, like I'd be that clichéd if I had a choice of excuses for why you have to be at work tomorrow."

Margot chewed on her bottom lip and thought about what ailment her character could come down with so she could leave with Jax the next day. Bert was thrilled she was going and had flown out earlier that morning to spend time with his family before the reunion activities began.

Since Jax had just started opening up about her childhood, Margot was dying to know about the people she'd spent her formative years with, and with any luck she'd meet her family. There were a few things she'd love to say to Jax's mom for what she'd done to her.

Then there was the girl she'd left behind, because Margot was sure there'd been one. She hadn't asked about that yet, not wanting to push Jax more than she had already, but there were things still left unsaid, and Margot simply knew they were to do with lost love. Whoever that woman was, Jaxon had left her behind and didn't seem to think of her much. That was a win, but she was still curious.

"There's no way I could take the weekend?" Even if she missed the events happening during the week, she could still get to the big bang on Saturday night. Margot drew on some of her acting classes, trying to sound as pathetic as possible. The laugh coming from the other end of the phone told her it hadn't worked.

"Don't even try that with me, young lady. What's so important about this weekend?"

"Jaxon's class reunion is this weekend, and I really wanted to go with her." She glanced around to make sure Jax was still in the bedroom. Usually she didn't like talking about her private life, but she trusted Judith. "I wouldn't bother to ask, but remember what we talked about? There's something about what she's not saying that makes me think I don't want to miss it."

"Sorry, kid, but Frank wants to work through the weekend to make up for lost time. You'd swear his father owned the studio and it's his life's mission to save the old man money." Judith whispered something under her breath, and it sounded like a lot of cursing.

"I have it on good authority that his father works in an accounting firm somewhere in Ohio."

"Figures, and the little dweeb always seems to forget that he has the number one show on television. If the cast starts to hate him, that might not be the case." Judith groaned and exhaled deeply. "You know, I'd love nothing better than to tell you to take off with the love of your life, but this industry is all about the money. Emotion went out when the silent movie died. Back then it was necessary. Get here before one, and tell Jax to have fun."

Margot hung up and slumped in her chair. Life just sucked sometimes. "Shit."

"If we had a dog, you'd look like someone just ran off with it.

Bad news?" The tray in Jax's hands was loaded down with her culinary efforts, and Margot did her best to smile.

"They fixed the plumbing on the set. I'm sorry, honey, but I have to go back to work today." She was in Jaxon's arms the moment she put the tray down. "I wanted to go with you."

"How about I stay home? I could be waiting on you all weekend, and I'll even volunteer to pose for the cameras if you want to go out." Jaxon kissed the top of her head and rubbed her back.

"I don't want you to miss this. All I want you to promise me is that you'll try to have a good time and reconnect with those friends you thought were worth it back then. They'll be thrilled to see you. If I have to miss you for a week, then you'd better make it worth it."

"There weren't many of those, and I was only going because Bert begged, and you'd be at my side."

"Listen to me, okay?" She got on the bed and pulled Jax with her. "You never want to talk about your family except for your brother, your cousin Tully, and your grandmother, and I'm glad you've shared some this week about the rest. They're still there, and they love you, so why not go stop by and see them?" She thought the way forward with Jaxon was to heal her past. It was hard to love someone, giving them your all, knowing you weren't ever getting all the way in because of walls that had nothing to do with you.

Jaxon held back—she knew that. It was her nature. At first Margot had taken it to heart, and it had taken her a while to learn that she'd have to wait Jaxon out. There was something in Jaxon that had never healed from all those years ago, and it had only festered with time. It'd always been there because she realized Jaxon hadn't let go, not really, but she was patient. Margot wanted everything her parents enjoyed together, but the only way to get it was if Jaxon's emotional bleeding stopped. The only thing that would stanch it would come when Jaxon shared whatever that hurt. Dragging all the secrets out into the sunlight would allow her to claim all of Jaxon.

"Thank you for not pushing me, even though you probably want to. I know you're a woman who loves talking about everything." Jaxon lay back and held her. "My upbringing was a lot like yours, in some ways. My father was in the army, and he wasn't around much. My mother thought moving children around wasn't wise, so we stayed home and waited for him. Even though it was my dad in the service, my mom was as strict and by the book as any drill sergeant."

"Your mother and mine sound like they have a lot in common." She moved until she was close to lying on top of Jaxon, so she could see her face.

"Patty Sue and my mother are nothing alike. I didn't mind the rules and curfews, really. No, our problems began when I met Iris Long in high school."

"The old girlfriend, huh?" She pinched Jaxon's side and smiled, glad Jax smiled back. She'd known this would come up and was glad it would be sooner than later.

"Actually, she was the girl who made me feel like I wasn't crazy. I was so tired of hiding from everyone except Bert, and I thought I'd love Iris for the rest of my life, as you do when you're seventeen and can't imagine what life will really look like." Jaxon sighed. "We spent so much time together it made my mom suspicious, and that's what made her finally ask. By then Iris and I had been together three years, and I didn't want to lie. I mean, what could be the harm, right?" Jax laughed, and it sounded bitter and almost angry.

"I know what your mom's reaction was, but what happened with Iris?"

"I didn't have anyplace to go, so I ended up with Bert's family. The shock was still fresh when I called Iris and told her, but my mom had beaten me to it and talked to her mom. My mother thought everyone involved deserved the truth."

"God. So what happened?" She studied Jaxon's face. Her jaw was tight, and she seemed to be clenching her teeth.

"Iris asked to meet me, so she could tell me all the plans we made weren't going to work out. She kissed me good-bye and blew me off." Jaxon inhaled deeply through her nose. "The only thing I could think to do was graduate and get the hell out. I had scholarships that covered college for the first four years, but then I had to take a year off to work and save enough for my master's."

"What did you do for a year?" This was like discovering a thrilling book on her nightstand, but instead of titillating, it was a story that made her heart ache.

"I worked offshore as a driller for Delacroix Oil. I'm shocked I still have all my limbs, but I worked twenty-one and seven for fourteen months, and would've worked it straight through if they'd let me. I stayed with friends on my seven days off, and that helped me save enough to pay for my first year at UCLA. Then I was lucky enough to get fellowships to cover the rest.

"Working summers helped me keep my apartment." Jaxon's voice got softer, and Margot kissed her. "When I left after that last argument, my mother told me not to come home, and I didn't. That last day was *the* last day. I haven't been back, and I don't think I will this time either. The family reunion at the beach was more my father's idea, but that didn't work out either."

Margot rose to look at Jax. "Listen. What your mother did was wrong. What you've accomplished is beyond incredible, and I'm so proud of you. It still bothers you, though, and it's okay to admit that." She put her hand over Jax's mouth when she opened it. "No, listen to me. I want to be your family—I am your family. I want all your days, and there's no way I'm ever letting you go or leaving you behind. But I want you to know it's okay to let all that go. That might take going back and cutting those ties."

"You don't think I can do that now?" Jaxon spoke around her fingers, and it made her laugh.

"Think of it this way. You know how you remember something that happened when you were little, and it's huge?" Margot combed Jax's hair back, trying to relax her. Jaxon nodded. "Then you go back as an adult, and it's really not."

"You think my family drama is like that?" Jaxon laughed without humor.

"Don't joke. I can see the pain you still carry, and I love you too much to not want to help you." She untied her robe and pushed Jax's shirt up. "Start with what Bert said. Go back and rub it in their faces how well you've done." The touch of all Jaxon's skin against hers would never get old. "I'm only sorry I won't be there to see it, but you can come with me to my class reunion."

"Honey, I'll be happy to take you wherever you want to go, but I can tell you that what happened is as done as it's going to get. Going back will probably make it worse, not better."

"If you don't want to go, then we'll be okay."

Jax sighed. "We will, but I'll give it one more chance. It's not going to work, but I'd like to see Granny, and Bert won't forgive me now if I abandon him."

"Are you sure?" She nodded again and kissed her. "You have to promise that you'll call me often and come home if you want to. Do you promise you will?"

"I promise, but I'm sorry I won't get to dance in my old high school gym with the girl of my dreams." Jaxon placed her hands on her hips and tickled her for a second. "I'm going to miss you. Make *me* a promise?"

"Whatever you want."

"Don't spend the whole time I'm gone worrying. I'll be okay, and I can stand anything for a couple of days. The other thing that should make you feel better is I'll still have Bert if I can't have you."

"You're telling me I can be so easily replaced with Bert?" She bit Jaxon's shoulder but smiled, liking that Jax was attempting to cheer her up.

"Are you kidding me? Under that cool math genius exterior beats the heart of a wild man I could never handle." Jaxon stopped talking and kissed her with the kind of passion she loved. "Never think anyone could replace you. You're one of a kind, and you're mine. Not to mention you have the most popular hair in America. Who can compete with that?"

"Shut up, you." The way Jax held her made her want to cry that she wasn't going to be there when Jaxon needed her the most. "You've never danced in that gym with anyone?"

"Nope." Jax kissed her as a way to get away with the one-word answers she knew drove her crazy.

"Not even at your prom?"

"I didn't go to prom." Jaxon tapped her on the nose and smiled. "I saw your prom picture, though, when your mom proudly showed it off. You're the only person I know who could pull off pink taffeta."

"Oh my God." She covered her face with her free hand and laughed. "My mother is toast, and when you get home, we're going somewhere that has dancing. I'll even wear pink taffeta for you."

"You don't want TMZ catching you in that, so let's say that you'll owe me a dance at your twenty-year class reunion."

"You have a deal, and don't forget where home is when you're done."

❖

Sean Gravois locked the door to her room and walked to the window. The view from her second-floor space looked out at the sidewalk and the street all the way to the large oak in Mrs. Hopkins's yard. The old tree blocked her view of the corner, but it didn't matter. She and Adeline were alone for the rest of the afternoon. Her father was working, and her mom was at the gym decorating for her reunion.

"Did your mom tell you the biggest news that's ever happened in the history of this fucking town?" Adeline asked as she lay on the bed. "My mom and their friends have been talking about it nonstop. You'd think they went to school with someone famous."

Sean kicked her shoes off and dropped next to Adeline, smiling when Ade took her hands and straddled her waist. "They sort of went to school with someone famous."

"What does that mean?" The way Ade lowered her upper body and ran her tongue along her bottom lip made her want to forget the conversation. "If this chick is famous, I've never heard of her."

"Have you heard of Margot Drake?" Ade nodded. "That's who Lavigne lives with. She's gay and landed Margot Drake. Can you believe it? Forget about that right now. Look what I found." She had to move Ade so she could get up and stand on a chair to reach the box at the back of the closet where she kept things that were important to her. She guessed her mother had piled all her stuff in the attic as a way to forget about it, and she'd used afternoons like this to sift through it all.

"Is this your mom?" Ade pointed to the person in the picture who was turned enough so you only saw a quarter of their profile. The shape of her mom's face was unmistakable as she stared up at a girl who had a big smile. "It's weird—it's like it's a young her, and she's looking at you."

"There's no way in hell that's me. That," she said, flicking the picture, "is Jaxon Lavigne. At least, that's what it says on the back. That's been freaking me out for the last week." She studied the picture again like she had for hours since she'd found it, and it answered so many questions. Her problem was that her mom wouldn't give her any more than she had, and that was nothing.

"Why the hell do you look just like her?" Ade seemed not to be able to take her eyes off the picture. "It's, like, kinda spooky."

"My mom never wants to talk about it, and believe me, I've asked more than once. Does your mom ever tell you anything?"

"Babe, they're best friends. Your mom must've told her to keep her mouth shut because she tells me to stop being nosy." Adeline massaged her shoulders. "They come down on us like they don't know what fun is, and they're keeping all these secrets. That you look like this chick is one big secret that had no chance in hell staying secret." Adeline put the picture on the nightstand. "Right now, we don't have that much time. How about we work on a plan later?"

She held Adeline and kissed her softly. They'd grown up together and had been in love since the sixth grade. Ade gave her a sense of belonging in the world. That was important because she didn't have that sense in her own family. With Adeline there'd never be a time they wouldn't fit. When she got out of here in another year, she was taking Adeline with her, and they weren't ever coming back.

"Do you think we have time to…you know." Adeline pressed her hips down again and kissed her.

"My idiot brother will be home in no time, and there's no way I'm letting him hear anything we do." She ran her fingers through Adeline's red hair that was the same shade as her mother Nancy's, but unlike Nancy, Ade was gorgeous. That was something Danny never failed to mention, and she was sure it was to piss her off.

"Think you could come over this weekend?" Ade pressed the heel of her hand into her crotch, and it made her breath catch.

"I doubt they'll know I'm gone. This weekend they'll be up each other's ass trying to pretend they haven't changed since they were in high school." It was only Tuesday, but tomorrow would start all the craziness that came along with the reunion's long weekend. "I'll ask, but it shouldn't be a problem."

"What are you going to do about that?" Adeline asked about the picture.

"The easiest way to get what I want is to talk to her, but I doubt I'll get a chance."

"Do you want me to jump her and tie her to a chair for you?" Adeline traced her eyebrows with her index finger, and it drained all the anger right out of her.

"I don't know. Maybe. Let me think about it."

"Then let's talk about something else," Adeline said and lowered her head again. "Or we could stop talking."

"Great idea."

CHAPTER NINE

The next morning Margot made time to take Jaxon to the airport. "Don't forget to call me, and remember everything I told you." Margot waited to inch along with the line of cars trying to get to the curb.

"I'll remember, and I'll call as soon as I land. If you're on set, I'll leave you a message." She reached across the seat and ran her thumb along Margot's cheek. "You remember to behave, and don't go anywhere alone. If something happens to you because I'm out of town, your father will go into a rage that'll end with me in the hospital with two broken legs."

They'd gone to dinner at Margot's parents', and she'd received another lecture from Wilber about Margot's future and how he saw it. Having something happen to Margot because she was mobbed at the airport would not bode well for her future in the Drake family.

"I'm planning to use the car service Judith set up, so you concentrate on having a good time. When you get home, we'll have a long conversation about your formative years and how I plan to help you put all that behind you by making you blissfully happy." Margot leaned over and kissed her, making it hard to get out of the car.

"You already do, and I thought I'd already put all that behind me. I'm going to this event to make you and Bert happy, but there are certain things that are set in stone. I still have a knot on my head from beating against all their narrow-minded beliefs." The line moved slowly, and if she missed her plane, she'd take it as fate.

"Are you sure you don't want me to go in and wait with you? I have time."

"Honey, you know how you attract crowds. I'd be crazy to let you walk back to the car alone. Go home, and take it easy until it's time to go to work, and I'll call as soon as I'm there. It's a direct flight, so I'll have time to grade some papers and think about you." They finally made it to the curb, and Jax got her bag from the trunk, then turned to hug Margot.

"I'm going to miss you."

"Not as much as I'm going to miss you. Please be careful, and I'll come back if you need me for anything." She kissed Margot once more and helped her into the car. "That includes needing me to take out the trash."

"I'm always going to need you, Jax, and you'd better start walking before I say to hell with it all and demand you come home with me." Margot tilted her head up for one more kiss. "I love you."

"I love you too, and I'll see you late Sunday. Don't worry about coming back to get me—I'll get a car."

Jaxon waved as Margot drove off, then grabbed a coffee after going through security before she boarded the plane forty minutes later with a briefcase full of essays. Her students sent everything electronically, but she loved reading while holding a paper copy and a red pen, so she had Viola print everything. She posted her grades but also handed back the red-splattered papers, so they could see why they'd received the grade they had. A few hours later, her lips still tingled from Margot's special kind of sendoff, and she'd gotten through about a fourth of the essays with plenty of red ink to attest to the fact she had read them. But the closer she got to her destination, the less she was able to concentrate, and she finally gave up.

The attendant was happy to bring her a third cup of coffee, and once she'd put her stuff away, she glanced out the window. They were flying over the beginning of the vast and lush Mississippi River Delta. The start of the little rivulets that ran where they pleased and left behind their rich silt deposits as well as river pollution that accounted for the dead zone at the mouth of the river. The way nature carved the land in such random patterns always reminded her of a vast and complex cobweb. This one spelled out a special welcome home, much like the extraordinary Charlotte had for Wilbur, in E. B. White's classic novel.

She rubbed her chest, trying to keep her apprehension down. All her protests that she'd never come back were promises meant to be broken. She'd wanted to forget all those years of her life that had brought so much pain that she wondered how she'd survived them, but family had a strong pull. The people who shared your name and blood somehow earned second chances when it was best to leave it alone.

Intellectually, she knew it was a lost cause. Her mother's stance wasn't going to change, but her heart always hoped that it'd get better. There'd be some epiphany and the apologies she was owed would come. Of course, that also made her an idiot, but she wanted to be honest with Margot going forward, so she'd try.

She handed over her empty cup when the announcement about landing was made, and she was glad the bag she'd packed was overhead. New Orleans had a new airport, and Bert had called to say getting a rental car now took time and patience. To beat the crowd, she'd packed light and so made her way outside quickly. There was no answer at her brother's office, so she left a message for him to get back to her with a time they could get together.

Unlike all her fellow California travelers, apparently new to New Orleans, Jax removed her coat before stepping outside. Louisiana weather was like a Southern woman—unpredictable, temperamental, and, overall, exasperating at times. Her sleeves were rolled up by the time she'd taken the shuttle to the rental car complex, and forty minutes later she was on the highway into the city in a black Yukon. That choice she had Margot to thank for, and it was her lover's nudge that it was time to retire the truck.

She connected her phone to the media center in the vehicle and gave the command to call Margot. "Hey," she said when Margot answered.

"Hi, baby. Are you okay?" Margot sounded echoey.

"Just got on the road." She sped up and merged onto the interstate.

"Tully called and said she's waiting for you, so don't think of blowing her off. Her words, and I'd take her seriously," Margot said of Jax's cousin, Tully Badeaux, an attorney in New Orleans. There was someone screaming in the background, and it made Jaxon wonder how Margot or anyone else on that set ever got any work done.

"She just wants to brag about her college sports days." Jax smiled as she wiped her brow, not believing it was already this hot, then concentrated again on the conversation. Tully was not only her cousin but had been a good friend back then, and her mom, Alma, had also been a comfort. She'd taken plenty of phone calls when Tully's first partner Jessica had run off with some asshole, but at least the story had a happy ending when Libby came into Tully's life. Tully had run from her small town as well but had ended up a little closer, in New Orleans with a wife and three kids.

"She wants to brag about how wonderful it is to have a wife and kids. Make sure you take notes. I want a full report when you get home." Margot laughed and it made her smile. "Seriously. She and Libby are both waiting at their house, and they promised they're coming here to visit us this summer."

"I miss you even though you give me a hard time." She took the downtown exit and kept quiet about how nice a ride the SUV was. Margot had a talent for being right but was nice enough not to rub it in her face. "I miss you."

"I miss you too, and you can tell me all about how much you enjoyed the Yukon when you get home. We'll have fun when we go shopping for one next weekend. I've already talked to the museum about taking your truck."

That made her laugh. "Try to have fun today."

"You too, baby, and call me later. I should be home by eight."

It had been a few years since she'd been to Tully's Uptown house, but she remembered how to get there without the GPS. This wasn't UCLA, and New Orleans was worlds away from the small towns they'd grown up in. The two small havens hadn't been all that different, aside from the fact she lived a little north of where Tully did, but that's where the similarities ended. When she compared their families, it was like night and day. Tully had come from a brood who loved and accepted her for who she was and who she loved. Jax's aunt loved Libby, Tully's wife, as much as she loved her own children, and that made her wonder if Alma and her father were really related.

"Get out here, and let's see how much you've aged," Tully yelled from her front porch.

They hugged and Libby stood by and shook her head. "What she means is, we're glad you're here," Libby said. "Come inside."

They entered, and Jaxon had to smile at all the toys strewn around the main room. Tully and Libby had added another little boy to the two kids Tully had with her first partner Jessica. "How are the kids?"

"Great," Libby said. "Bailey's preparing for LSU, and Ralph's busy trying to fend off every girl at school. I have to peel this one off the wall every night because of all the dating going on around here. Ralph likes to play the field, and Bailey's got a girlfriend. Thank God Henry only seems interested in *Sesame Street*."

"Where is the little guy?" She followed them to the kitchen and sat at the island with Tully.

"Day care," Tully said. "Libby pries him out of my arms every morning and pushes me out the door so he can play with kids his own age."

"With your immaturity level, I'd think you'd make the perfect playmate."

Libby laughed as Tully made a rude gesture. "Sure, make fun of me, and I'm so sorry Margot couldn't make it. We wanted to tell you guys together." Tully smiled as Libby came and leaned against her. "We have another one on the way."

Jaxon closed her eyes momentarily as a surge of jealousy coursed through her at the news. She was happy for them, but she was ready to admit that she wanted that with Margot. "Congratulations. Margot's going to be sorry she couldn't make it."

"It's time for you to put a ring on that girl's finger," Libby said. She moved to the stove to check on lunch. "If you need reassurance that the age difference isn't a problem, ask your buddy there."

"I'm not that old," she said, and Libby laughed. "Did Margot call you and give you some pointers on bending me to her will?"

"Libby and Margot are smarter than both of us, so I'd listen to them." Tully squeezed her shoulder and pointed to the front of the house. "I'm glad you're here, but I'm shocked. You've always said it would take a death to bring you back here, so what changed your mind?"

Tully seemed to understand her better than anyone else when it came to this subject. "The same argument that landed you in the land of diapers again. Margot asked me to come to try to put some stuff to rest." She scrubbed her face with her hands and sighed. "I would've given it a pass, but I didn't want to disappoint her. I'm happily whipped."

"I totally get that, and if you want, Libby and I would love to come with you if you need some friendly faces. Think about it before you blow us off. Besides, Granny would love to see Henry." Tully sat forward and threw a few trucks in a toy box.

"Did Margot ask you to do that?"

"Are you going to get pissed if I say yes?"

She smiled and shook her head. "I'm not sure how I lucked out there, but she does stuff because she loves me. I don't think I've been truly mad from the time she dragged me out on a date. She looks at me, and whatever's bothering me flies out of my head."

"You're a faster learner than me, then. It took Libby whacking me in the head a few times when she was doing things for me for my own good, and I wasn't cooperating." Tully laughed, and Libby joined her when she came in and handed them each an iced tea.

"I'm not so crazy that I'd ignore Margot's advice. She's got the pinch from hell."

They sat down to lunch and talked about growing up along the bayou as well as their days at LSU, making Libby laugh. She and Tully, as well as Bert and a few other good friends, had a good time back then even if they didn't exactly fit in with the majority of students. It was fun to reminisce, and if this had been the reunion she was coming for, she'd gladly do it more than once a year.

The horrible years of high school had been balanced out when she'd gone to college. It was hard remembering all those good memories since the bad had a louder drumbeat. She needed to bring Margot here and share this with her. Margot wanted to know her past, and this part of it had been the beginning of her survival. She'd felt alone for most of her life, but when she thought about it, she hadn't been, not really. There'd been family like Tully and her friends, and that had been enough.

"I guess I should get going," she said a few hours later.

"No way," Libby said as they sat outside with coffee. "Margot canceled your room for tonight because you're staying here. She wants new pictures of Henry, so stop pouting." She had to smile when Libby pressed on her lip. "I think it's a test to see if you actually know how to hold a baby. Besides, one day with us might be more fun than the reunion you're driving out for."

Libby kissed Tully before leaving for a few minutes to pick Henry up. It gave them a chance to talk privately about all the things that she tried her best not to freak out over on a daily basis. Marriage, children, and keeping Margot happy had a tendency to panic her, but it was hard to deny how happy Tully appeared. Her cousin had taken a chance and was happy to tell her it was time to do the same. They rounded that out with her latest stories of Wilber.

"I'm sorry Libby lost her parents young, but I'm also lucky I don't have to sit through that every week," Tully said, laughing hard enough to wipe her eyes.

"Sure, laugh at my expense. If I ever go missing, make sure he's questioned extensively by the police, and check the trunk of his car for my blood. But I'd rather face Wilber every day than go to this thing."

"Are you sure you don't want us to come with you? I have the time, and Henry loves to travel," Tully said.

They heard the front door open and the squealing of a small child. Henry seemed to be full of energy, and it made her feel good when he ran to her and gave her a big hug.

"Believe me, if this was golf and good times, I'd be helping you pack. I'm going so I don't disappoint Margot by being a coward, but I'll be fine on my own. I'd like to see Granny and my brother again too. It's been a while since we've been in the same space, and I'd like to think he's a little more evolved than the rest of the family." She accepted the truck Henry handed her and rolled it back to him when he moved away.

She wasn't a masochist. Having Tully and Libby there would make the weekend easier, but then she was stuck. If it got to be too much, there'd be no escape, so going it alone was the best option. She didn't think anything would change—that was a given. This time would be the last time, though, and it would be her family who'd cut the bonds between them. They'd have to live with that, and she'd finally have her closure.

"Will you at least promise to come by with Bert before you leave?" Libby asked. "It's been ages since we've seen him, and it'll be nice to have both of you over for lunch or something."

"That I can do. I'll call Sunday morning and let you know when we'll be here."

They went out to a local place close to the house for dinner and Henry kept up a conversation of mostly babble as Bailey and Ralph took turns pushing him in his stroller. The night was a good reminder that not all things from the darkest period of her life were horrible. Tully and her family's acceptance had given her hope that there was a path forward she could not only embrace, but also be happy with.

The next morning, they had breakfast, and she enjoyed the easy conversation about their upcoming day. She and Margot spent most of their mornings like this as well, but the rings Tully and Libby wore spoke of a permanence she didn't have. Of course she didn't only because of stubborn pride, and she'd have to work on that. She was successful at what she did and would've lived comfortably, albeit with nothing like the home and lifestyle Margot's success brought them. It was hard sometimes not to feel kept, but that was on her and not Margot.

But also, she was damaged. Her mother had said it repeatedly, and on some level the message had sunk in. She had friends and some family, but she'd never thought to commit to anyone, not wanting to give them the power to hurt her when they saw what her mother had seen. It was ridiculous to think no one would ever love her because she was unlovable, but that hurt kid who'd withstood the barrage of angry hurtful words wasn't completely gone.

"Call if you need some friendly faces to survive the weekend," Libby said as she held Henry, who was waving wildly. The kid looked just like Tully and had that same rambunctious personality.

"I will, but concentrate on keeping an eye on this one. It's a good thing she tells me you're the best attorney in the firm. Keeping her out of trouble should keep you busy until you're ready to retire." She hugged Tully before doing the same with Libby and the kids.

Margot had called the night before to talk to Libby for a while. It was funny that she and Tully were family and spoke maybe once a month, but Libby and Margot spoke weekly, if not more. Tully often joked that the two of them were planning her life for her as well as trading tips to keep both of them in check.

"I didn't have a chip inserted in her ass for nothing," Libby joked. "And get back early enough on Sunday so I can take you shopping. There's a great jewelry store in the Quarter I'd like to show you. There are some antique rings that I think Margot would flip over."

"I'm starting to see a pattern emerge in Margot's orbit of people. Don't fuss—I'm not going to disappoint."

"I'll hold you to that, and I have someone Bert might want to meet." Libby handed Henry over when he started squirming too much.

"How does he feel about chest hair?"

"I have no idea, why?" Libby appeared confused.

She smiled and shook her head. "Call Margot and ask. Bert's inherited none of the luck of the Irish."

"I thought his family was French," Tully said.

"Precisely."

Jaxon was able to catch Margot while she was still at home and talked to her for most of the trip to Chackbay. She had to thank Margot for rearranging her schedule to stay with her old friends as a way to lift her spirits before she went home.

"Remember one thing, honey," Margot said.

"What's that?" She turned off the main highway onto a two-lane road that would take her back not only in time, but off the beaten path.

"You're a badass who teaches at one of the most prestigious schools in the country. Don't take any shit from anyone."

Margot's delivery was fierce, and it made her chuckle. "I thank God for you every day, my love." She concentrated on the road as she talked to Margot and enjoyed the scenery along the way. The old cypress homes raised off the ground dotted the right side of the road, while Bayou Lafourche stretched out on the left. It was like stepping back in time in more ways than the obvious. Some tourists flocked here to see this simple way of life, but to her it was like a visual migraine. She wanted to lock herself away in a dark room and sleep until it was over.

"Back at you, lover. Be careful and call me later—my ride's here."

"Have fun, and if there's any kissing scenes, give me fair warning."

"That's a deal, and let's hope the writers do the same for me. Go find Bert and bring me home some pecans."

She moaned at Margot's pronunciation, *pee-cans*. "Babe, it's *pa-cawns*." She said the word like everyone in her hometown, the accepted way in Louisiana.

"Thank God I'm not standing close to you, or you would've marked me with that famous red pen of yours. Love you, honey," Margot said before hanging up.

Jaxon stayed on the same road, and eventually it gave way to marsh and swamps. The swamp was as timeless as the culture of the people who lived along its cusp. It never really changed except it wasn't as green in the winter, but the moss still hung from the cypress trees growing up out of the water, and the palmettos clung to the very little land.

She still remembered the smell of the mud and how mad her mother got when she and Roy got home covered in it when they went on their adventures. The swamp was full of beauty but also had its share of deadly things. It'd been a good training ground for life.

The people were a lot like that Spanish moss in the trees. They clung to their faith as well as traditions, and change came slow, if at all. In her experience Louisianans were born, lived, and died all within a ten-mile radius of the Catholic church they attended every Sunday and holy day, out of obligation. Sunday mornings were spent sitting on hard oak pews, trying to forget the sins of Saturday nights, and thinking about the football or baseball game they'd watch when the priest quit his droning.

Jax often wondered what life would have been like had she not been so eager to leave the little town that was almost like a museum of a bygone era. As fast and as far as Jax had run, there were still some things she'd learned growing up that she'd packed and brought with her. Margot loved that she greeted anyone who made eye contact with her whenever they went out. An older woman in Beverly Hills had once shoved a twenty in her hand after Jax had said good morning, as if thinking it was the appropriate response. Southern ways didn't always translate well in LA.

Despite the little things Jax had taken from the small town of Chackbay, it was never a place she felt a part of, even though her family was active in the community. It had been a lonely existence growing up, as she tried to find a sense of place as elusive as a snowy day in the South. That first glimpse of what the world could be hadn't come until the day she walked into Miss Eugenia Landry's English class as a senior.

Miss Landry understood Jax and saw her potential. Aside from Bert, Eugenia was, at the time, her one true friend. That last year of school, Eugenia had opened a new world of poetry and classics to Jax by lending her young protégé the priceless books she had collected through the years. She'd treasured their afternoons together, talking about the written word and the meaning of all those classics.

With careful guidance in those long months of Jax's senior year, Eugenia had taught her how to think like a scholar, and Jaxon knew her teacher considered that the crowning achievement in her long and fruitful career. Jax still had the letter Eugenia had written her when she'd graduated from LSU, telling her just that, and that she believed in her. Eugenia had written eloquently about how there was nothing she couldn't accomplish if she simply worked for it, and there would be plenty of students in Jax's future who'd give thanks to have spent time in the classroom with her. That letter had been the catalyst that had gotten her through her doctorate on the days she wanted to quit and take up some job that required no thought.

The familiar landmarks were starting to appear, and Jax smiled, remembering her theory as a child that paint was a precious commodity in Louisiana since some people used it so rarely. She hadn't cleared the first traffic signal in town when she saw the flashing blue lights in the rearview mirror. The light had been green, so it couldn't be that, but the deputy believed in using not only the lights but the siren. The damn thing sounded like it was on some sort of booster that made people stop and stare. She took a breath, knowing her appearance wasn't going to sit well with a small-town cop. Sometimes small-town also translated to small-minded.

"Shit." The grocery parking lot was the safest place to pull into, and Jax kept cursing until she turned the ignition off. "Who the hell knew they still made mirrored sunglasses? Those look like a collector's item."

She muttered the question when the deputy used the radio to warn her not to leave her vehicle, and to show her hands. "Thanks, baby, I must look like a drug kingpin, driving this thing." She lowered her window and waved her hands out. Officer Professional was still on the radio announcing her license to whoever happened to be in a five-mile radius.

The thought of spending her reunion in jail for some unknown traffic violation might be fate's way of telling her this was all a big mistake. She waved her hands to remind him she was still there in an awkward position. It'd been years since she'd been here but not long enough to forget it was never a good idea to get out and make any sudden movements.

Unless there'd been major changes from her time here, this crack team of law enforcement officers were still required to have a high school diploma of some variety. The other two boxes they had to check were being able to walk and to fire a gun. Those high standards always explained the exceptional recruits they armed and turned loose on the streets. It also explained why it was fairly easy to get away with pretty much anything if you liked to dabble in illegal activities.

"Step out of the car." The people shopping in the grocery must have heard the command blaring out of the bullhorn speakers on the cruiser because they'd come out into the parking lot and stopped to watch. "And keep your hands where I can see them at all times."

The blue polyester uniform was stretched to the limit when the officer stepped out of the car with his hand on the butt of his pistol. The uniform's problem wasn't that he was overweight, but because he used it as a way to try to seem fitter than he was. He tried to emphasize that by not putting his arms down, as if he couldn't because of the muscles in his chest. It gave him the appearance of carrying two milk pails.

With her hands in full view she tensed the muscles in her face so as not to smile at the caricature he presented and fought the urge to check her reflection in his ultra-shiny shoes. She straightened her shoulders when the guy unsnapped the pepper spray on his utility belt. "What seems to be the problem, Officer?" The standard question when you weren't speeding or breaking any other traffic laws that she knew of.

"This car's a rental."

She was raised to respect law enforcement, and not that she was pulled over often, but when someone started like this, all bets were off. "I'm sorry, is that a statement of fact, or a question?" Jax looked at the guy and tried to place him. He looked weirdly familiar, and not being able to remember him was frustrating. Her brain was chasing down memories, but the guy's fidgety hands made her concentrate.

"Just give me your license, and stop trying to be such a smarty-pants."

It was the use of the term *smarty-pants* that brought it all back. If there was a reason not to come back, here he was. On the other hand, seeing him made the trip worthwhile and was a big boost to her ego. "This is too good to believe," Jax said softly as she slowly reached into her front pocket for her wallet. "Daniel, how are things?"

Daniel Gravois, or D-Boy as everyone called him in high school, was the captain of the football and baseball teams. A Greek god in his day, who, aside from all his athletic accomplishments, lived to make Jax as miserable as possible as often as he could. He did that by being as cruel and obnoxious as his little mind could conjure up. That explained the tight shirt and sunglasses. A peacock never changed their peacock ways.

The wonder of the football field never could accept that Jax ran faster and threw farther. The main thing he took offense at was that she smoked him in the classroom even though she was three years younger. All that paled when it came to one thing. They'd clashed over it again and again until it had built a mountain of hate between them. She'd never added to the pile, but Daniel couldn't let it go. He wanted Iris Long, and he'd been willing to crush her to get what he wanted.

Daniel had picked Iris from the first day she'd started high school, and any other girl probably would've creamed her panties at that distinction. That delightful expression had been his, not hers, but Iris had made her own choice that day. His problem was that Iris hadn't chosen him. That truth was why he'd hated Jax from the day he'd laid eyes on her.

"I'm doing better than you are right now, but nice effort trying to be my friend. It ain't gonna get you out of a ticket today."

There was no doubt she was getting a ticket today, so there was no reason not to poke the bear a little. It'd be worth the couple hundred bucks this was going to cost her. "How's Iris?"

He frowned a little, looking at her like he was trying to place her. "Ah, you know the old ball and chain too, huh? Oh, I get it. You're here for the reunion, and you think that's giving you a free pass. That's not happening. We got speed limits for a reason." He laughed, and that same condescending smirk she remembered hadn't changed at all. "Hand over your license, and let's see who you are, hotshot."

Jax thought of Margot's reaction should the phrase *ball and chain* slip from her lips for any reason, referring to her or any other woman. Margot never confessed to knowing any kind of combat moves, but saying that would give her an up-close demonstration of how to maim someone using just your hands.

Daniel held the license at arm's length, and his squinting meant he still couldn't make out the small letters. He exchanged his sunglasses for the half-moon readers in his shirt pocket and still held the license out at arm's length. She smiled at the sour look that overtook his face when he was able to decipher the name.

"Jaxon Lavigne," he said. "I didn't think you'd have the guts to come back. Now that I look at you, you haven't changed all that much."

It's so comforting to know you're blind but choose to wear those nifty shades instead of the glasses that'll allow you to actually see the world around you. D-Boy, you must make a fabulous cop. Jax tried not to laugh out loud as she tried to figure out if he was getting tired holding his arms away from his chest like that.

"True, I'm just a teacher and nowhere near the success you've made of yourself, Deputy D-Boy, but I get by. Why don't you start writing, so I can get on my way? I'd like to check into the B and B and start on all the fun. Do you need help with anything?"

"It's Officer Gravois to you, asswipe—get that part committed to memory." Daniel glared at her before throwing her license on the ground at her feet, then shifted his utility belt as he puffed out his chest even more. Without another word he got back in his cruiser and drove away.

"I can't believe they gave that idiot a gun, and here I thought it would've been Wilber who plugged me full of holes," Jax mumbled to herself as she got back in the car. "Welcome home, Jaxon Lavigne," she said her name the way Daniel had.

She had to remind herself why she'd done this. People like Daniel were like sharp rocks you banged up against at times that inflicted pain. That was their whole purpose, and they didn't care what damage they left behind. If all the abuse he'd heaped on her when they were in school had left scars, she'd be covered in them, but like Margot said, she carried them under her skin. Being back on familiar ground, all those scars had become raw again.

❖

The large old Acadian home at one end of town had been converted into a B and B a few years ago by some young people who'd graduated from the culinary school that was now world renowned. Tully had told her about it, so Margot had changed her reservation from the Marriott two towns over. It was Margot's way of keeping her close to the action and not sitting somewhere avoiding everyone.

"Welcome to The Oaks," a young woman said, standing on the front stairs. "Do you need help with your bags, or a drink maybe?" What an interesting thing to say. "Do I look like I need a drink?" she asked, laughing.

"Maybe I'm projecting," the young woman said and smiled. "Sorry, I hope I didn't insult you."

"You're actually a mind reader, and if you can point me to the front desk, then the bar, I'll be in your debt." She shouldered her bag and took the overnight duffel off the back seat. "A word to the wise, don't let anyone talk you into going to a class reunion."

"And now I know why you need a drink." The jokester handed her a valet ticket and walked her inside. "Enjoy your stay, and let Meg know what you like to drink. She's working the bar today and pours a mean Sazerac."

"I'll have to eat something before I attempt one of those." She wasn't thrilled to be here, but it was hard not to like this kid.

"You've come to the right place. We're not huge, but the kitchen here is first rate. Is there anything else?"

"That'll do it, thank you." She handed over a tip and accepted a key from the front desk attendant. Her room was on the second floor and had a good view of the cane fields on the other side of the bayou that seemed to run all the way to Bayou Lafourche. The crop had a few months to go, but it was tall enough to blow in the wind, and she found the sight comforting. It used to relax her at night when she watched a small patch outside her bedroom window.

"I wonder how long it'll take the gossip mill to reach my mother?" She spoke softly, knowing that Margot was right. It was time to put the past to rest.

CHAPTER TEN

The front door slammed open, hitting the wall behind it. Iris was tired of repairing the drywall when the knob went through it. Before she could say anything the door slammed closed, and Danny was on the stairs. "No running!" Iris yelled but it was as if she was talking to the new hole in her wall. The next door to slam was on Danny's bedroom. "For the love of God, no door slamming!" The cursing she kept in her head, but it was tiring to repeat herself constantly.

The only response was the loud music that started, and it made her shake her head. "Was I this obnoxious when I was a teenager?" She kept picking up clothes off the floor of Sean's room so she could start the laundry. She'd already picked up in Danny's room, and she stopped briefly by his door, contemplating asking him for the clothes he was wearing. "No loud music, do your homework, kiss your mother hello," she said, ticking off the list she'd started when he was six. "And would it kill you to show that cute face around the house other than when you demand food?"

She stopped in the kids' bathroom to pick up all the towels hanging off the counter and lying on the floor to add to her growing pile in the laundry basket. As she glanced around the room again to make sure there wasn't any underwear hiding in the shower, she had to sigh. When had she become the maid service?

She walked down the hall shaking her head. "I wonder if it'd be okay for me to run away from home. Jesus, I've turned into *my* mother." The memory of her mother saying that on a daily basis came to mind as she went down to the washer.

"Nah, your mother never had an ass like this." Daniel snuck up on her and slapped her on the butt before kissing her hello.

"Keep telling me things like that, and you won't be able to afford the therapy bills. I didn't know you made a habit of checking out my mother's ass."

"It's hard to miss, sugar." He put his gun and utility belt in the cabinet she'd cleaned out for him in the kitchen. That he reached for a beer next meant he was off duty. "What'd you do today?"

With the wash going she checked on the chicken stew she'd started when she got home from school. "The same thing I do every day, Daniel. I went to work as a secretary at the same high school we went to, then came home to pick up after you and the kids, then I cooked dinner. My life is so full." She threw her hands up, already aggravated with this day. "You'd think one of you would know what a towel bar is used for."

"That over-the-top sarcasm is something you definitely got from your mother." He took a sip of his beer and wiped his mouth with the back of his hand. "I bet I could tell you something that would brighten up your obviously horrible life."

She turned after he stopped talking and pointed to his feet on the table. "Come on, Daniel, I don't need Danny following your lead on this too."

He was complaining about her sarcasm, but that's exactly how he talked to her lately, and she was getting tired of that too. His passive aggressiveness meant he was waiting for her to beg. She'd only fallen for that once, so he should've learned by now that he'd be waiting until that beer can welded to his hand before she did it ever again. When he didn't move, she couldn't help but take one more shot.

"Is your big news that you're going to call someone to fix the toilet that keeps running?" She changed her tone to syrupy sweet, and that seemed to bug him more than her being flippant.

"I already fixed that." He put his can down with a bit too much force.

"I'm sorry, let me be more specific. I realize you *fixed* it," she said making air quotes. It was something else he loved about her. "Now, when are you going to call someone to come and do it right? The water bill is going to be a doozy, and we need to start thinking of Sean's college expenses."

"Keep ragging me like that, and I'm not going to tell you what you want to know." He pointed at her and smiled as if he held the answer to all her problems.

She turned and stirred their meal again, stopping to taste it to see if it had the proper amount of seasoning. "Either spit it out or wait until later. I have laundry to do."

"Lover girl is back in town, and she even asked about you. I stopped her ass out by the Piggly Wiggly and was generous enough not to give her a ticket. Just for old time's sake, you understand, and because I'm such a generous guy."

It was a good thing she still had her back to him, so he couldn't see when she closed her eyes and balled her hand into a fist. There was no need for him to elaborate on who he was talking about. Jaxon was close now, closer than she'd been in sixteen years, but right now she had to let that go. Denying her feelings would maybe avoid the fight that had started on the day Sean was born. Over the years, it had been the only real point of contention between them. Aside from that major thing, they'd been happy together. But that was about to be put to the test.

"I don't know who you're talking about." She left the room when the dryer buzzed, and she started folding clothes, well aware that he had followed her.

"Come on, Iris, don't bullshit me. You've been waiting for this from the day she drove away. Hell, I know that's why you got yourself put on that planning committee for the reunion." He moved closer to her, but his voice got louder. "Did it give you shivers when you licked the invitation closed and dropped it in the mail to the high and mighty professor?" He took another swig of the beer and licked his lips as he slapped her ass again. "I know that's what all the dieting and exercise was for the last couple of weeks. It certainly wasn't for my benefit."

Iris put her hands on the washing machine and leaned forward a little. "Jaxon and I were only friends—why can't you accept that? She isn't here anymore, but you are. I'm not married to her—I'm married to you. Don't you get it? If you don't, I'll explain it to you in a way you'll understand once and for all. You won, Daniel. I married you, that means you won, so give it a rest."

"I've heard that before, and you might think I'm an idiot, but I'm not. She looked down her nose at me today, and all I could think of was how you'd be salivating all over her the first chance you got. That's a fact, but the fucking thing I can't stand is that everyone in this fucking town knows it too. It's embarrassing to hear them still whispering when I walk up. But why would that be different from any other day? Thanks to you I've been nothing but a laughingstock in this town since that bitch left."

She didn't move from the front of the washer, but she turned her head to look back at him. "What in the hell are you talking about?"

"Come on, don't play dumb now—you know exactly what I'm talking about. How long are you going to wait before running over there? How long before you start pulling out photos of all she missed out on?"

"Did you start drinking before you left work? I still don't know what you're talking about."

"She left before you could show her your special little project," he said with as much venom as he could conjure up. When he was this angry, she knew venom was never a problem for him. She loved him, but he could be trying when his manhood and ego were challenged.

"Spit it out, or stop talking." God, would this day ever end? This was the millionth time they'd had this same argument, and it was never going to be put to rest, so it was a waste of time.

"Iris, stop fucking lying to me and to everyone else. You know exactly what I'm talking about, and I'm going to enjoy all the shit that's about to blow up in your face when she sees Sean. The downside is that all your lying is going to take me down with you." He crushed the can and threw it toward the trash can and missed, making it clatter across the kitchen.

When Iris's eyes widened, he stopped talking and turned around. He punched his palm when he saw their daughter standing in the back doorway. From the look on Sean's face, she had heard every word of the fight. Without saying anything, Sean ran to the back of the house and slammed her bedroom door.

"Honey, wait," Iris called after her, but for the second time that afternoon she didn't get a response from one of her children. When she glared at Daniel, he put his hands up.

"Don't you dare blame me for this. All this is on you. I'm not the bad guy here."

"What you should've done was leave me a long time ago if you felt so wronged. I didn't marry you to make your life miserable. Actually, it's not too late." The tears she was tired of shedding in private came again, and she wiped her face impatiently. "The way you talk to me and constantly blame me for everything that's wrong in your life means you'd be happier without me."

He sighed, his shoulders dropping as he relented. "Don't give me that shit. What we need to agree on is that we made this bed and we're stuck with each other. We can spend the years we have left having this same fucking fight, or put a bullet through it." He lowered his voice and came closer. "All I've ever wanted was for you to admit what you did. What you did to us, to yourself, and more importantly, what you did to Sean."

"I was young and stupid, and I apologize...again. Sometimes I don't acknowledge what you did for me, but I've always appreciated it." She lowered her head, thinking not for the first time how lucky she was. Daniel was often an ass, but he'd come through for her. He liked to remind her constantly that he'd done that, but he'd been what she'd needed.

"What I've always wanted was for you to *love* me for it, Iris. That's it—it was all that was important to me." He rubbed his forehead. "You can't bring yourself to say that, can you?"

"Daniel, if you don't think I love you, then we really are over." She motioned between them. "Neither of us ended up with the life we wanted when we were young and stupid. You thought you'd go to college and play, hoping it would lead to something else, and I thought I'd go to college and be something more than a secretary."

"We gave that up for Sean." He put his hand on her shoulder and she nodded. "I'm sorry. Sometimes it makes me mad, but not about Sean. You were both worth it."

"Thank you, but you remember how they talked about that woman I graduated with, when they found out she was pregnant before we graduated? Anywhere else in the world it wouldn't have been a big deal, but this place thinks we're still living in Victorian England. I panicked." Her tears fell faster, and she didn't protest when he held her. It had been years since that moment she found out she was pregnant, but it still brought with it that sense of dread. That still surprised her, considering pregnancy had been part of a convoluted and ill-thought-out plan to bring Jaxon home.

"What we are as a family isn't going to change. We'll get through this together, and what happens in the next few days will decide for us how everyone will treat us from now on." He kissed the top of her head. "I don't know about you, but I'm damned tired of all these assholes talking about us and our kids. No matter what, we handle this with our heads up and tell anyone who doesn't like it to fuck off."

"I agree, but I don't think Sean's going to accept us not talking about it—really, me not talking about it. She wants out of here, and we have a year to change her mind about staying at least a few more years, until she's really ready." Their daughter had been bright from the moment she was born, and Iris understood everyone thought that of their children, but in this case it was simply fact. Sean was leagues ahead of everyone else, and the only reason she wasn't graduating this year was because they didn't think she was ready emotionally to be away from them.

"I don't think we can," Daniel said bluntly. "Sean isn't going to be happy here no matter what, and she's ready to see what's out there for her. I'm sure Adeline is packed already and pushing her out the door. Keeping her here will only make her miserable. It hit me like a two-by-four when she let us know that, by the way."

"You've evolved," she said, laughing. "She's been saying that for months."

"I don't want her to hate me more than she does already. I'm not happy she's in love with that girl, but only because her life will be hard. Maybe living somewhere else will make it so she's happier." He gave her a sad smile. "We know the kind of regrets that can lead to."

Sean was their daughter, but she was Jaxon in every way, right down to her looks. She was smart, driven, and ready to fly. She didn't need propping up, and it was hard to change her mind once she'd set it on something she wanted. That she was smart would help her in college, but letting her go wouldn't be easy. And Iris had already known how important it was for Sean to go, but the relief she felt at Daniel accepting it made it far easier.

"Thank you for this. Let me go check on her."

Daniel held her tighter. "One thing," he said in a flat tone. "Jaxon Lavigne has nothing to do with her. I mean that, Iris. She's my kid, and I expect you to respect that."

She had no response because she didn't know how she'd handle this. It wasn't about Jaxon and her anymore, but about Sean and what she needed. "We'll see," was all she could say.

❖

The people next door waved when Jaxon went out on the porch with a book, and she smiled at the woman who put a drink on the small table next to the rocker she'd picked. She couldn't quite make out the neighbors and briefly wondered if they recognized her. If they did, the gossip network that worked overtime in this town would be in overdrive, eventually reaching her mother. Her promise to Margot was something she took seriously, but facing her mother for a talk she in no way wanted to have might take a day. Despite time and distance, there was no doubt in her soul her mother hadn't changed her mind.

It was a weird concept to wrap her brain around, that the person who loved her enough to bring her into the world would find her so lacking that she'd throw her away. On the days she wasn't busy enough, the things she thought about were the pictures that lined the hallway of her childhood home. They were proof of all the things she'd done in her life, leading up to her high school graduation. Her mother wanted them on display for all the world to see what great people she'd raised. They'd probably all been taken down now.

In the span of a life, those early years were infinitesimal when you compared them to what came next. College, licking the wounds of first love, a career, and then true love. All that overshadowed the years at home trying her best to make her parents proud. Once she'd been sent away, though, there'd been no parents scrambling to the front to take a picture, not when she'd finished at LSU, and for no other achievement since.

"How could I be so unforgivable?" she whispered, closing the book and concentrating instead on her drink. The most amazing thing in all this was that Margot loved her. But there were still moments she felt unfit to be her partner. Hell, if her mother had found her that depraved, shouldn't the rest of the world?

That small bit of the little kid that still lived in her had a fantasy that her parents would show up one day and beg her forgiveness. They'd made a mistake when it came to her, but then she was too much of a pragmatist to not know that line of thinking was as stupid as it was delusional. When she'd started teaching, she'd study the gallery, often searching for her father's face. He'd been the reader in their family, and she suspected he would enjoy some of her lectures. She wanted to think that he'd be proud of her for the job she did with her students.

She shook her head and took a sip of her drink. It wasn't until someone was standing right in front of her that she glanced up. The sight of her old English teacher made her smile and stop the train wreck of morbid thoughts. Eugenia Landry hadn't changed all that much, and Jax stood to hug her.

"Miss Landry, it's good to see you. How are you?" There was some guilt that she hadn't been in touch in a long while.

Eugenia held on to her after kissing her cheek. "Jaxon, either you start calling me Eugenia, or I'll be forced to start calling you Dr. Lavigne. Don't tell me you've forgotten your manners already. Ask me to sit." Jax laughed as she waved her to the rocker next to hers and got the bartender's attention through the front window.

"How about a glass of the pinot?" The bartender kissed Eugenia as well, which meant there was another generation who appreciated her for the great teacher she was.

"That would be lovely, and don't forget about the book club next week. You missed a good one last time, so don't fall too far behind."

"Yes, ma'am." The bartender saluted before going to get Eugenia's wine.

Jax smiled, remembering those gentle reprimands, and they'd kept her engaged when she'd been subjected to them. The main reason she was sorry Margot couldn't make it was not being able to introduce her to Eugenia. She'd been such an influence on her that Jax attributed most of her success to this small but fierce woman.

"Still giving everyone hell, I see," she said and smiled when Eugenia reached over and took her hand.

"If I had to guess, I'm not the only one. Bert's the best gossip in the world, and he's told me about your classroom antics. He tells me there's not an empty seat, and the kids love you."

The pride in her mentor's voice was hard to miss, and she had to swallow the lump in her throat. All the emotions of coming home were starting to build to the point of embarrassment.

"It's okay, honey. I didn't come to upset you. How are you really?"

"I'm good, and I'm happy. I'm sure Bert told you about Margot." Just mentioning Margot's name made her smile.

"He did, and she sounds like a lovely girl. I realize coming back isn't something you're wild about doing, but I'd like to meet her. That said, I'm glad I get you all to myself for a little while." Eugenia smiled as the bartender put her wine down, and they clinked glasses before she took a sip. "I wanted to thank you for all those great notes you've sent through the years. It's amazing that I blinked, and you became the best writer I know."

"After all the authors you introduced me to, I doubt that's true. I have tried to make you proud, though." She didn't mean to admit that last part, but Eugenia deserved to know just how important to her she was.

"I've always been proud of you. Of all my students, you were the most memorable. That you became an educator makes me think my life has had some meaning. But enough mush for one day."

"Thank you," she said, toasting Eugenia again. "An overflow of tears puts dents in my cool facade." She took a sip of her drink and exhaled. "How have you been?"

"I'm tired, and the school board is pushing me to retire. I think after this year I might give in to their wishes and enjoy what's left of my life."

To know Eugenia wouldn't be in a classroom giving kids the start they'd need to fly one day saddened her. "Is the board as clueless as it was when I was here? If teaching is what makes you happy, they should leave you alone."

"I'm not retiring because of them, Jaxon. I'm retiring because there's a few things I'd like to see and do before I die. The first might be coming to visit you, so you can introduce me to your wife." Eugenia winked and laughed.

"I'm not married."

"You should be, and from what Bert tells me, Margot Drake is madly in love with you. Only books should be put on a shelf, Dr. Lavigne. If you love her, then prove it to her."

They'd never discussed their private lives, but she never remembered Eugenia with anyone. She'd never married, and if she dated, she didn't do it in Chackbay. "I do love her, and I'm working on it."

"Love is a precious thing." Eugenia held her wineglass and stared off into the distance. It was like she was flying back in time remembering something precious, from the expression on her face. "Don't ever forget that."

"What, or who, was your great love?" Curiosity was a central part of her personality according to Margot, but this might be pushing the limits. Most Southern women didn't like being asked personal questions. It was like a combination of asking what they weighed and how old they were. That was none of your business no matter who you were.

"We have a great deal in common, my friend. I should've left here years ago and lived the life I truly wanted, but there was plenty holding me back. That we don't have in common." Eugenia reached over and patted her hand, and Jaxon held it. "You ran out of here like the devil himself was chasing you, and look at the life you've built. I lived for weekends and holidays when I could get away."

"Where'd you go? If you don't mind telling me. I don't want to upset you."

"It's a finished chapter, and telling the story now isn't going to make a difference to my life. I'd drive to Baton Rouge to spend time with Dr. Elle Taylor. She wanted it to be permanent, but she understood my commitment to my parents."

"Wait a minute. Dr. Taylor and you?" If she had a favorite teacher after Eugenia, it was Elle Taylor.

"Yes, and she spoke of you often and the notes you sent her until her death last year. I took a sabbatical to take care of her, and she left you something. Stop by the house before you go, and I'll give it to you." Eugenia wiped away the tears that fell steadily, and Jaxon moved to hold her. "It was a different time when I was young, just like it was when you were growing up."

"It sounds like you weren't together all the time, but you were happy."

"We were. Our summers were always full of adventure to exotic places, and memories of our weekends are what help me make it through the days now." Eugenia kissed her cheek and pushed her back to her rocker. "That's why you need to show that girl of yours how special she is."

"Like I said, I'm working on it."

Eugenia nodded once and took another sip of wine. "Now that I've spilled my secrets, let me tell you the real reason I'm here. I want you to do me a favor."

"You can ask me anything—you know that."

"I've been teaching for years now, and with Elle gone, I was looking for a sign to finally let it all go. This year that finally came, and I think it's time for my protégé to leave her own stamp on my students."

"I'm not sure what that means, but I'll help if I can." She only loved mysteries in books.

"Come and teach my junior honors class on Friday. A few of my kids need a taste of what a big-city education could do for them."

Jaxon laughed and shook her head. "Wouldn't your seniors be better candidates if you want them to aspire to college and beyond?"

"Believe me, I know what I'm doing. There are fourteen kids in the class, and I get them at ten in the morning. You can pick the assignment, and I spoke to the teachers who get them after me, and they said they don't mind you cutting into their class time if you go over." Eugenia drained her glass and patted her hand again. "I'll be waiting for you." She handed over a card with her information on it. "When you think of something for them to read, call me, and I'll email them all with the information. Don't be late, and don't cut them any slack. You may not believe me, but some of these kids need to see you."

"See me?" If she didn't know any better, she'd swear she'd had a lot more drinks than her one.

Eugenia nodded. "Nothing in life is better than a living, breathing example of what could be if only you took the chance. Fear should be reserved for things like charging bulls, Jaxon, not being the person you are."

"Words to live by, I guess." She was confused by this whole conversation, but it wasn't an unreasonable request.

"They are, and I'm leaving before you come to your senses."

For a woman in her late sixties, Eugenia was spry enough to take the stairs faster than Jax would've thought. Her departure left her with the thought she'd been bamboozled, but telling Eugenia no wasn't in her DNA.

"And people think I'm an odd duck." Jaxon signaled for another drink and called Margot on her way up to her room. She got her voice mail, so she grabbed her journal and headed across the street to the bayou and the Adirondack chairs set up to take in the view.

She remembered the old dock someone had built at the back of her grandmother's property, and how many hours she'd spent staring at the lazy flow of the dark brown water. Those gentle ripples had been one of the first things that had stirred her imagination to put words to paper. The ocean and the view from their backyard at home in California had opened her mind to bigger and better things, but a different view of this same bayou had been her humble beginnings.

The journal sat forgotten on her lap as she continued to reminisce until her phone ringing woke her up. She smiled at how the muddy water still had the ability to put her to sleep as she fished her phone out. "Hello."

"Do you miss me as much as I'm missing you?" Margot sounded whiny, a sure sign she'd had a crappy day so far.

"Who is this, Viola?" She loved teasing Margot and got a raspberry for her trouble.

"And why am I missing you?" Margot laughed then made a kissing noise. "How's it going?"

"I started missing you the moment you drove away." She was glad she was the only one out here, not wanting anyone to overhear her conversation. The sound of slamming car doors meant other guests were probably arriving, and some, if not all of them, were probably old classmates.

Margot hummed for a moment then sighed. "You do have a talent for redeeming yourself, Lavigne. Now answer my question. How are you?"

Trying to learn from her past mistakes, Jax gave her a full account of what had happened from the time she'd left Tully's, including her encounter with local law enforcement. "This guy took bullying to a whole new level for the two years I was subjected to him, and it's good to know he now wears a gun for a living. The bright spot of my day was a visit from Eugenia." Margot knew exactly who Eugenia was from all her old stories.

"Are you going to do it?" Margot was making plenty of noise on her end, but Jaxon couldn't figure out what she was doing.

"I'd fear for my life if I didn't show up. What are you up to?"

"We got let go early, and I'm tired of takeout. I'm making stir-fry, and I promise to freeze you some. So, what award-winning lecture do you have planned?"

"I was thinking of the short story you argued so passionately about."

"'The Ones Who Walk Away from Omelas' is a great choice, sweetie. That day of class will always stay with me, and I use it sometimes when I have to conjure up a good image of man's inhumanity to man. Makes me cry every time."

The short story written by Ursula K. Le Guin was, in Jaxon's opinion, a masterful use of words. It described the utopian city of Omelas, where there was no poverty, sickness, or problem of any kind. The city's dirty secret was these blessings depended on one child being locked in a closet and singled out for a life of misery, and most of the city's residents accepted this atrocity as the bargain they'd made with some unmentioned being for the lives everyone else got to lead.

"It's not very long, but it's a great teaching tool to make you consider your actions, going forward in life. I'd like to believe I'm putting not only educated people out into the world, but decent ones."

"True, but some of the opinions people expressed in class still shock me. I blame those idiots for electing Trump. It'll be interesting to see what a younger group thinks."

"That story makes you wonder if a sacrifice of one person for the good of everyone else is something you could live with. It works unless you or your child is the sacrifice."

"But it was a child, honey." It took a minute for Margot to go from calm to indignant over the subject.

"Sweetheart, the story wouldn't work if the one singled out was some evil killer rapist. It has to be a sacrifice you have to have second thoughts about. Looking in on that kid surrounded by darkness and dirty mops should make you examine yourself as a person if you're able to turn away and not have a problem with it. And we've already had this argument." She stretched and cracked her neck from sleeping in an awkward position for so long.

"Uh, I loved and hated that assignment. How can you be so blasé about it?"

"Because I've taught it for years, but our initial reactions weren't all that different. They pay me to be more objective about it. Calling those who'd have no problem with it heartless assholes isn't acceptable, according to the dean."

"Hey, I'd find that a totally acceptable response," Margot said and laughed.

Remembering Margot screaming that at the top of her lungs at some asshole sitting behind her made her laugh as well. "How's work?"

Margot took a deep breath, which meant it wasn't good. "It smells like someone died on the set, but Judith was right. The furniture dried like new, but I've done everything possible not to sit on any of it, so my butt doesn't smell like mildew. This week's episode will look like someone followed us around holding dead fish under our noses. All that matters is that we're on schedule. Those assholes would've walked away after seeing that poor kid and bought everyone a round of drinks."

"I'm sorry, but if you're on schedule, you should have the weekend off. It's not worth the flight for just a Saturday night thing I probably won't be at for long. Take some time to go see your parents, and save me the trip," she said, teasing.

"You know Daddy would be disappointed if I showed up without you." Margot blew her another kiss and sounded better. "Sorry, I didn't mean to call you just to bitch. I'm pissed about work and because I'm here and not there. Go get something to eat, and promise you'll call me later. If I can't go to sleep with you next to me, I can still go to sleep with you."

"I promise, and have the driver stop for some mints before you go in tomorrow. It'll help with the smell. I love you, and I do miss you."

"I love you too, honey, and try to eat something that doesn't come in a grease-stained bag. If you clog your arteries while you're out of my sight, you're in for a lecture that'll make you reexamine yourself as a person when I get you home."

She laughed at that. After moving in with Margot, *hot dog* had become a dirtier word than *fuck*. "I'm eating with Bert and his parents, so not to worry, my cholesterol will be the same when I get home."

"Good, and I love you too."

She changed for dinner and drove to Bert's after stopping for a bottle of wine. The delicious meal both his mother and father had put together made her lethargic by the time they were done. Going to bed so full was a bad idea, so she took a walk after getting back and enjoyed the way her footsteps echoed on the sidewalk. Los Angeles was never this quiet, and she'd forgotten there were still places like this in the world.

She remembered nights spent eating with her best friend's family like she had tonight, then climbing into Iris's room after her parents were asleep so she and Iris could kiss. All those memories made her smile. Those had been some of the last times she'd not been consumed with guilt, worry, and angst over what had happened when the people she'd loved knew the truth of her. The pain had made her strong, but she had no desire to relive it.

Seeing her parents again was important, but she'd walk away for good this time, not allowing the hurtful things they probably still thought to get past her defenses. Time had taught her that everyone was entitled to their opinions, but it didn't make them true. It had taken plenty of hard work to carve out a life she was proud of, and nothing anyone said would make her love Margot any less.

In the end, that Margot loved her was all that mattered.

Iris put a bag of oranges in her shopping cart and pushed it forward, but she accidentally bumped the cart in front of her. "I'm so sorry," she said, putting her hand up. She was trying to rush home and change to meet Nancy and the girls. The pre-reunion cocktail party was the next afternoon, and she was trying to finish putting all the food and mixers together, so she could relax for the party.

"Iris, it's been a long time," Eve Lavigne said. The woman always managed to make her name sound like *Ooh, I have dog shit stuck to my shoe.*

There was no one else in her life who'd spoken to her like they were shooting the words down their nose in disdain. They hadn't had many interactions since Jaxon left town even though they lived about a mile from each other, but she'd bet everything she owned that Eve blamed her for what had happened.

Roy had told her a little of how his mother had reacted to learning about Jaxon's sexuality and the hateful things that dug an ocean between mother and daughter, one neither of them was willing to cross. Eve most probably made herself feel better by making Iris the villain. In her version of reality, Jaxon was fine until Iris seduced her into a life of sin and perversion.

"Mrs. Lavigne, I apologize, but I'm in a hurry." She tried to go around Eve, but she moved her cart to block her way.

"Is it true Jaxon is back for the weekend?"

Iris barely heard the question Eve had asked so softly. "She sent in her response that she was coming, but I haven't seen her. I'm sure she'll call you when she gets to town." Sean picked that moment to come back with two cases of Coke she'd sent her for. The way Eve stared at her daughter made her uncomfortable. "Hey, could you pick up a couple bottles of cranberry juice for me?"

Sean glanced at Eve before heading to the other side of the store without a word.

"Is she yours?" Eve asked, following Sean with her eyes.

"Yes, she's my daughter. If you'll excuse me, I really need to get going." She turned and moved around one of the displays to get away.

What had happened wasn't one person's fault. She bore the majority of the blame for being a coward, but what Eve had done didn't help anything. It had taken a wedding and having a baby for her own parents to forgive her for something they didn't understand or accept. Her mother had told her Daniel was the best thing that could happen to her, followed only by Jaxon leaving for school. It would make all the gossip die down, her mother had foolishly thought.

"Who was that?" Sean asked. She put the cranberry juice in the cart and stood next to her.

Iris had been surprised Sean had volunteered to go shopping with her, but no one would ever guess she wanted to be there from the way she walked with her hands shoved deep in her pockets. "Eve Lavigne," she said, going down the chip aisle and picking up a selection. "She's the mom of someone I went to school with."

"Jaxon Lavigne?" Sean asked. The name fell off Sean's lips quickly, and the way she didn't look at her meant she wasn't expecting an answer.

"Yes, Jaxon was a friend in high school, but I haven't seen her in years." She headed for the registers and placed her hand on Sean's shoulder when they stopped in a line. When had she gotten so tall? "How would you like to go to New Orleans for a long weekend next week? Just you and me."

"Why?" Sean gazed down at her with her usual noncommittal expression. It seemed she was never truly angry but not happy either.

"I think we need to talk, and I'd like to spend time with you. I'm not forcing you to go, but I'd like it if you said yes." They worked together to unload their cart, and she saw Eve was behind them, her eyes still on Sean. Eve seemed to drink her in like someone who'd wandered the desert before finding an oasis.

"What's her jam?" Sean mumbled, turning her back on Eve.

"She's not the nicest person," she said softly, and the cashier nodded, having obviously heard her. "Don't worry about it."

"Can I go back to Adeline's once we're done here?"

"Sure, I'll drop you off on the way home. Are you spending the night again?" They finished, and she laughed when Sean turned and waved to Eve as they were leaving. That produced that pinched face Iris was very familiar with.

"Thanks, Mom, and thanks for thinking of next weekend. I didn't think you understood where my head is at."

There were times when she looked at Sean and swore it was a young Jaxon standing before her. They were so alike in so many ways it sometimes scared her. It caused a pain in her chest that felt like someone was filling her with pressure at the thought of Sean leaving and never looking back. Eve might've been that stupid, but she'd never let either of her children down that way.

"I know exactly where your head is at. Compared to you, I'm ancient, but I still remember what it was like to be your age." She hugged Sean once they loaded the car and got in. "The days you spend in high school seem endless, but one day it'll be over, and you'll be free to do whatever you want."

"That's what Miss Landry says all the time." Sean set a bag of groceries in with a sigh. "Most of the people in my class are jerks, but it's cool. I know I'll only be seventeen next year, but I'm going away if all my scholarships come through. You're okay with that, right?"

Conflicted, Iris smiled to hide her feelings. "I want you to do what's going to make you happy. All I want is for you to not push us away." God forbid she pushed her away completely when she knew the truth.

"That'll never happen, no matter what," Sean said as if reading her mind. "Maybe it's time I told you some stuff too."

"You're my child, Sean, so I know all I need to. No matter what you do, who you love, or where you go, I'm your mother, and I love you. I always will." She'd no more damn her child to a life she didn't want than she'd force her to stop seeing Adeline.

Life threw enough regrets and pain in your path, and her job was to make sure Sean and Danny could navigate each one. It's what her mother should've done for her, and she'd break the cycle in this generation. For the first time in a long time, she had hope that this might work out, and she'd do what she needed to so Sean wouldn't turn her back on her.

Chapter Eleven

G ood morning, everyone. I hope you've all had a chance to read the assignment." Jax opened her bag and took out her notes.

The low grumbling and the tapping of feet were the most familiar things Jax had heard since arriving. Her classes started much the same way until she was able to encourage the reluctant learners out of their shells with either the assignments she handed out, or with the large stick Margot liked to call her wit. This was a little over their grade level, but Eugenia had assured her it was a great choice.

Walking through the halls of the old school brought on a mild case of claustrophobia that eased as some as her old teachers stepped out of their classrooms to say hello. There weren't many of the old guard left, and she'd seen plenty of fresh faces who appeared extremely new to the job. What Jax quickly figured out was that many of the new teachers had been students here and had plans to be in these classrooms until they retired.

That could've been her fate, and only her mother's rejection had saved her from the life of a high school English teacher in a town that never would have accepted her. That was the silver lining in the whole fuckup, and it made her smile. As happy with her life as she was, it made her equally happy to see the eagerness in these people who were responsible for the next generation. If there were any more kids like her sitting in their classes, she hoped there were future Eugenias who would shepherd them to where they needed to be.

When she put her papers down and looked up, there were thirteen kids staring back at her as if trying to decide what would happen next.

There was one kid in the back with their head down, and she wasn't in the begging mood. You either paid attention or you didn't. The rest of them, though, stared at her as if trying to figure her out.

They'd probably never seen Eugenia show up to teach in jeans and a bright pink pullover shirt. She really needed to pay attention to what Margot was placing in her suitcase. Except for the few gray hairs sprinkled at her temples, and the laugh lines around her eyes, she thought she resembled the new teachers she'd met today. She had Margot to thank for that with her healthy diet choices and all the other things she did to take care of her.

"How's everyone doing this morning?" Her question got her crickets. She smiled and tried again. "I know we just started, so you can't be bored yet."

"Good morning," they said, not exactly in unison. Not exactly enthusiastically, either.

"Trust me, guys, you'll thank me for this when you're a senior in college and have to read this same story. I've always thought it's a sort of sociological study professors conduct to see what kind of insanity we're about to release on society. You're only semi-crazy now, but believe me, it gets worse when you go away to school and pickle your brain with the evil that is alcohol." The laughter was somewhat expected, and it was the signal she had their attention.

An hour later a few of her old teachers came and sat in Eugenia's classroom to listen in. It made her smile that no one had looked toward the clock. She'd known plenty of students whose attention was forever glued on the time to see how close they were to escape.

"The most important thing when it comes to this story is how it made you feel. Intellectually it should make you think of the possibilities." She wanted to start wrapping up before the lunch bell rang.

"What's to think about?" a guy sitting in the second row asked. "I say, heck yeah."

"So you'd be okay with it? You think it's all right to let some kid sit in a dark room in their own mess, eating slop, just so everybody else can have a perfect existence? Remember that same child, who at one time knew love and carried with them the memory of warm hugs from their mother, has had that and everything else ripped away. You'd be okay with that being the payment for a deal struck for everyone else's benefit? Is that what you're saying?" Jaxon asked in return. All her questions were meant to make him think about what kind of person he wanted to be.

Pretty much all the students were engaged in the lecture, and she did her best to wring out every emotion from the story. That one kid in the back was still staring at whatever was on their desk and hadn't moved from the time she'd started. She couldn't figure what was on the kid's mind, but the favor Eugenia had asked was for one lecture. Delving into the problems of postpubescent teenagers wasn't her responsibility.

"No," the boy said, and it sounded a lot like a question.

"Is it no or yes?" She threw the question back at him. He had to pick an answer. The story deserved a cut-and-dried response.

"Why shouldn't it be yes?" a tall redheaded boy asked. He was sitting on the front row dwarfing the girl behind him. "Doesn't the good of the many outweigh the good of the one?" That was his comeback when she still was silent. "Kids die every day in war, or their parents kill them trying to get them into this country illegally. They either die in the desert, or they get sold into sex rings. It's why we need the wall—to save kids like this one in the closet." The boy was firm in his convictions—she gave him that. "That way only one goes through all the crap, and the rest of us would be good."

The kid appeared ready to slap himself on the back, and Jax tried to keep her horrified expression in check. "Okay." She had to take a moment to think of something to say that didn't include the words *Neanderthal*, *fuck*, and *you*.

It was amazing that some of the people in this town were still spilling their shit onto the next generation. What this little asshole was basically saying was if the kid was brown, they were dispensable. It was only an added bonus if they could cure all the world's problems. If that was true people like him would line them up for torture.

"A *Star Trek* fan, huh?" Jax almost laughed at the blush that made his face resemble his hair. "Okay, so you have one person willing to suffer for the rest of us. That sounds like a good thing. No more illness, crime, hate, xenophobia, the list is mind-boggling, right? What a great thing to be able to sleep with whomever you want without shame, or take drugs or drink without ever becoming addicted. All because you keep this kid locked up in their own dark hell."

He cut in as she opened her mouth to go on. "Yeah, I mean, I could live with that. I'd have been one of the people who would've been perfectly okay with the situation when they showed me that room. The ones who walked away from perfection were a bunch of idiots." He turned and looked around to his peers to back him up. "I mean, Christianity is kinda the same thing. The woman has basically plagiarized the story of Christ."

Jax looked at him for a long moment, making his blush deeper. She was somewhat impressed with the analogy he'd used to articulate his point. He was like the majority of people she'd known growing up who sat in those pews every Sunday religiously, but invoked Christ to defend untenable positions. "Plagiarism is a bit harsh, but consider this—Christianity is based on a volunteer. The Son of God knew what he was up against and what was expected of him."

"Maybe," the kid said, clearly not ready to let go.

"The story *I* made you read was about an unknowing innocent who's made to live all the misery life meant for the rest of us, and I mean *all* of it. A pact with some evil source makes it so, but the problem is, the kid's not going to live forever. The sacrificial lamb needs to be constantly replaced by some other unsuspecting soul, so when are you ready to go?" Jax tried to keep her voice calm, knowing it was her job to push all their buttons, not the other way around.

"What do you mean?" The redhead's face went from embarrassed to confused.

"The suffering of the one, mainly you, will be great for the many, that would be us. So I ask again—when are you ready to go?"

"I don't want to do it."

She inflamed his anger when the others sitting around him laughed. Jaxon was having fun now, and Eugenia was laughing with her from her seat at the back of the room. "Okay, you don't want to go, how about this. Do you have an annoying younger sibling?"

"Yeah, I've got a little sister, why?" He appeared wary now.

"When can we pack her up and shuffle her off to the basement?" The kid just stared at her and didn't have any other comeback. He wanted what the luckiest of Omelas had, but he didn't want to pay the price. No one ever did.

"Okay, I get it," he said, not as enthusiastic as before.

"I picked this story for a couple of reasons, and most of them I'm willing to admit were selfish. Life will teach you many things the older you get, and none of those are lessons you'll learn in a classroom. I think most of you realize that, since who you are and what you already know came from the whole of your life's experiences up to now."

This was the reason she added this assignment to her curriculum every year. The lessons were things everyone learned. Through trial and error she'd done the same, and she would've appreciated someone giving her a hint when she was this age—it might've saved her a lot of angst. Knowing that pain didn't last, that being alone didn't have to be your fate, and that you could be the architect of your life made things bearable.

"That means you know there is no place as perfect as Omelas. The real question is this: Is Omelas perfect? I don't think it is, because you can't build your life on the misery of someone else. The things which make life sweeter are the things you earn along the way on your own merit."

She had them now. They all looked at her as if she'd cast a spell. "Some of you will go on to be what society defines as highly successful, and some will be content with a job that will put a roof over your head and food on your table. Does it make those people who chose a different path failures?"

A lot of the kids attending school here would go on to trade school, then to jobs offshore, or for one of the manufacturers that built everything from boats to oil platforms. People worked with their hands and were proud of it. Those jobs had become a tradition of sorts, and there was absolutely nothing wrong with them. This lesson was for them as well as for those who'd walk away in search of something different—especially for those who'd walk away.

"The moral of any story is what you perceive it to be. The important lesson of any story is how you can use it to learn something about your own life. The lesson Omelas should teach us is that life is perfect because it has flaws. Everything we do carries risks and consequences, sometimes good, sometimes bad—it just depends on the paths you choose. Things like health are sometimes beyond our control, but nothing will bring you greater satisfaction than taking all that life or fate throws at you and achieving victory anyway."

"But wouldn't we be better off without disease?" a young woman asked, still not ready to let go of the idea of total utopia.

Jax nodded and pointed at herself. "I personally don't like being sick, but when I am, it makes me appreciate my healthy days that much more. Think of it this way—Omelas is the name of the city in this story, but in reality it can be anywhere."

The girl smiled at her with what seemed to be a touch of infatuation. "What do you mean?"

"Most of the people I went to school with, their picture of perfection was here." She sat on Eugenia's desk and patted the surface. "Why would you want to leave a place that embodies everything good you've ever known? There's hardly any crime when you compare it to the big cities, and you can walk down the street and recognize probably nine out of ten people you see."

"Yeah," the redhead said. "Our parents want us to think that and stay close to home no matter what."

"You need to make up your mind about that, but listen to the advice they give you. Chackbay might have its dirty little secrets locked away in even the nicest homes along the bayous, but overall it's home. For some of us, though, we opened the door and looked in on those ugly hidden things and walked away, and kept on walking until we found our own ideal Omelas. A place where it's easier for the newcomer to justify the nameless kid in the basement, afraid of the dry and crusty mops. No matter where you end up, no place is perfect, and what counts is that you're happy. Everywhere has its problems. You have to find the one where you can overlook the bad, or even work to make it better, as well as live the life you want to lead."

She glanced back at Eugenia, glad to see her nodding. The seniors had set their course by now, but her old teacher wanted her to open the horizons of those kids still making those future plans. They had this year and next to decide what would come next. It was plenty of time, but having a plan you believed in would help with those parents who wanted to keep their chicks in the nest. What she was trying to do was give these kids a permission slip, making it okay to want something different. She wanted them to feel good about picking a course that would make them happy.

"I'm back to reflect on all those choices I made when I decided to walk away. You're just starting out, so don't feel bad for whatever you decide when it's your turn to walk to that basement door and look in. In the end, we all end up in a city named Omelas." She paused and let what she'd just said steep for a moment before she wrapped up for the day.

"If no one has any questions, I want to thank you for your attention and participation. I'm thinking you'll all make wonderful college students if that's where you're headed. If it isn't, well that's okay too, but don't forget to keep reading even after they hand you the sheepskin. Life can teach you plenty, but don't knock the power of a good story."

The students came up and thanked her and shook her hand, asking questions about the next level of their education, and that was the best reward of the day. The teachers in attendance were next, and by the time the mutual admiration was finished, she was hungry. Jaxon declined the offer of the school cafeteria experience and headed into town to one of the local cafés.

"Hey, baby, I just finished, and I'm headed to lunch. Call me when you're free. Have a good day, and I love you." The day reminded her of all the things she loved about teaching as well as all the things she didn't miss about this place. That redheaded kid either had to evolve or spend the rest of his life with friends who also enjoyed dragging their knuckles on the ground.

"Lunch?" the woman at the diner asked.

"Yes, please, and it's just me." Thankfully that wasn't true any longer.

❖

The Formica-topped table had been cleared of the fried catfish lunch Jaxon had ordered. A platter of cholesterol wasn't her usual fare, but there were some perks to being in south Louisiana. The food wasn't good for you, perhaps, but it was good. The waitress hadn't minded her occupying a table for a couple of hours, so she'd ordered coffee and was on her third cup. She'd split the time watching the world go by and grading papers.

She circled the C she'd placed in the upper right-hand corner of the page and was writing some notes in the margin when she heard someone clear their throat, a sound she'd know if she was locked in a dark room. Her mistake was relaxing out in public and not in her room where there was a lock on her side of the door. "Mother, I didn't think you ate out in town."

"I never will figure out where I went wrong with you. After not seeing your family for years, that's the only thing that comes to mind when you see me?" Her mother sat across from her and wiped that side of the table with a napkin. "We could all be dead, and you'd never know it."

"I'm not sure I understand." She stacked the essays and pushed them aside. "You told me sixteen years ago to leave your house and you'd washed your hands of me." Her mother opened her mouth, and she recognized the expression of a woman who loved to change history. "Don't even try it. Those words are branded into my soul. I'd forget my name before I forget what you said."

"Always so dramatic," her mother said as if they were talking about the weather.

"No, Mother. I gave you what you wanted, and I'm sure you've played the martyr to the hilt from the moment I left. The one who could've been dead was me. Everything I made of myself from the second I left has nothing to do with you. Why are you even here?"

"Why are *you* here? What's so important that you came back now?"

The waitress held up the coffeepot out of her mother's view, and she smiled and shook her head. Leave it to her mother to have this conversation here, of all places. But at least she could get it over with.

"You've proven you care nothing about your family and our wishes."

"What exactly is that supposed to mean? You asked me to leave, and I left. I did exactly what you asked." What was wrong with her mother? Would whatever afflicted her affect her and Margot's kids? Not that she could get Margot pregnant, but thinking about that was better than whatever the hell this was.

"You don't think people here talk. They see you in those dreadful papers with that woman. Have you no idea how embarrassing it is for your father? After all the years he spent serving his country, he deserves better." It was amazing how much emotion her mother could put into a conversation without ever unclenching her teeth. "What I did was to help you see that what you were doing was wrong."

"That woman has a name. It's Margot Drake, and I love her. I'd say I was sorry that you don't understand, but I'm never going to apologize for my feelings. To answer your question, the reason I'm here is because of Margot."

"What does she have to do with it? I'm sure you've filled everyone who'll listen with vile lies about me and your father, but that woman doesn't know me or my family."

"She wanted to see if we could work things out. I came to try, but it's no use. You won't ever admit you're wrong, and I'm never going to bend to your will. That means it's a stalemate. It's not all bad. Once I leave this time, I won't come back. You can be happy that I've given you what you wanted." She rubbed her hands on her jeans, trying to let out some of the tension building into a headache.

"You think I want this?" Her mother acted as if she had no idea why she was upset.

"You're the one who asked for it. That you came here to berate me for both not getting in touch and for being here at all, as well as for having the audacity to be in love with someone who ends up in the news, tells me all I need to know. You have no desire to have me in your life. Or is it that you'd like to add to the gossip supposedly still going around about me?" She placed her hands on the table and thought about flying home that night if she could get a flight. Her promise to talk to her mother had been fulfilled, and there was no going back.

"Do you hate me that much?" Her mother finally showed some cracks in her armor.

"No. You don't get to make this about you. I've never hated you. What you can't face is that I'm your child, and you threw me away. I wasn't going to conform to what you wanted, and it made me defective. You threw me to the wolves, so they'd tear me to shreds, and I'd have no choice but to come crawling back." Margot was right. Getting all this out in the open was cathartic. "But I made it without you, and I'm successful and happy despite your desire to break me. You're going to have to live with that—I've made my peace with it."

"If that was true, you wouldn't be here." Her mother wasn't one to give up easily.

"Think whatever you want. I'm here for a fifteen-year class reunion. It makes no sense to me, but that's all it is. There is no hidden agenda, and you can feel better about yourself for listing everything I'll burn in hell for, and for making sure I feel less-than. Well done."

The deep breath her mother took made her think she was preparing for a second round, or had learned to spit fire, but she gripped her purse and left, her head held high. So much for touching reunions and seeing the error of their ways. Nothing here was ever going to change. This town was as timeless as the ancient oaks that'd stood guard over the land for hundreds of years. In people that quality was only honorable or beautiful if they evolved.

Her mother proved they had not.

CHAPTER TWELVE

D o you mind if I sit for a minute?" The girl sounded both shy and uncertain.

Jax lowered her hands enough to be able to see her. Her mother's visit had made her want to scrub the frustration off her skin. She was about to tell whoever this was she wasn't in a social mood when she really looked at her. "Jiminy Cricket."

It was like looking in a mirror and seeing your younger self. It was disconcerting. Who was this, and who exactly were her parents? The two twigs on their branch of the Lavigne family tree were her and her brother Roy, so unless he was holding out on her, the kid's looks were a major coincidence.

"Uh, sure." She pointed to the seat across from her. She couldn't stop openly staring, but the kid seemed to be doing the same thing.

"I didn't want to bother you, but I'd really like to talk to you." The kid shrugged and Jax lowered her eyes to the jacket she had on. The letterman jacket had symbols for softball, track, basketball, and volleyball.

She had to laugh at what ran through her head. If this kid had to share her face, it was good she wasn't just smoking behind the gym. "Uh, okay." She made a quick mental note to stop saying *uh* so much.

"I've been waiting for the day you'd come back. My girlfriend told me you were here, so I hope you don't mind me running over. If you're in town for the reunion, I don't have a lot of time."

The speed of the words made Jax want to tell her to take a breath before she passed out. "Is there anything in particular you need?" She blinked after saying that, wanting to add, *aside from stealing my face, that is?*

"I was in Miss Landry's class today when you taught."

"Ah, the kid in the back who never looked up. Did you think of something you wanted to ask me?" Thankfully this kid hadn't raised her head. If she had, Jaxon would've forgotten her own name, much less the lecture she'd prepared. "It's okay—I don't mind. If you have a question, I'll be happy to answer it."

The girl shook her head, still having trouble making eye contact. "No, I wanted…" She started but didn't finish.

"Let's try something easier. What's your name?"

"Sean."

"That's funny." She cocked her head to the side and wanted to rush through the list of questions she needed answers to. "Not a lot of people know this, but my middle name is Sean. Nice to meet you, Sean. What can I do for you?"

"I wanted to know if you'd tell me about you." Sean raised her head for a second and quickly lowered it.

"That's a broad question. Can you narrow the scope a little? What did you want to talk to me about? And I'm guessing it was me specifically." She kept her voice low, so as not to draw any attention to them, and Sean's head came up, and she opened her mouth. She closed and opened it again, but nothing came out. Jax could tell she was upset when she saw her eyes, glassy with unshed tears. "Hey, hey, kid, what's the matter?"

"My dad knows you. He talks about you sometimes when he drinks and thinks my brother and me aren't listening. He blames you for why my mom is the way she is. He doesn't like you, and because I look like you, he doesn't like me either. It made me want to know you."

"I'm not sure I follow."

"I didn't either. Some asshole at school saw your picture in the trophy case, and they gave me crap about it. I found my mom's old yearbooks and saw when you graduated. I asked Mom, but she doesn't like to talk about you at all, so I thought maybe you'd talk to me." Sean spit it out in a quick ramble before she dropped her head back down, her chin hitting her chest. The kid was going to have neck problems before she was twenty if this kept up.

Jax took a deep breath, making her cheeks balloon out before letting it out in a slow stream. Unless she'd unknowingly slipped into a coma, she didn't have any other family in this area aside from Roy. That's who she figured Sean needed to be talking to. If he'd gotten some woman pregnant and left the child to be raised by some idiot, she'd be pissed with her brother, but it had nothing to do with her. "Okay, I'm not sure what you're talking about, so let me ask you something. Who're your parents?"

Jax needed confirmation before the headache that was taking root at the base of her neck could blossom into something totally miserable.

"Iris and Daniel Gravois."

Of course. If there was someone who wouldn't like to raise a kid who looked like her, it'd be Daniel. Now if only a benevolent fairy would fly through the window, land on her shoulder, and tell her why he and Iris had a kid who looked like her. Jax escaped into her head a minute before thinking of something to answer all the questions Sean had.

She could try to work between the lines and give Sean some answers, but the girl deserved better. The root of this problem didn't actually rest with Daniel, but with Iris. "Ah, yes." To think, she got paid to sound smart.

"Do you know them?" Seeming braver, Sean lifted her head and just stared, appearing to be trying to memorize every line on her face.

"Iris and Daniel? Yes, I do. I ran into your dad the day I got here when he stopped me for some reason. I thought I'd be fined, but he let me go. We weren't great friends in high school, so I'm not sure how much I can help you with your questions."

"How about my mom?" Sean appeared glued to that seat, and she wasn't moving until she got through all her questions.

"Iris and I were friends," she said, and Sean leaned closer. "We lost touch when I left for LSU, then to California for grad school." She took the picture Sean held out. It was of her and Iris lying in the grass. It was a selfie taken with an old camera before people even used the term. She remembered the picture and where it was taken, but she couldn't piece together why she was in this conversation. "I haven't talked to her since a week after graduation."

"Did you like my mom when you lived here? And I mean *like* her."

"I'm not sure what you're going for here, but like I said, that was a long time ago. The answers you're looking for are out there, but you have to ask someone who was actually here." The wheels of the train had not only left the track but fallen off a cliff. She had the urge to glance around to try to find the hidden cameras, so they could all laugh at how they'd punked her. Now she needed answers the same way Sean did.

"I don't look like my dad or my brother. At first I never thought about it, but when I was ten, I started feeling like I didn't fit in. I started asking my mom, and she kept putting me off. She's still doing that." Sean's lip trembled but she didn't cry. "I didn't think my dad would like it if I asked him. Tossing it in his face like that wouldn't be a good idea."

That Sean wasn't anything like Daniel was a cause for celebration. He was all Sean knew, though, so it was time to be the bigger person, something she was sure Daniel would never do for her. Perhaps she was maturing after all. She pressed her fingers to the table and tried to think of something to say to help the girl out, but she really didn't have a right to tell her anything.

The only consideration she took into account was what she would want if she was Sean. "I have to agree with you on that. Your dad and I were never friends, but I left. Any animosity should've ended when I took off sixteen years ago. Your mom and I were friends, and that ended as well. If you're looking for answers, you need to talk to your mom. It's not my place to tell you things she's not ready to tell you."

"Were you her girlfriend? Is that why I look like you?"

She smiled and shook her head. "I'd like to think I'm a good teacher, but I don't have any talents you might call extraordinary. Passing my DNA on that way isn't in my wheelhouse."

That finally made Sean laugh and relax somewhat. "Thanks for not telling me to get lost. At least you were willing to talk to me." Sean kept her head up now.

"I wish I could help you. Hopefully you and your mom get along better than I do with mine. If you really want to know, then don't demand, but ask. If you don't push, maybe she'll be more open to answering your questions." The new waitress refilled her cup and put one down for Sean.

"Can you tell me about the last time you saw her?"

"Your mother?" she asked, and Sean nodded. "It was right before

I left for LSU, and I met her on the bleachers of the football field. She'd told me she needed to talk to me, but it turned into a good-bye. We had that talk, and it was the last time I saw her or had any communication with her."

"You never called her?" Sean sounded almost accusatory.

"There were plenty of things we probably left unsaid, but that might have been for the best. She got married and has a family, so I hope she's happy. Your mom was a good friend, a good person, and she deserves it."

"My birthday is about seven months after that. You would've still been together."

The implication made her laugh. Leave it to Iris to bring a child into the world who didn't belong to the peacock she married. Considering the kid's looks, Daniel must've had a hard time not giving Sean as much shit as he'd given her from the moment he laid eyes on her. Sean implied as much, and it was a selfish act on Iris's part. She had to give it to her, though. Sean filled the role of the baby she would've left behind if she'd had the power to get Iris pregnant then skip town. But the implications of that made the headache begin to pound at the base of her skull.

"I'm sorry—I'm not laughing at you. This is hard to wrap my head around, and I hate to sound repetitive, but I'm not sure what I can tell you." Sean nodded and looked almost antsy for Jax to keep talking. "Your mom and I were close growing up, and with me looking the way I do, it made people talk about the true nature of our relationship."

"So, she *was* your girlfriend?" Sean leaned forward and smiled.

"The secrets of our relationship will be forever between your mother and me," she said, smiling in return. "It doesn't matter that it's her daughter who's asking. Unless, of course, she decides to tell you herself."

"But I thought you said…" Sean fell back again, as if in defeat.

"I don't remember saying I'd give titillating details." Jax arched her eyebrow and waited Sean out. If she wanted any more, she was going to have to accept what she was willing to share. She wasn't here to revisit old subjects that deserved the burial she'd given them.

Sean sighed and nodded. "Okay."

"Listen," she said, not having the strength to leave this kid hanging. "Your father was a year ahead of us and fell in love with your mom the first time he saw her. That's what I've always thought, anyway. When he sized me up as his competition, he wasn't the nicest person. That didn't stop your mom and me from being friends." When the pleading expression crossed over to irresistible, Jax laughed and added, "Okay, *really* good friends."

"Why hasn't she heard from you in all these years? I can tell she still thinks about you. Shit, they're still arguing about you."

How bizarre, to think Iris and Daniel had thought anything about her at all in the sixteen years she'd been gone. Bizarre, and sad. "Sean, honey, there'll be people who come into your life who make it seem like you'll never be able to live without them." She paused, not wanting to give Sean the impression she didn't care about what sounded like the most important thing to her.

"She wasn't enough for you?" Sean asked and glanced back at the waitress who'd brought their coffees. "Then you really didn't love her?"

"Don't put words in my mouth," she said, shaking her head. "The truth is, someone fills up something in you that you might need in that one fleeting moment, but then that piece of you grows empty again, and you have to let go and keep on searching." She paused to make sure Sean understood what she was saying, though she probably sounded a little like a vague fortune cookie. "Your mom and I were like that. I needed something more, and she wanted to stay here and make a life where she felt she belonged. She turned me down and waved good-bye. I've never blamed her for that, and I'm glad she has two children and someone in her life. It's not perfect in every way, maybe, but what family is?"

"Did you find something to make you stop wanting more?"

Margot's face and her laughter came to Jax's mind. "I found a something and a someone, yes. Now instead of wondering if that part of me will grow empty again, I worry if I can make enough room for the gift love can be." She'd been an idiot for not making Margot believe that, and it was time to correct her behavior.

The truth, now that she thought about it, was that maybe Iris's rejection had affected her more than she had allowed herself to admit. To her shame it'd been Margot who'd unwittingly paid the price in her attempt to protect her heart. But then again, her first relationship hadn't exactly ended in rejection. It had been more of an inability to compromise on both their parts. Enough years had passed for her to admit that.

"My mom didn't ever find that, not really. My grandmother always says something about lying in the bed you make. I want to know where I came from because I don't want to end up in the same situation. I've heard your name all my life, and I sometimes wish I did belong to you." Sean was talking fast, to either get it all out or because of nerves. She couldn't tell. "I know I can't biologically belong to you, but when you're a kid, wishing's all you got."

"Have," Jax corrected.

"What?"

"Wishing is all you have. I'm sorry, you didn't come to see me for an English lecture, but I can't help myself. You should sit with your mother and try again. Up to now she might've thought you were too young. If you're planning on college, you have one more year at home, so she might be willing to tell you what you want to know."

Sean looked down to her hands pressed to the tabletop, dragging out their time together with her silence. Jaxon couldn't help but notice that their fingers were shaped the same.

"Will you talk to her and tell her the same thing? If you don't want to, that's cool, but she might listen to you."

She blinked and the only thing on her mind was fantasizing about beating Bert until he cried. There was no way he didn't know about all this, and he'd still encouraged her to come. "Sean, tonight I'm going to a cocktail party with a bunch of people, and all I have in common with them is the year we graduated. The next night it's off to the gym to talk about what I'm sure they'll describe as the good old days."

Sean nodded but did appear confused. "What does all that have to do with talking to my mom?"

"This town wasn't the best place to grow up, not for me. Hopefully you've had better luck even though your house isn't the ideal situation all the time." She thought about being in the same position as Sean and what she'd truly want from someone she thought held all the answers. It wasn't the same, though, and she didn't want to get sucked in. "To tell you the truth, my parents weren't thrilled with me either, and that hasn't changed."

"Was that your mom, before?" Sean pointed in the direction her mother had disappeared.

"It sure was, and she hasn't changed her mind about me. Your mom, though, I can't imagine would ever do that to you. The girl I knew back then would understand what was best for her children. You need to give her a chance to do that."

"So...you're not going to help me?" Sean's eyes watered, but the kid held firm.

"After this weekend I'm going home, and I'm not coming back. Standing up for yourself and the things you want isn't always easy, but it's something you'll be doing long past this issue. If your mom doesn't tell you what you want to know, it must be for a good reason." She didn't know why, but she felt the need to defend her old friend just a little even if she didn't deserve it. "I didn't say that as a copout. Try to believe me. Just be patient with her. Iris may surprise you if you don't push too hard."

Sean nodded and looked at Jaxon for a long moment again. "Thanks for not just telling me to get lost. Have fun at the reunion." The beginning of her good-bye didn't sound very enthusiastic, but Sean seemed not to want to overstep too much. "See you around, but I doubt it, huh?"

"Hold on." Jax reached out and put her hand over Sean's. When she dropped back into the booth, Jax fished through one of the side pockets of her bag. She took out one of her cards and wrote her cell number on the back. Sean held it like it was a lifeline when she handed it over. "I didn't mean to sound like a bitch who doesn't give a crap. If you want to talk again, just give me a call. You're a junior, though, and you sound like you should be done already."

"How can you tell?" Sean looked at her as if her answer would make a difference.

"You sound much more mature than your age, and you wouldn't be in Miss Landry's class if you couldn't pull your weight."

"I was able to advance a year but could've skipped a couple more. My parents, though, thought I was too young to go away to school yet. It was no biggie. I didn't want to leave Adeline behind either." Sean glanced at the waitress, and it dawned on Jax that she had more in common with this kid than just looks.

"I see. Good for you, but what are your plans after next year? Don't tell me you're wasting that brain by not pursuing something."

Sean opened her book bag and put her card away. "I want to go to college, that I'm sure about. I'm not sure about what I want to study yet. There's a good chance I'll get a softball scholarship, so I have a way to go no matter what."

Jax smiled. This kid really was her a million years ago. It was hard to remember exactly what it was like to be so ready to hit the road, not caring that she didn't have a complete roadmap for her final destination. The need for escape was enough to make you swallow the fear and jump in even if there were rocks you could crack your head on. "Enjoy college for a while, and what you want to be when you grow up will come soon enough."

Sean surprised her when she stood and hugged her. "Thanks." When Sean walked through the swinging doors of the restaurant, Jaxon noticed she wasn't the only one watching.

The guy wearing an apron picked up the carafe of coffee and approached her table. He picked up another cup and sat without asking. "Do you want another one?"

"I have a three-cup limit, but thanks." Jax started packing her bag, wanting to retreat back to her room at the B and B. If there were any other surprises waiting to ambush her, she wasn't interested. Her mother and a kid who apparently shared her DNA were more than enough. "Thanks for letting me sit. I appreciate the space to work, but I've got to go and change."

The man put the carafe on a rag he had in his pocket and shook his head. "You don't have to leave if you have more work to do. It's too early to get ready for the cocktail party tonight."

"Thanks again, but I've taken up enough space here this afternoon."

"Do you mind a short chat? I'm sure you've had your fill of uninvited guests for today, and you're not dying for another one. I promise to keep it brief."

"Sure," she said, closing her bag and trying not to let her wariness show. Now what? "Jaxon Lavigne." She held her hand out.

"Oh, I know. You haven't changed much from high school, and I doubt you remember me, but we graduated together."

Jax smiled again, wondering if this was the café of past revelations. "No, sorry. I can't place you, but I do know who has the most popular hair in America." The emotions of the afternoon started to pile up on

Jax, and she started laughing, stopping with difficulty when the guy didn't join in with her. "I'm sorry, it's been a while since I've come back here, and it's been a hell of a day so far."

"No problem, and I doubt many of our classmates will recognize me. I had much more hair back then, but that, along with my waistline, are distant memories. Pete Lyons," he said. The answer made her lose her smile. "I know we weren't friends in high school, and if you tell me to fuck off, I will."

Pete was Daniel's best friend even though he was a year younger. While he didn't treat her the same as Daniel, he sat back and laughed at her misery. This was just the day that kept on giving. "Pete Lyons, how have you been?" She wanted nothing to do with this guy, but she'd withstand a brief visit.

"I'm sorry, Jaxon. There's no excuse, but I was a kid back then, and I wanted to fit in. All that stuff doesn't matter now, but I'm really sorry." Pete ran his hand through his thinning hair and laughed. "All the shit I saw you go through is coming back to haunt me because my kid is going through the same thing now. It's piled on the shame of my actions higher than I can deal with sometimes. I've always wanted to tell you I'm sorry."

It didn't really matter to her now. This asshole, along with his friends, had taken pleasure in their tormenting of her and people like Bert, and a quick *I'm sorry* years later wasn't going to make up for that. It wasn't important enough to fight over, so she simply nodded and smiled. "Can I help you with something?"

"My daughter Adeline is Sean's best friend…Well, she's her girlfriend, really." He smiled and glanced over his shoulder at the doors to the kitchen. "I bet she was a surprise today, so thanks for not blowing her off. That kid's been waiting on you it seems like all her life."

"Sounds like your pal Daniel won't be thanking me for talking to her. It actually sounds like he wasn't too thrilled at all." She wondered if shit like this only happened in small towns.

There was a certain level of drama you didn't have in big cities. Not that places like Los Angeles were perfect, but there was some comfort in that her neighbors didn't give a shit about her business. Perhaps this was why Tennessee Williams was never short on subjects to write about. Crazy was a state of being perfected in the South. The heat probably had a lot to do with it.

"Daniel and I haven't been close since high school. I married Nancy, and I see Iris, since they're still best friends. Daniel never comes over with her, and I'm good with that. Nancy told Iris she should've talked to Sean before now, but she hasn't budged on the subject." He stared out the window as if he too was having trouble keeping eye contact.

"I don't know what the kid's story is or why Iris has kept it from her. The thing is, I'm not sure I want to know." Her fingers tingled from pressing them into the table trying to prove to herself she was awake. This made no sense, but admitting the most obvious truth made her chest hurt. Her brother and ex-girlfriend had driven a knife through her belief in both of them.

Pete chuckled and shook his head. "You can't have changed that much in sixteen years. You asked more questions in high school than anyone else, and from what Adeline tells me, you still have that quality. She was in your class today too, and she hasn't shut up about it." He drummed his fingers on the coffeepot. "It's good for the girls to see that someone like them can make it out of here, be happy. You know?"

It was good to hear the girls had parents so different to her own, but she still wanted this conversation to end. "The truth is that I have changed plenty in that time. I had to in order to survive. The scars this town left taught me to be more resourceful than if I'd breezed through." She shouldered her bag but didn't move. "Why hasn't Iris talked to her?"

"I'm not sure, but you can ask her at the reunion. She's on the committee with Nancy and a few others, which means she's going." He held his breath, puffing out his cheeks. "I'm not sure, but it sounds like she's been waiting a long time to talk to you as well."

Fan-fucking-tastic. She held her hand out to him, glad when he instantly took it. "Thanks, Pete, and thank you for the apology. My teenage self appreciates it. I'll see you and Nancy tonight then."

"Thanks, and if you stop by before you head home, I'll treat you to a meal."

"I appreciate it." Jaxon walked out to her rental, wanting to escape before anyone else stopped her for a walk down memory lane. That street seemed to be loaded with landmines and lively ghosts with an abundance of chains to choke her.

Her first look at Sean had thrown her off balance, and after their talk the planet seemed to tilt off to one side, knocking her on her ass. The only explanation as to why the girl she'd loved in high school had a kid who bore a strong resemblance to her lay with her brother. Sean must be right—Daniel wasn't her father, since he and Iris shared similar coloring. Coloring that was on a different end of the spectrum from hers. This was a secret Iris had not only managed to keep, but it was also the only link to the one family member she still spoke to. She'd come back to replace one set of hurts for another.

Jax hadn't lied to the kid. Twenty years ago, Iris was all she could think about. How many hours had she lost back then, daydreaming about the life they would lead together? The fantasies of inexperience, which centered on a house and kids. She'd stood up to her family and to anyone who thought to condemn what she felt for Iris. The pressure her mother had put on her had been blistering, and she'd put it all on the line because she loved Iris.

Being cut off had been worth the gamble because she refused to deny what she felt and, more importantly, who she was. In the end Iris had repaid that grand gesture by coming by one afternoon to tell her she was staying. Her explanation had been she couldn't leave her family, and she wasn't college material. Iris had been tearful when she told her to go. She didn't want to hold her back, but she did love her. What a joke that had been.

In the end what had surprised her wasn't Iris's cowardice, or her total lack of wanting anything more than Chackbay could provide, but how quickly she'd gotten over the hurt. For someone who supposedly loved her, it sounded like a month after she'd left for school, she'd walked down the aisle with Daniel, of all people.

She parked in the small lot and stared at the porch of the place where she was staying. Bert was waiting for her, and she shook her head when he stood up as soon as she was out of the vehicle. "What?" he asked.

"Tell me you didn't know about Sean Gravois. If you did, and you still talked me into coming here, I'm never going to forgive you." She stopped at the bottom of the steps and had to take a couple deep breaths to control her anger.

"Who the hell is Sean Gravois?" Bert asked with his hands on his hips.

"Iris's daughter." She was clipping her words, and she couldn't help it. Bert had been kind through the years and not mentioned the one person above all others who'd gutted her. Keeping this from her, though, was one thing. Letting her walk into it blind was something no friend did.

"What does that have to do with anything?" Bert seemed confused.

"Come on, buddy. You've been visiting your folks for years, and the subject never came up? You never ran into her in the diner or the store?" She balled her hand into a tight fist and Bert raised his hands.

"Look, I'm not sure what you think I do when I come to visit my parents, but it's not to gossip. We go out every so often, but I seldom run into any of our classmates. If I have, I didn't recognize them, and I wouldn't have given a teenager a second glance." Bert came down and stepped closer but didn't touch her. "All I knew was who she married, but I never asked anything else about it because I wasn't interested. She broke your heart, and she didn't deserve any space in my head. You've known me all my life—I'm not lying to you."

"Okay, I believe you." She walked up the steps, wanting to be alone, but that wasn't in her fucked-up cards today.

"Did something happen? I know you were at the high school today. I wanted to come by to see how it went."

"Fine, and I have some stuff to do, so I need to get upstairs." It was the first time she'd turned away from him, and the guilt made her stop. When she was alone at LSU and wondering how she was going to make it through, Bert had been there for her. He was part of her family of choice, and he'd never disappointed her.

"Tell me what's wrong." He placed his hand on her shoulder, and she stopped. "Something happened, and it's hurting you."

"I'm sorry I snapped at you, but I can't talk about it right now." She faced him and wrapped her arms around him. "Sorry, it's been a weird day, but I do have some work I wanted to get finished before tonight's fun starts."

"You know you can talk to me about anything."

"I know, and I love you for it. Right now, I need to be alone, so I can concentrate." She took the steps two at a time and entered the big house without looking back. Why the hell had she for one moment thought this was going to be a good idea?

Her phone rang and she recognized the ringtone. "Hey, darlin'."

"Hi, baby, I have about five minutes, so tell me quick how today went. Did the kids like your lecture?" Margot, as always, sounded upbeat and harried all at the same time.

"I think I got my point across and pissed a few of them off. It was a good day." She thought of how easily Margot made her heart lighter.

There were still things in her past she needed some answers to, but her future was something that paved the way to being able to put that all aside the moment she left. She'd gotten over Iris completely, and Margot's love showed her just how far she'd come.

"Are you okay, honey?" Margot asked.

"I'm fine. I miss you, and I ran into my mother today. Sorry, I couldn't hold my tongue, and in no way did it go well. We'll talk about it later."

"Are you sure?" Margot said softly. "I can ask for time if you need me."

"I always need you, but it's fine. Go back to work, and I'll talk to you tonight." She dropped her bag and lay down on the bed. There was a small water stain on the ceiling, and she stared at it as she listened to Margot breathing. "I have that cocktail thing tonight, but call me when you get home. You'll probably be saving me from a long night of conversations I really don't want to have."

"Will you forgive me?" Margot sounded truly apologetic.

"For what, exactly?"

"For talking you into this. I thought if your parents got to see you again, they'd be sorry they ever let so much time go by without you in their lives. As for everything else, I thought you could put all that to rest as well. There's something that haunts you, and you don't have to tell me, but I want all of you, Dr. Lavigne. No more holding back on me."

"When we get home, I owe you a few long conversations. I'll admit there are things in my past that make me overly cautious, but it has nothing to do with you." She sat up and opened her bag to take out her journal. "Go to work, and don't worry. I'm not cracking up on you."

"Believe me, I know you well enough to put you back together. Try to have fun tonight, and I'll call you when I'm done. Remember that I love you more than life."

She smiled as she took out a pen and stuck it in the journal. "I love you too, sweetheart, and I can't wait to get home."

Home held new meaning now. It rang with more of a permanence than she'd ever considered. This place had still held some sway over her, but not any longer. It had become more of an unknown she didn't care to explore. A few thousand miles away, she had a woman who loved her, a home, and a job she adored. It was enough to be truly happy about if only she gave herself permission to accept it. She would, and she'd never take it for granted again.

CHAPTER THIRTEEN

Iris stood outside, talking to a few people who'd come from out of state, catching up on what they'd been up to in the last few years. These old classmates were regulars at the reunions who used the excuse to come as a way of visiting family in the area. Most of the couples who'd married out of high school had children and, like her, were planning for the years ahead as their kids left for college.

She listened and commented when she had to, but she'd kept her eye on the door the whole night. The cocktail party was hosted by Molly and Mike Voisin every time, since they had the largest house with a backyard backing to the bayou. So far she hadn't seen Jaxon or Bert, but her mother had told her he was also in town. She also knew Jaxon had taught Sean's class today, but Jax hadn't stopped by the office, so she'd missed her there as well.

"How's Daniel?" the man she was talking to asked.

"He should be here in a little while. Work kept him later than he expected." She spotted Bert heading for the bar and excused herself. "Hey." She tapped him on the shoulder, and he turned around with an expression she couldn't quite make out. "Everything okay?"

"Sorry, it's been a strange day." Bert gave her a brief hug that made her think he'd rather lick the bathroom floor at a dive bar than touch her. "It's been years. How are you?"

"Okay, I guess. Is Jaxon coming tonight?" It was rather pathetic, but she needed to lay eyes on Jaxon.

"I stopped by the bed-and-breakfast, and she didn't seem in the mood," Bert said cryptically. "I know we haven't seen each other since graduation, and I don't really know you, but I'd ask you a favor. Leave her alone, Iris. Whatever's on your mind, it's years too late. Do you understand me?"

"All I want is to talk to her." She needed to tell Jaxon the why of everything, even if she had no idea how to do that.

"This time maybe think about what she wants instead of what you want," Bert said before he turned away from her.

She didn't want to be the drama everyone remembered about the night, so she took a deep breath and went inside. Nancy was waiting with a glass of wine and led her to the bathroom close to the kitchen. She leaned against the sink when Nancy locked the door.

"What happened?" Nancy asked.

"Nothing yet. I went home to change, and Sean walked by me like she wanted to hit me. Something happened to her today, but hell if she was going to share it with me." She took a sip of her wine, but there was no way she could afford to get even slightly drunk. Losing control of her senses and her mouth was not a good idea.

"Pete told me Jaxon had lunch at the café after she'd given her lecture at the high school. She sat for a few hours grading papers and drinking coffee after that, and as she was getting ready to leave, Sean showed up." Nancy held her hand and grimaced in sympathy. "Adeline must've called her and told her Jaxon was there. They had a forty-five-minute talk, and Pete told me Jaxon appeared shell-shocked."

"Jesus Christ on a crutch." If she had the chance to talk to her younger self, the lecture would be memorable. "Was she angry? I already know Sean is."

"Pete talked to her afterward, and she didn't seem overly pissed, according to him. He took the time to apologize for all that crap in high school. I doubt Jaxon was interested, but she seemed to understand it was important to the idiot I married to make amends. He seemed relieved when he got home." Nancy sat on the closed toilet and crossed her legs so she could rest her drink on her knee.

"You want to know, don't you?" Everyone in town wanted the whole story. A child that looked like the girlfriend you didn't acknowledge in high school was something you couldn't hide.

"I *know*, sweetie, and I've known you well enough not to have to have it spelled out for me. You were in love, but in the wrong place and time." Nancy squeezed her fingers and smiled. "It was hard to miss back then. The way you looked at her made it plain."

"You're right about that, and my mother called me on it. Granted, Eve Lavigne called her after what happened with Jaxon and spelled it out, but she knew way before then. She convinced me it wouldn't last and that there was no reason to implode my whole life for a fantasy." She took another sip. "I don't blame her, though. I blame myself."

"Iris, you were seventeen years old. Who thinks straight at that age?" There was a knock at the door, and they both stared at it.

"Everything okay in there?" She recognized Molly's voice.

"Sorry." She kissed Nancy's cheek. "My zipper got stuck," she said, opening the door. "Need any help with anything?"

"The caterers have it under control, but Daniel is looking for you. He just walked in a few minutes ago."

Molly left them alone again, and Nancy smiled. "Don't back down this time. Talk to her, and I'm sure she'll understand."

"That's wishful thinking. She's going to be pissed, but there's no going back, my friend." The thought of Jax hating her was something she accepted, even though it made her ache inside.

"For you and Jaxon, maybe, but it's not too late for Sean. You know she needs something going forward, and she's not going to find it with you or Daniel. It's none of my business, but you've kept her waiting long enough." Nancy kissed her cheek and they walked out to the party that was now in full swing.

"Hey, I'm glad you could make it," she said, kissing Daniel quickly on the lips. Adding a pissed-off Daniel on top of Sean and Jaxon was too much to think about. "Would you like a beer?"

"I'll get it. You go ahead and mingle. I'm sure you're excited to see all your old friends." Daniel winked at her and smiled. "Some more than others."

"What's that supposed to mean?" This was getting ridiculous. She wore his damn ring and slept in his bed every night. "Never mind. I don't want to hear it."

"Calm down. I don't want to cause a scene." He took her hand and led her outside. There were people standing around, so he walked almost to the water. "What happened today with Sean?"

"Nothing that I know of. You know what she's been like lately.

We weren't much different when we were young." God, she should've pressed Sean before she left the house. The anger Sean had would only grow if Jaxon had told her anything about what had happened. She doubted that, but the thought of what Jaxon must've thought when she saw Sean terrified her.

"Are you lying to me, Iris?" Daniel said sighing.

"I was at work, and she asked to stay at Adeline's—that was the extent of our talk. She'll be there for the weekend, so they can finish some assignments they have." That was the truth as she'd known it before she talked to Nancy. This wasn't the time to get into it.

"I can't keep you from something you've wanted from the day you left it behind, but I told you I refuse to let my kid get in the middle of this cluster you've created." His voice was low and cold. "I wasn't the brightest guy in high school, and I waited for you to graduate because I wanted you. When I saw Sean, I knew instantly she wasn't mine, but I didn't care. I raised her, and she's my daughter. My love for her has nothing to do with DNA."

"No one is saying otherwise." She took his hand and stepped closer to him. "To be honest, I do want to talk to Jaxon before she leaves, but not for the reasons you think."

"What do I think?" Daniel turned and stared at her as if he could see right through her.

"That I want to rehash something that's dead. I know you well enough to think that's what it is. What you can't seem to understand is I'm happy with my life. I love my family, the family *we've* built together." She didn't touch him and didn't look away.

"You lie well, Iris. What you can't seem to understand is that she's been here the whole time. From our very first night together, Jaxon Lavigne has been there with us like a ghost in an old house." That last statement sounded like it hurt to say. "That you're so anxious to see her again cuts a hole right through me."

"Daniel, you're an honorable man, and I respect you. That you doubt that makes me sad, but what I'm doing isn't for me. It's for Sean. She needs someone who isn't either of us to help her make that next step."

He laughed, but it sounded bitter. "And you think Lavigne is the answer? She's got the counselors at the school and us if she has any questions about school and her future. Over my dead body, Iris. You do that, and you're on your own. I'm not sticking around to be humiliated again. I've been the butt of every guy's joke in this town, and I'm not reviving the old rumors to make you feel better."

"Daniel, it's more than school. I know it hurts you, but Sean is a lot like Jaxon, and she can help her because of the experience she has with what comes next. I don't want our daughter to suffer if she doesn't have to. I think that Jaxon can—"

He put his hand up to cut her off. "Tell me you understand, because I'm not fucking kidding."

She hesitated but nodded. "I understand."

❖

The lazy current of the water moved pieces of debris like it had for hundreds of years, but the sight failed to provide Jax with any solace. She walked across the street to sit by the water after Bert had left and was still there as the sun started to set. The journal sat on the arm of her chair, but she couldn't get her thoughts together to put a word in it. All she could think about was Sean and what her existence meant.

Her phone rang before Jax had figured out how the hell to approach things, and the ringtone left no doubt she'd answer it. The sound made her think her plan to leave in the morning was as sound as passing on the cocktail party tonight.

"What's wrong?" Margot's question sounded as if she'd put an exclamation point on the end.

Despite the day, Jax smiled and stretched out her legs. "Hello, pretty lady, it's nice to hear from you."

"Honey, I don't have time for niceties. After I talked to you, all hell broke loose around here, ending in a fire. A fire that unfortunately didn't touch any of the furniture that smells like Satan's crotch. We're having to work late now, and the evil spawn who is our director is about to ring that goddamn bell summoning us back to the set in a minute, so tell me what's wrong."

"Ah."

"And, Jax, honey, think very carefully before saying your usual *nothing*. I know you like to work these things out on your own, so I won't worry about you, but let me warn you. If that's how you want to play it, that's fine by me. But I promise, I'll set up a driving vacation for two weeks with you, me, Mom, and Daddy. A trip where I'll gladly sit in the back and let Daddy give you directions for the three-thousand-mile trip I'm planning in my head. If there really is a world's largest thimble, we're going to see it."

Jaxon stayed quiet but did do a full body shiver at the image of being trapped in a car with Margot's parents for that long. "I went to teach Miss Landry's class today."

"Let's dispense with the stuff I already know."

She laughed. "You know, the two guest appearances on that law show make you annoying at times."

"Think how annoying I'll be if you don't start talking."

Margot listened as Jaxson launched into the tale of her day. The only interruption for the rest of what she had to say was Margot uttering *uh-huh* a few times as if reminding her she was still on the line. It was a bizarre situation, and there weren't words in existence that would make the situation in any way plausible. Hell, plausible was living in a land far away and was inebriated on drinks that came with fruit and umbrellas.

"Of all the times for me to be stuck in this stupid trailer," Margot said as she sighed. "I'm so sorry, my love. That's a shitty thing to go through alone."

"There's nothing to be sorry for. I wanted to blame Bert, but he swears on his life that he didn't know anything about this."

"Why is she not talking to your brother? If she looks like you, that has to be the answer." There was some banging from Margot's end, and it signaled the end of their talk. "Okay, I heard you the first time. Give me a minute," Margot yelled, presumably at whoever was banging. "For fuck's sake, you'd think we're working on a cure for cancer."

"I'd ask him that, but the shit's not answering his phone. Believe me, I called a few times this afternoon but no luck." She wanted answers, but taking a swing at Roy was also on her mind. "The thing about that theory, though, is that he and Iris never got along, but I don't have anything better." She kicked at the grass. "But Occam's razor applies. The simplest explanation is usually the best."

"Don't you have a function tonight?" Margot sounded like she was on the move.

"Yeah, but I don't feel like going. If you don't mind some

company, I was thinking of flying home tomorrow." She sighed, and Margot echoed it. "I'll even come to the studio and watch you work."

"All I wanted was for you to make peace with your past, and more importantly yourself, but if you want to come home, I'll be here waiting on you. What happened years ago isn't something you can blame yourself for, and I hope if nothing else you can let all that go now and put it behind you. I love you and I miss you, but stop and see your grandmother before you leave. Tell her I can't wait to meet her."

"Thank you. It's hard. I never expected all this." She wiped her face, shocked that she was crying. She never cried, but this all was too much. "I just want to leave. If that makes me sound like a coward, I can live with it."

"I know, baby, but that's in no way you. If anyone in this world should scare you, it's Daddy, and yet you go into that study every time." Margot paused as if trying to find the right words. "No one would've handled this without a lot of confusion, so stop beating yourself up."

"I might write a screenplay when I get home, and have you star in the movie I have playing in my head."

Margot laughed, and it sounded like a gift from the gods. "I'll be happy to convince you to give me the role on your casting couch. I have to go, so let me know what you decide."

"I thought we decided," she said, laughing.

"Don't take this as me pushing you, but you're there. Get answers, especially now that you have even more questions that'll drive you insane in the coming weeks. I love you no matter what, but I think it'll make you feel better if you rip the Band-Aid off and start demanding answers."

"Babe, this is like a Band-Aid stuck to my pubic hair. It's going to be a bitch to rip off."

"Ewww," Margot said loudly. "That's quite the mental image. I can't wait to get you home, but think about what coming back early would mean."

"Okay, you convinced me. I'll go to the reunion, talk to Roy even if I have to hunt him down, and finish the total disaster this trip has been. Then I'm out of here." She exhaled and swatted a mosquito on her knee. It was time to go in and order something to eat and watch some television or something. Roy and Iris had been on her mind all afternoon, and it was time to stop the infinite loop of escalating thoughts.

"You don't sound done, baby. I know you like to organize your thoughts before you start talking, but I'm crushed for time. Just this once can you cut me some slack?"

Margot had always told her being careful and not blurting things out was an admirable trait she'd admired in her. They'd had their arguments, but hurting Margot needlessly was something she'd tried never to do. "I just wish there was something I could do to help the kid. She looked so lost, and no one seems to want to help her understand anything. I've got experience with being the kid who doesn't belong. I guess that's the best way I can put it."

"You did a beautiful job, love. You have a way about you, Jax, and it makes people feel cared for in your presence. Sean has your number, so I'm guessing she's feeling like she's acquired an ally right about now."

"Thanks for saying that, but you didn't see her. She's as skittish as she is lost. I doubt I'll ever hear from her."

"I'm just telling you the truth. So, what are you going to do with yourself this evening now that you're ditching Bert and the rest of your classmates?"

She pulled the phone from her ear and looked at it. "Did Bert call you?"

"You just said you didn't want to go, so answer the question, Lavigne, and leave poor Bert out of this."

That answer meant the little shit had called Margot, who was doing her best to keep him out of trouble. "I'll see if I can find Roy, then go and get something to eat. Since I already talked to my mother, I'm not wasting time on that. Maybe tomorrow I'll take Eugenia out to lunch after I go and visit Granny. If I see both of them, I can pin them down on coming to visit us if you don't mind. It's time you finally met them both."

"I'm looking forward to that, but right now I've got to go before one of these guys has a stroke." Margot made another kissing noise. "I love you."

"I love you too, so go have fun. Don't worry, and I'll call you tomorrow."

"Honey, that's my job. I love you, and I worry about you. If you're not used to it yet, work on it. And if you're lucky and I get off early, I'll call you, and we'll have phone sex. If it's on your bucket list, we'll go ahead and check that off."

Jax tapped her phone against her hand after they'd said goodbye. She took a deep breath as she started to dial, hoping she'd sound halfway coherent. Before she could finish punching it in, her phone rang and she didn't recognize the local number. The urge not to answer was strong, but maybe it was Sean.

"Jaxon?" It was a woman, but she sounded more mature than Sean.

"Yes, can I help you?"

"It's your grandmother, child. How can you not recognize my voice? I got a new phone, so put this number in yours, and don't forget to use it."

She had only one living grandparent, and that was her father's mother. Birdie Lavigne had lost her husband six months before Jaxon was born, and in a mood of sentimentality her father had named her after him. He'd said the name fit even if she was a girl, and it deserved to live on in honor of the greatest man he'd ever known. Her mom's parents had died long before, so Birdie had been her one grandparent growing up.

"Granny, it's so good to hear from you." She actually talked to her grandmother every couple of months. "I was coming by tomorrow."

"Jaxon, don't try to sweet-talk me. I should've been your first stop."

"I'm here, and I wasn't leaving without seeing you, I promise. My class reunion is tomorrow, but I wanted to stop by in the morning and have coffee with you." It had been interesting growing up with her mother and grandmother, and it made her smile. If Sean thought *her* family dynamic was strange, she had no idea.

Her father had been gone for months at a time, and the only help her mother had back then had been Birdie. But they couldn't stand each other. Her granny had often commented on the stick her mother had up her ass, and her mother thought her mother-in-law was the spawn of the devil. She and her brother knew, though, that no matter what, Birdie would be there for them. She had deep pockets, an open mind, and a loving heart. It was a great combination in a grandmother.

She'd ignored her grandmother's numerous calls the first couple of years at LSU because she thought she was going to pile on, but Birdie had finally driven down and sat in the stands at one of her softball games. After the win, she'd pulled her ear so hard, Jax thought it would detach. She'd followed that with a long talk about acceptance. Her grandmother thought she was perfect simply because she was Jaxon, and what she decided to do with her life was perfectly okay with Birdie. She'd offered to pay for the rest of school, but by then it had become a mission of pride to do it on her own, and Birdie had understood that as well.

"Uh-huh. You should've been here way before now. How did it go with your mother?" Birdie wasn't known for subtlety either.

"How do you know about that?"

"Please, child. The gossips in this town are professionals. I didn't get the particulars, but I do know she found you in the café." Her grandmother stopped and let out a disgusted sounding grunt. "I've talked until I'm blue in the face, but your mother's head is a cinder block stuffed with cotton. I'm not sure who the hell she's trying to impress, since she rarely goes out. Throwing away your child over something so stupid is something only a fool does. If I had more energy, I'd put my son over my knee for going along with this."

"Time hasn't blunted the message, and I'm not interested in listening any longer. As for Dad, he goes along to keep the peace. He has to live with her, not me. Are you going to be home tomorrow?"

"Come early, and I'll make you pancakes to go with the coffee. You remember the way, right?"

She laughed. "Yes, ma'am. I'll see you then, and thanks, Granny."

"Bring that beautiful girl in the pictures you sent me. It's time I met her and told her some stories about how cute a kid you were."

"Margot had to work, so maybe you can come with Eugenia for a visit. The house is big enough for you both."

"We'll talk about it tomorrow, so sweet dreams, baby."

The call made her feel better about the day, and her shoulders finally relaxed. Conversations on the phone weren't enough, but her grandmother gave her some sense of home. She'd come to California a few times, but that had been before Margot. Now that the two most important people in her life had called her, it gave her the courage to try the call she'd wanted to make again.

"Sir?" she said when the line connected.

"Ah," Wilber said, sounding shocked to hear from her. "Jaxon, where the hell are you?"

"I'm back in my hometown for my class reunion, sir. Not to worry, though, I'm coming home."

"That's too bad. What's on your mind? Be quick before my wife comes back in here and whacks me for giving you a hard time. My wife and daughter are under the impression you're a pansy, and I'm beginning to believe you are if you need that much backup." The sound of a slamming door made her guess Wilber was now safely in his study so Patty Sue couldn't run interference for her.

She started and spoke from the heart, and she was glad he didn't interrupt until she was done. This was something she'd wanted to do in person, but not having to face him staring her down was easier. Maybe that did make her a pansy. She didn't hesitate to answer his questions and tried her best to put him at ease. They spoke for an hour, and he, like her grandmother, didn't consider her feelings when telling her what was on his mind.

"You do this then back out, and I'm going to hunt you down and feed you to my dog."

"You don't have a dog, sir." She massaged her chest to ease the tightness in it.

"The pound will have one I can adopt and train to rip your throat out."

"Duly noted, sir, and thank you." The length of their talk surprised her, and she smiled when it ended. It hit her that she was trading one crazy family for another, but Margot deserved her all.

CHAPTER FOURTEEN

The big house surrounded by cane fields was still beautiful, and Birdie was waiting on the porch, making the picture complete. Her grandmother never seemed to grow old in Jaxon's eyes, and she cried when she wrapped her arms around her. There was never anything that could top the embrace of someone who totally loved you, warts and all, as Birdie always said.

"Granny, I've missed you." She held on a few minutes more before letting her go and taking her hand. "I know, I know," she said when she got the eyebrow. "It's my own fault."

"You hurt my feelings, baby. Not calling or visiting makes me think you're lumping me in with your mother, and that"—Birdie pointed at her—"is unacceptable. I'm bitchy, but I'm not that bitchy."

"I know, but this town gives me a case of depressed with a pissed-off chaser." They went inside to the large kitchen in the back.

It was amazing how the smell of a place could flood you with memories that served to remind you of happy times. Spending summers here had cemented the kind of person she'd become. Afternoons with Birdie had been spent reading in the library at the center of the house, then talking about the books along with long conversations about life. Those talks had given her the permission to be who she was without apology. Unfortunately, that realization didn't come until she was on her own.

"I can understand that, but you're over thirty now. It's time to stop hiding from the piece of yourself you left here." Birdie poured two cups of coffee and brought them to the chrome and Formica table that had been in this kitchen much longer than she'd been alive.

"What do you mean?" There was a nostalgia about drinking French press coffee with fresh cream and plenty of sugar. Margot would have a stroke at how much sugar, but it was hard to ask someone who owned thousands of acres of sugarcane to use an artificial sweetener. It was a good way of getting run off the property by Birdie and her shotgun.

"Eve called me last night and had plenty to say. For once, though, it had nothing to do with you. She was at the grocery yesterday and ran into Iris." Birdie stopped and took a sip of her coffee while staring at her over her cup.

"I haven't had the pleasure yet, and I'm not sure I want to. Margot had to talk me into staying last night. My plan was to come and spend the morning with you, then drive back to New Orleans and fly home." The sight of Sean was still fresh in her mind, and she still couldn't wrap herself around what she was feeling. "I'm going tonight, but I still think it's a bad idea."

"Does Iris's daughter have anything to do with that?" Her grandmother stood and took the chair next to hers so she could hold her hand. "Eve was upset when she called, but even she couldn't understand what she was seeing. I think that kid sent her into a real tizzy."

"Think of me in high school, and you've seen Iris's daughter. I don't understand either, and that's okay, since I'm not planning any return trips here, but what isn't okay is that the kid doesn't understand." She put her arm around her grandmother when she leaned against her and kissed the top of her head. "We both know it's Roy, but that he would betray me like that is hard to take. And how none of us could know after all this time…"

"Remember that every story has multiple sides. You have to realize that before you let go of that hot temper of yours. He's your brother, and there has to be an explanation."

"He knows exactly what happened to me when I wouldn't back down to Mom. He was the golden child after that." She spit the words out, which was immature, but she didn't care. When you filled in history with facts, you didn't always get the answers you sought.

"Don't make assumptions," Birdie said, standing up and heading to the stove. "Roy hasn't been in your mom's good graces for a while now. He's older than you, he's not married, and he hasn't started a family. In your mother's opinion, those are sins of the highest order. If what you're telling me is true, then maybe he started a lot earlier than any of us thought."

The butter in the frying pan sizzled, and she watched her grandmother pour the batter. "You can't know what the first couple of years were like when I left here. I lost so much, and while I made peace with giving up on Mom, losing Iris hit me in the gut. The plans we'd made seemed so concrete, and she threw all that away in a five-minute talk." She finished her coffee and smiled at the sludge of sugar at the bottom.

"I was a phone call away, so that pain was self-inflicted, but let's forget that part for now. Pain, my mother used to say, gives us the nails we use to build character, and you survived. I had no doubt, and I've forgiven you for not letting me in back then. The older I get, the more I think of the history of our family and what the future looks like." It didn't take long for Birdie to put a plate of pancakes in front of her with cane syrup. "You need to come back here with your girl, but right now I want to forget all this stuff, so you can tell me about Margot."

"She's doing great, and the show she's on has become a hit. The best thing about her is she's in love with me, and it's hard to accept, but I try my best."

"Of course she loves you. What's not to love?" Birdie pinched her cheek and laughed. "Are you finally ready to settle down and make this permanent?"

"I am. Fear has held me back, but I'm not going to let it rule me anymore."

"Will you do something for me if I ask you?"

She finished her breakfast and nodded. "You know it. Name it."

"I want you to bring her back here, and I want you to take this. I've held on to it for you—it's part of your inheritance." Birdie handed her a box and closed her hand over it.

"Birdie, it's going to be a long time before you have to think about inheritance." She leaned over and kissed her grandmother's cheek. It was hard to imagine a world where Birdie Lavigne didn't exist.

"My spring chicken days are behind me, cher. I doubt you'll ever live here again, but this house should go to someone who'll appreciate it and won't immediately put a For Sale sign in the yard." Birdie grabbed her plate and started making more pancakes.

"How about Roy? He doesn't seem to be leaving for bigger things. From what little he tells me, his practice is going well, and he's happy here even if he hasn't procreated to make our parents happy. Or not that we know of, anyway." She turned and stared out the window and watched the cane blowing in the wind. It reminded her of a gentle dance with a bit of danger mixed in. Cane plants were beautiful, but they were razor sharp, and a walk through the neat rows was an invitation to be cut to shreds by a million small cuts. It was a good analogy for her life the longer she stayed here. "He's usually in town. He's not answering his phone, and I have one guess as to why."

Birdie seemed to be lost in thought as well and took a deep breath when she put a fresh stack in front of her. "You were the one who loved the history of the place, and all I ask is that you keep it. Who knows, perhaps one day you'll have a kid who wants to be a cane farmer and enjoy all the headaches that come with that."

"Is there something you're not telling me?" She stopped her fork halfway to her mouth.

"No, I'm old and have oodles of time to think morbid thoughts. I have a scattering of ducks, and I want to put them in a row before I forget who I am and why the hell I'm here."

She had to laugh at her grandmother's sense of humor. "I promise I'll make you proud."

"That's the last thing on her mind," Eugenia said when she walked in. That she hadn't knocked or announced herself meant she visited often. "You've been making both of us proud for a long time, and we don't see that changing."

Birdie kissed Eugenia's cheek and started making more pancakes.

"Did I get you into trouble with my lecture?" She figured the back and forth with the students might have been talked about around some dinner tables.

"There were a few parents that got their panties in a wad, but the kids appreciated what you did." Eugenia leaned over and kissed her cheek before sitting down. "It's funny that I sit with parents year after year and remember the things they said when they were my students. All of them told me as students that when they had children, they'd be different and give them the freedom of making their own choices for the future."

"Doing that means letting go of your control, and some people have problems with that. They want to make sure their kids stay in their lanes and out of trouble. I understand that up to a point." She finished her second stack of pancakes and placed her plate in the sink. Any more and she'd go into a sugar coma. "I don't run into that too much in my job, but there's a few."

"Are you going tonight?" Eugenia asked.

"Yes, and then I'm going home. Since you two seem to be good friends, I'm expecting you to come visit."

"We can do that now that Eugenia is retiring."

They spoke for another couple of hours, and she laughed for the first time in days. Eugenia excused herself and came back with a gift bag. "Elle asked me to give you this and made me promise to be sure you understand how much she appreciated your time with her. You were a joy to us both."

She took out a small book of Robert Frost poems and instantly recognized it. The book was a first edition of Frost's first published collection, and her old teacher had treasured it. "Are you sure? This was so special to her."

"I want you to use it as an incentive to start your own collection of short stories so I can brag I have a first edition of your work. Like I said, she made me promise, and I don't want to go back on that."

"I'll treasure it," she said, holding the book as if it was indeed made of gold. "And thank you both. I feel better than I have since I got here."

She promised she'd come by again before she left to see her grandmother one more time, but she was planning to drive by Roy's house to see if he was screening her calls. The reunion was hours away, and she had to be in the right headspace for that. Her call to Margot on the way back to the B and B went to voice mail, and she hoped that didn't mean a long weekend of makeup work because of any other gremlins on the set.

The only thing she wanted from the whole trip was for Sean to call her. Whatever Iris had done, for whatever reason, she wasn't abandoning the kid who seemed to want to connect with her. That meant staying tethered in a way not only to Iris but to Daniel as well. She'd think about that later...much later.

❖

Daniel stood in the closet of their room putting on a fresh uniform. Iris watched him like she had for years and could describe his process in detail, from the way he tightened his tie, to the way he put on the utility belt. He was meticulous in how he put each piece of the outfit together, which was surprising since he did nothing but complain about his job when he wasn't doing it.

"We need to finish the talk we started last night," she said when he stepped out with his boots in hand.

"That conversation is done. I'm not telling you what to do, but if you go behind my back, I wasn't kidding about what I'll do." He sat and almost ripped his socks when he started putting them on. "I'd like to think that my kid will come to me if she needs to talk to someone. This job isn't what I'd planned to do forever, but I remember what it was like to have dreams. If she needs advice, I've got plenty to give."

"I'm not going behind your back, but I'm also not going to stop Sean from doing what she wants. Jaxon was invited to give a lecture to her class, so they've met."

His fist was so tight that his whole hand turned white. "When were you planning to tell me that?" He raised his voice, and she was glad the kids weren't home.

"I didn't know myself until it was done." She told him about Sean's visit to the café and for a second thought Daniel would have a stroke. "I'd like to think we're strong enough to survive this, but I'm tired of fighting you on a subject that doesn't matter to either of us."

"Are you so clueless? A subject that doesn't matter? It's all that matters, and now you've dragged our daughter into it." He laughed, but it sounded like a rabid barking dog. "Why did Sean go to see her?"

"She wanted to talk to her. You know how the kids are. Adeline told Nancy that their classmates noticed the pictures in the trophy case at school, and they've given her crap about it." She sat on the bed and thought about staying there for the rest of the day.

"Kids are assholes." He finished putting his shoes on. "And I know there's not much I can do about all this. You're going to do whatever you like, and so is Sean." He smoothed down the front of his shirt and glanced back at her. "I'm not proud of how I've acted in every moment, but I love her."

"I know you do, and more importantly, Sean loves you." She stood as well and put her arms around Daniel. "You might not believe me most days, but I do love you. It might not seem like it, but it'll be okay." Daniel left, and she pulled the stairs of the attic down. To make Daniel feel better about himself, she'd hidden her memories away years ago and rarely looked at them. It was hard to face proof of your mistakes. The boxes weren't exactly where she'd left them, and she figured it was Sean. When she wouldn't answer her questions, Sean must have started trying to find the facts on her own. She opened her senior yearbook, and Jaxon was waiting for her on the tenth page.

How could she have walked away from her? Jaxon had been perfection in every way that counted. She'd loved her so much that she was still shocked that Sean had survived Iris's grief. After Jaxon had left, it was so final, and it had broken her heart. There was no one to blame but herself, but by then she'd made the decision for herself that wouldn't be easy to navigate. She neatly restacked the boxes and left the attic.

Her phone rang as she ran her hands through her hair to get it into some kind of order. "Hello."

"Iris," a man said, and she had to think to place the voice.

"Roy?" Great, that was all she needed.

"Hey, it's been a long time, but I hear my sister is in town."

He sounded nervous, and it made her question how he and Jaxon could be related. If it wasn't for Eve's air of superiority, she'd swear Eve had stepped out when it came to conceiving Roy. "That's what I hear."

"Look, I'm stuck in New Orleans on a case and wanted to know if you're going to tell her about Sean. She's called me a few dozen times, but I wanted to talk to you first." He'd been reluctant all those years ago but had given in after she assured him all she needed from him was what Jaxon couldn't give her.

"I haven't seen her—"

"Oh, thank God," he said before she could finish.

"Sean, though, found her, and they had a long talk. Don't worry about anything. I'm not about to ask you for anything." This was getting ridiculous. She started downstairs and grabbed her keys. "I have to go."

"Wait," he said loudly. "Don't do anything stupid."

"Way too late for that."

❖

Jax headed back to the chair across the street with a Diet Coke and her journal. She'd tried Margot again and got voice mail, but she wasn't worried. The one who appeared relieved was Bert when she stopped by and apologized. He'd told her about the cocktail party and his run-in with Iris. All she had to do now was survive the night, and she'd get back to her life and her girl. She opened her journal, and unlike the day before, the words came easy.

Sixteen years...a fucking long time. She didn't usually use such simplistic language since it was frowned upon by some of her peers. Some of the older professors had told her that people with doctorates in English who taught other people the wonders of literature didn't need curse words to do it. This, though, was the account of her life, and she used the word *fuck* liberally and in all forms. Life was, after all, a fucking mess, and there was nothing you could do but be honest.

The footsteps behind her meant she'd have to share the space, but hopefully whoever it was wasn't in the mood for conversation. When they didn't come closer, she capped her fountain pen and sighed when she glanced back. The woman rooted in place a few feet behind her made her question her judgment about venturing outside. If all these drama-charged scenes had been landmines, she'd have stepped on every single one.

"Jax." Iris pressed her hands together as if in prayer.

"Iris." It was a stupid response, but it was all she could think to say.

"You haven't changed at all." Iris wasn't moving, so she turned back around and waited. It was immature, but this wasn't her show.

"I've changed plenty." The sight of Iris made her want to release sixteen years of rage and make her hurt like she had. She was due, and the intensity of the rage surprised her. She'd thought it was long gone.

"You didn't come last night. I was disappointed that you skipped it."

The hand on her shoulder startled Jax into knocking her drink off the wide arm of her chair, spilling the soft drink on the pavers. It wasn't that Iris's touch was unpleasant—it was her voice. She remembered the way Iris spoke that caused her skin to tingle. Of all the things she'd tried to forget about Iris, that's one thing that had seared into her mind. When she'd been seventeen it had driven her to distraction.

"I try to limit the amount of reminiscing I do about things that upset me. I don't celebrate and embrace those years as much as other people. High school is better left in the hole I dropped it in, lit on fire, and covered with as much dirt as possible. Hopefully you had a good time, but I doubt anyone missed me." She had to stop and exhale in an effort to stem the overflow of emotions.

"Aren't you going to say hello to an old friend?" Iris opened her arms, and Jax almost snorted when she laughed.

"Have a seat if you want." If Iris had been waiting for some great reunion, she was sixteen years too late. "I doubt you're here for the view." She bent and picked up the empty can to set it next to her chair.

"I wanted to talk to you," Iris said softly. "Can you at least look at me?"

"What do you want?" Why did anyone have to do shit they didn't want to once they were over thirty? At a certain age, you should be able to pass on things that aggravated you. The thought of tattooing *stop* on her palm popped into her head again. Just lifting her hand on occasions like this was something to consider.

"Don't be cruel." Iris lifted her hand but stopped before she touched her. "I've been waiting for this a long time."

She laughed at that. "Iris, I don't mind talking to you, but skip all the crap, okay? Sorry, I don't want to be rude, but what you did…I can't wrap my head around it. You could've just said you used me to get to Roy."

"That's not true, and I'm sorry." Iris reached over this time and put her hand on her forearm. "I really am."

"Save it." She stared at Iris's hand until she removed it. "*I'm sorry* isn't going to cut it, but you're not the first to try. Whoever told every kid in this town you can treat people like shit, torture them for years, but follow it up with a big *sorry* lied to you. What you did when you were seventeen isn't anything you have to apologize for. You did me a favor."

"I wasn't as brave as you, but I am sorry, even if you don't believe me."

"I would believe you," she said and laughed at how ridiculous all this was. "The problem is that I don't think I'd even reached Baton

Rouge when you were married. Do you have any idea what I went through because of you? I put it all out there because I believed you, and I lost everything."

"Your mom made my life just as miserable."

"Stop, just stop. You want to talk to me, then tell me the truth." There was no reason to get angry now, and some of the rage drifted away. Iris had hurt her, and it felt good to look her in the eye and say so.

"I need you to know how sorry I am." Iris started crying.

She didn't want to fall into whatever trap this was. "Don't," she said, not moving. "I just realized I've wanted to blame you all these years for what happened, but I can't anymore. You and I wouldn't have mattered even if we'd only been friends. My mother will never accept that she raised someone she finds lacking her dented moral compass." She couldn't keep her eyes on Iris as she spoke. The pain was something she'd numbed through distance and amnesia. Now she was hip deep in memories and possible betrayal, and yet Margot was right. It needed to be done.

"If you think I haven't agonized over this, you're wrong. Letting you go broke something in me that isn't ever going to heal." Iris's words were barely understandable because of her tears. "There were so many times I wanted to pick up the phone and call you, so I could beg you to forgive me and come get me. The only thing that stopped me was that I was married, and I didn't see a way out."

"Stop crying, please." She'd never learned to deal with crying people. "You aren't to blame any more than I am. That means you have nothing to apologize for, and there's no reason for you to be here." She had a life to get back to, and she wanted to leave with only the bag she'd brought.

"I left you all alone, and that was a mistake. After that, the mistakes didn't exactly get easier, but I'd committed. I was stuck."

"Why don't you tell me about Sean?" The question was like opening a black hole and voluntarily jumping in. The truth was going to suck the life out of her, but hey, why not.

Iris's mouth opened and closed with a click. "I can't. I thought I could, but I can't."

"Your daughter came to see me." She stood and walked to the edge of the pavers close to the water. There was no way the water was going to relax her today unless someone surfaced and shot her with a tranquilizer. "Whatever all this is about, I have to tell you it's a little messed up. She's confused, and she thinks Daniel hates her. I'm not a parent, but I think there should be a chapter in parenting books about not raising a kid your husband is wired not to like." Her patience had run out. "Who does she belong to?"

"She's mine—that's all you and everyone else needs to know."

Jax dropped her hands to her sides. "I'm sorry, did you not hear me? Your daughter came to see *me* asking questions I had no clue how to answer. One look is proof enough that she doesn't belong to Daniel. If you don't want to tell me the story, then fine, that's your business, I guess—although I'm going to have a chat with my brother. I don't want to be involved beyond that, but at least talk to her."

"I don't know how to do that." Iris covered her face with her hands and cried harder. "Daniel accepted it, and he loves her."

"You haven't listened to her, then. It sounds like Daniel sees me when he looks at her, and he's been vocal about how that's not a good thing. If you and Daniel have tried to keep those conversations private, you should've had them somewhere other than your house." She didn't raise her voice, but she wanted to. Taking her own advice, she stayed calm. This spot was private, but a screaming fight wouldn't stay between them. "Daniel has been pretty up front about his feelings, and Sean has suffered for it. I think you owe her more of an explanation than you've given her up to now." She dropped back into her chair and slapped her hands down on her knees. "Jesus, Iris, what did you do?"

"You wouldn't understand."

"Try me." She softened her tone and briefly reached over and touched Iris to get her out of her self-pity and back to the conversation. "She seems like a sweet kid, and I enjoyed my time with her yesterday. It sounds like she's made some plans and has found someone who loves her."

"Thanks." Iris smiled and wiped her face. "She's everything I wanted, and she's so smart."

She smiled back and nodded. "Tell me about her. I do want to understand."

"Sean's a gift I gave myself." Iris's tears started again but without the hysterics from before.

"How does Daniel fit into all this?" The statement of a gift Iris gave herself didn't make sense, but hopefully they had time to get to it.

"I knew you were leaving, and about four months before you did, I decided I couldn't go with you. Way before your mom called mine." Iris dropped her head as if not able to make eye contact while she spoke. "I couldn't tell you until that very last day, and I let you go. It was like I couldn't wrap my head around the fact that you weren't coming back, so I did something to fill the hole that left in me."

All she could do was nod, since it was starting to make sense. Iris didn't see what she'd done as a betrayal. She'd clearly used her brother as a way to keep a bit of Jaxon with her. It was like a hot spike was being driven through her head. There was something trying to crawl out of her chest and choke the life out of her. It was nothing to do with her, but Iris's choices had dragged her into something she didn't want.

"So you had Roy's baby, and gave her my middle name?" She couldn't help spitting the accusation at Iris. "I can almost understand that. What I can't understand is Daniel. Why not stay with Roy?"

"There was no Roy, Jax—there'd been only you and me. Daniel was the way I could do it without embarrassing my family. You were gone, but my mom was as relentless as yours. Unlike you, though, I had nowhere else to go."

"You did well in biology, so there had to be Roy. And you had me, Iris. You threw me away, but you had me." She raised her voice and had to mash her teeth together to stop.

"I was seventeen going on eighteen and wasn't thinking straight. I couldn't go with you because I was scared and knew I'd have nothing to offer a world so big. The truth is, here people haven't evolved that much. You get pregnant without being married, and you're marked for life. I slept with Daniel after you left, and he offered to marry me when I told him I was pregnant." The tears fell faster, but Iris seemed to need to get it all out. "You should've seen the shock when I said yes. I know how he treated you, but he has been a wonderful father."

"Didn't he wonder about the timing of her arrival after the *I do*s?"

Iris laughed bitterly and shook her head. "We started having fights about Sean from the day she was born. He stayed with me, though, and we had another child. I'm sure he sees that as a consolation prize, but Danny's a good kid who is his father's image."

"He didn't figure it out? I'm not here, but my brother is."

"Daniel's never going to be as smart as you, but yes he did, and like I said, there was no me and Roy—it was a one-time thing and nothing more. I should've thought the whole thing out better, but I've never been sorry I had her. Sean was my way of keeping a piece of the life I let slip away. She was my way of hanging on to a part of me I had to let go to make everyone else happy." Iris wiped her face and turned away from her.

"I know this is going to sound harsh, but wasn't that a high price for the kid to pay?"

"I don't know how to answer that." Iris moved closer and gazed up at her. "You know, it's funny—I've waited sixteen years to have this talk with you, and it isn't going at all like I imagined."

"Are you kidding me right now?" The flip remark seemed to ignite Iris's anger, and her tears stopped cold. "Sorry, but I don't know what you're hoping for here."

"I'm not asking you for anything. The thought of calling you has crossed my mind more than a few times through the years, but I let those urges die away with a lot of other juvenile hopes I had."

"What in the hell did you do? And why didn't Roy help you with all this?" She put her hand up when Iris went to say something else. "Don't deny it. You and Daniel had as much chance of creating a kid who looks a lot like me as the kid actually being mine. Roy's been close the whole time, and he has to know about her. We might not be in each other's lives as much anymore, but he's not a complete asshole."

"You know how Roy and I felt about each other back then, and that hasn't changed much. I didn't want him involved. He was just a means to an end, and he was fine with the situation as it was. Like I said, I'm not asking you for anything. I loved you—a small part of me still does—so I wanted a reminder of what you meant to me. A reminder I thought I wouldn't have to share or let go of." Iris wiped her face with the sleeve of her blouse, and it smeared the little makeup she had on.

"Why in the world did you not tell me all this? I can understand that you were young, but you had to have some idea what the consequences were going to be." She had to stop talking, or she'd start screaming again.

"I didn't think ahead. I wanted a baby, and I found a way to do that and keep her. Only now, just like you, Sean is waiting for the day she can leave and not come back. She's got her scholarships lined up, and all that's stopping her is her next year of school." Iris stopped and took some more deep breaths. "I could have let her skip some grades, so she'd be done, but I thought sixteen was too young to be on her own."

"I don't know her well, but I can understand wanting to go. If that's all you're going to tell me, then what can I do for you?"

"I can help her with what she wants, like going to college. What I can't give her is the guidance she desperately wants because she doesn't fit in. At least, that's the impression she gives me, but she refuses to talk to me. I don't want her out there thinking I'm ashamed of who she is, what she wants, and who she loves. Sean needs someone like you to talk to, a mentor of sorts, and I'd like it if you would be that someone to her."

"How's Daniel going to take that? I doubt he'd like me talking to you, much less Sean."

Iris paused and seemed to think before putting her hand over hers. "Don't worry about Daniel—that's not why I'm here. I know I don't have the right to ask, but I'm thinking about Sean and what she needs. At this point in her life it's easy to go in the wrong direction and not find her way back. She's full of questions, and she's angry. I'm doing my best, but she's getting farther out of my reach."

"Are you afraid she'll go, or stay?" The way this conversation was going was like being on a hamster wheel. She was picking up speed but going nowhere.

"I can't answer that yet. I have time before she decides on a school. All I know is that in the last few months I've lost her. Something happened, and she won't talk to me." Her pain sounded genuine. "If I can't get her to talk to me…"

"What? She'd talk to me?" she asked when Iris stopped talking abruptly. "Your daughter is sixteen, so I'm not sure what a great idea it is for me to forge a relationship with her. For one, she needs answers from you, and then there's Daniel. What's so hard about telling her what happened? You decided to have a baby to make yourself happy, and that's what you did. She's not going to hate you for that."

"Sean wants the same things you did. It's scary how much alike you are. I've tried telling her that I'm fine with Adeline and what she means to her, but it seems to just push her farther away. I know it wasn't easy for you, but you might be able to give her insight I don't have. You know what it is to be a gay kid in a small Southern town who leaves it to see the world. I screwed up, but like you saw yesterday, she's a great kid." Iris gripped her arm and scooted to the front of her chair. "And don't let her fool you. Daniel wasn't that bad. He has his moments when the past overrides his mouth, but he didn't treat her any differently than he did our son."

"That he stayed when he figured it out says something about him." It made the bile rise in her throat to admit it, but it was true.

"Daniel and Sean see the world completely differently, but he's her dad, and he loves her. I'm not here because I think she needs another or a better parent. What I think Sean needs now is a teacher and a mentor in life. She's got the educational part down. I need to know someone will be there to help her get along after she leaves here. You can give her a place to go if she starts to get lost out there."

"I gave her my card in case she wants to talk again. Beyond that, I don't know what you want or expect from me. If that's not what you want to hear, you've got to understand I'm at a disadvantage here. The girlfriend who dumped me, and apparently knew she was going to dump me, had sex with my brother so she could have a baby that looked like me. Surreal doesn't begin to cut it." The enormity of the situation was starting to make her tired. She glanced down at her watch, wondering if she had time for a nap.

"Do you like your life, Jax?" Iris finally sounded normal as she stopped crying.

"It took me a while to find my way, but I do, very much." She thought of Margot and her urging her to do this. Did Margot have any idea what a mess coming back was going to be? "Why, don't you?"

"You may find it hard to believe because our expectations are so different, but yes, I do. I'm happy with my children and my job. My marriage isn't a grand passionate affair, but whose really is after so many years?" Iris shrugged.

"You're still young—if you're not happy, don't settle just because it's comfortable. Life's too short for that."

"I don't feel like I am settling. It took time and work, but Daniel and I are the best of friends, and I love him. When my youngest, Danny, started school, I started working as the high school secretary. It's not as exciting as your career, Dr. Lavigne, but I like it. What I'm trying to say is I could've had a completely different life by making different choices, but overall, I'm happy." Iris smiled and she did as well. "This is a mess, and I'm sorry."

Jax stared at the water for a while, pondering the situation. "Your apology really isn't necessary. I saw my mother while I was here, and she's still fussing about the same things. What I went through made me appreciate what I have now. With a little time, I think we both can see that what we had was that first puppy love, and it was nice but meant to end. And teenagers do stupid things." She reached for Iris's hand and squeezed her fingers. "I'm glad we both ended up where we were supposed to be, even if I am pretty pissed at Roy right now."

"Thank you, Jax. It might've been puppy love, but it was nice. Like you said, Sean found someone, and she seems happy, but we'll have to see where that leads. That's why I want you to be there for her if she reaches out to you. I want Sean to be able to say she's where she's supposed to be when she's our age." The request made Iris's eyes water again. "As for your mom, I should tell you I finally ran into her again. I know this town is the size of a postage stamp, but I really haven't seen her much."

"She shouldn't have any problems with you. If anything, you're the daughter she would've wanted."

"I've seen her in church and some other places, but I think this is the first time I had Sean with me." Iris cringed as if expecting a bad reaction from her. "I don't think she's ever seen her as a teenager."

"I'm sure you both got that trout-in-the-mouth look. Roy's life should be interesting for the near future. Tell me about Danny, your son." The request surprised her as she made it, but she wanted to keep talking to Iris now that they'd made peace. At least there was one issue she could put to rest.

Iris's laugh made Jax smile. "He's a lot like his father, only I've tried to teach him to be a nicer person. It's hard to keep him humble during football season, but I try my best. I told him I wouldn't tolerate a bully."

"I'm sure Sean and her girlfriend appreciate that."

"He idolizes his sister and has gotten into more than one fight when anyone gives her trouble." Iris reached in her purse and took out a picture of her son in his football uniform. "After school he wants to follow his dad into law enforcement, but I have a few years to work on him about that crazy idea."

"The world needs all kinds of people, and a career as a police officer isn't a bad choice. It's good that he and Sean get along."

"Danny's my party boy, and Sean's my bookworm, and she's the reason he does so well in school. He sits for her tutoring because he doesn't want to get benched. It's a blessing they'll always have each other to get them through the tough times."

"I'm happy for you, Iris. You might've thrown me for a loop with all this, but I'm glad I came back. If you don't mind my input, don't knock your life by comparing it to mine or anyone else's. You have a lot to be proud of." Jax held the picture up before she handed it back. "I'm also glad you went with your gut and stayed where you're the happiest. You might have some lingering doubts that you made those choices out of fear, but I don't think that's true."

"I'm not that noble," Iris said. "At the time they were totally out of fear. Please know that I talked to Daniel plenty before I accepted his proposal. I never forgot how he treated you." Iris dropped her eyes again and seemed to study the picture of her son. "Even then I felt like such a sellout."

"We both know he fell in love with you the day he saw you. I don't think it was an act, and I'm glad he's given you a good life."

"Can I ask you something?" Iris waited for her to nod. "Why didn't you come back before now?"

"I'm not proud of myself, but I didn't realize how angry I've been until I drove past the sign that welcomes you to town."

"I'm so sorry," Iris said.

"Stop saying that. I was angry for a lot of reasons, and there was nothing here that was going to make that better. Once I started teaching and met Margot, this stopped being home. I still talk to Birdie, and she's come out to visit like Roy has, but Mom and Dad haven't budged. It still hurts, but it has made it easy to let all that go." She laughed and pointed at Iris. "I should thank you for sending me that invitation. I'm not sure why you all think this five-year interval is a good idea, but it's taken this long for me to admit that keeping all that anger bottled up isn't healthy."

"I've missed you, and I've been curious about you. It's not often you see your old friend on the cover of those gossip magazines in the grocery store."

She laughed that her life sometimes revolved around trying to avoid the paparazzi. "Margot works hard but is also lucky. That show started off a little slow, but it took off, and her career went with it. It makes it hard to have a date night."

"I'm happy for you. All the pictures I've seen of you two, you look like you love each other." Iris closed her eyes as if building her courage. "Do you ever think about me?"

Jax could almost feel the thump on the back of her head Margot would've given her for answering the question honestly. The truth was, she had thought of Iris, but never with good intentions. She was sure that would change now, and there was no reason to be cruel. After all, Iris had gone through a lot, by her own design, to keep a semblance of Jax with her.

"I didn't hate everything about this place. You were a big part of the things I loved about that time. Sorry this is so late, but thank you for that, and for all those happy memories you gave me."

"Could I have a hug now?" Iris stood and held her arms out again.

Jaxon held Iris against her, remembering the last time she'd done it. That memory revolved around a painful good-bye. This time it was both a welcome and a farewell, and it brought with it a sense of resolve. What they'd shared never had a chance at success, but it did help shape the people they'd become. That could be counted as success enough.

"Promise me you won't turn her away if she calls, Jax." Iris squeezed her and pressed her face against her shoulder. "You would've loved watching her growing up, playing every sport we could sign her up for. She's talented, smart, and she has your adventurous heart."

"I promise I'll do my best." Her answer made Iris smile up at her. If Sean did turn to her, she'd give her all the advice she wanted, and part of that would be giving her the roadmap home if that's what it took to make her content.

Finding a niece hadn't been on her radar, and what Iris said made her wistful. What would it have been like to watch the kid grow up? There were plenty of clues of what it would be like now to include Sean in her life. When you added her, Roy, Daniel, and Iris, that meant messy and drama fueled, but they were adults. They should be able to find a balance to give Sean what she needed. She'd be sorry if she didn't at least try, no matter how long it took her. Like it or not, Sean was her family now.

CHAPTER FIFTEEN

Sean lay back on the stack of blankets Adeline had piled in the loft of the barn at the back of her parents' property. She had her arms around Adeline and was rubbing her back. They'd spent the afternoon in their private space after she'd heard her parents arguing again. It was ridiculous that they could never get past that one same fight. If they'd stop and realize what they'd done to her, they'd figure out how badly they'd failed. The shit she'd taken for her looks was ridiculous, and yet it'd always been about them.

"What are you going to do?" Adeline kissed the side of her neck, and whatever she was worried about didn't seem so horrible.

"She gave me her number, so I'll keep it in case I need it. The thing was, she had no clue about me. I could see that when I sat down. I've waited so long for the story, and she was my last chance." She moved her hands down to Adeline's hips when she sat up and glanced down at her. "It's weird that my mom was in love with her. I showed her that picture, and she remembered it, but I was a stranger. A stranger with her face."

"I can't blame your mom there, baby. Jaxon Lavigne looks so much like you, and I think you're hot. Your mom has good taste, but she's brave. Having a kid and listening to people give her shit about it must've been hard."

"My dad wasn't thrilled—still isn't." She didn't want to talk about it any longer when Adeline kissed her. "And you know damn well I've taken more shit than she has. We both have. I'm so lucky that you didn't do what she did and drop me for some guy to make your life easier."

"You think that's what happened? It could be Jaxon dropped her, and she was stuck. That'd be hard to talk about, and on top of that she was in love with a woman in high school a million years ago."

She had to laugh at that. "I didn't get the vibe that Jaxon was to blame. It's not like she could have gotten my mom pregnant, and that's the part I still don't totally get. You know my mother and my grandmother. Grandma probably hog-tied her in a closet until she worked all the gay out of her." She made a face. "Grandma isn't my biggest fan."

"Your grandmother isn't fond of anyone that I can see."

"I'm thinking now that she must see my mom's old friend when she looks at me. Whatever the hell it is, I just wish my mom would spill it already."

"It's a messed-up situation, but they're still willing to help you when we leave after graduation right?" Adeline's parents were pushing her to stay close to home, but they thought Baton Rouge would be enough space to get them used to the idea. What they hadn't told their parents was they really wanted to move out of state. "Living in a dorm for the whole four years isn't what I want."

"We'll be okay. I doubt my mom will cut me off. No matter where we're going. If they do get pissed that we're not going to LSU, I'll talk to Miss Landry and see what other scholarships I can get that would take us out of state." She went under Adeline's shirt and flattened her hand against her back. The first time she'd touched Adeline intimately, her life had finally made sense. Where she'd never had that sense of place, with Adeline she had that as well as someone who loved her for her.

"Baby, I'll follow you wherever, and if we need to get jobs, we will. All we have to do is promise right now that we'll make it. I can't lose you."

"I love you, and I'll dig ditches for a living if I have to if that's what it takes to keep you." She lifted her head and kissed Adeline. "How about your parents?"

"They said they'll support me no matter where we go. There'll be no ditch-digging in your future. Trust me—we're going, but I think there's another option," Adeline said, kissing her again.

"What?" She moved her hands up higher and unfastened her bra.

"I think you need to talk to Jaxon. My mom won't tell me the whole story because of your mom, but my dad told me a little while you were talking to her. She worked her way through school because her parents cut her off because she's gay. The history is already there, babe, and all we need to do is learn from her mistakes."

"I've met her mother. The woman's totally bitchy."

"If you fucking throw your kid away like they're a cat you don't want, you'd have to be." Adeline lifted up and stripped her shirt off. "Right now, I don't want to talk about that. I want you to show me all the things I know you can do right."

The tease made her laugh but her laughter stopped when Adeline threw her bra aside. They were young, and people didn't understand what they meant to each other, but she'd found the one person she'd be with for the rest of her life. If her mom had been in the same position and gave it up, she'd understand the misery she'd been in for a long time.

"I love you." That she was planning to do until her last day.

❖

Jaxon called Margot, and it went to voice mail yet again. The urge to talk to her was high, but she had to get ready for the night. She was about to take her pants off when someone knocked on her door. If it was another old classmate wanting to unburden themselves or show her another love child she didn't know about, she'd either have to start drinking heavily or take a nap.

"Hey," she said to the young woman who was at the front desk most afternoons. "Did I forget something?"

"No, but you've been checked out."

"Not until tomorrow, so I hope you didn't give my room away. If I have to sleep in my car, you're getting a horrible TripAdvisor review. I love writing them." She opened the door wider when the woman made a motion to come in.

"No, nothing like that. Birdie Lavigne called and took care of your bill, and she said you were staying with her tonight after the reunion."

"I guess if my grandmother says that's what's going to happen, I shouldn't argue."

"No, you shouldn't, since I'm not taking a chance to get on her bad side." The woman placed a drink on the desk and pointed to it. "She also said to drink that before you go. I wouldn't argue about that either, since I also graduated in this town."

"Thanks." She saw the woman out and locked the door. A hot shower relaxed her, and she stayed in longer than she'd planned. All she had to do now was get dressed, pick Bert up, and pray she didn't punch anyone in the face before they left. With Daniel on the force, she'd probably be driven to a swamp and strung up.

"You ready for this?" Bert asked an hour later as he stared at her bags in the back seat. "Or is your plan to make a run for it?"

"Birdie checked me out, so I can stay with her tonight, and one snarky comment too many tonight, and you'd better pray one of these guys drives for Uber. Besides, I was able to put a ghost or two to rest today." The drive to the high school brought back a slew of memories that revolved around getting there every morning and seeing Iris. They didn't have every class together, but it was nice to share all that time with her. If she could go back and talk to her younger self, she'd have to warn her about first loves and how painful they could be. She still wouldn't have skipped it, but having a glimpse of where she'd end up would've helped.

"Don't worry. I've been to only one of these, and no one talked to me. After thirty minutes of that, I headed home and sat with my mom and ate ice cream. The thing to understand is all those cliques that we knew in high school still exist. There's no changing them, but I'm glad I'm walking in there with you this time. I'm going to take your example. We'll tell them who we are and what we do, and then they can suck it." Bert straightened his bow tie, and she had to admit he looked nice. He cleaned up well when he decided to leave the pocket protector at home.

"I doubt anyone in there is as cool as you, buddy. Do they at least have alcohol?" The parking lot was surprisingly full, and she had to park on the street.

"Your question should be if they have *good* alcohol, and the answer is no. Whoever buys for this must think we're all still in high school and can't afford anything better than Mad Dog 20/20. That and keg beer are about as good as it gets." Bert laughed and followed her as she weaved through the cars to the door. "Also, the gym still smells the same, and that's not a good thing."

"That all sounds so enticing. I can't wait." The music was blaring when she opened the door, and it might have been a good thing that it would make it hard to talk to anyone. Whatever conversations were going on stopped when they walked in. "Wow, they seem so happy to see us."

A woman walked up and held her hand out. "Jaxon, it's good to see you again."

She took it but had no recollection of who this was. "Thank you."

The woman hadn't let go of her hand. "Nancy Lyons, I married Pete from the café. He told me he talked to you."

"Sorry, it's been a while. He did, and it's nice seeing you."

That was the first of many people who came up and introduced themselves. She took the opportunity to talk about Bert and what he was doing on campus. It was funny to see them glance to wherever Bert was and nod their heads. From what she could tell, their class had produced some attorneys, two medical doctors, and plenty of people involved in the oil field. The majority of their classmates didn't live very far away and really did hang out with the same friends they had in high school.

Once she got them engaged with Bert, she sat with a warm beer that must've been brewed in the colonial days. It was humorous to see their class bullies standing around Bert, listening to whatever he was saying. The way they were shaking Bert's hand and slapping him on the back made her think everyone had the ability to evolve.

She was happy to let Bert have his moment. At least they'd turned the music down to a dull roar to make talking easier. There was no one she was looking for but was surprised not to see Iris and Daniel in the group. She hoped they weren't staying away because of her. She allowed herself to contemplate the last few days.

Sean was now sixteen and had lived here for all that time. If she was a secret, she was the biggest open secret in the town's history. The only thing missing was a neon sign hovering over her head with an arrow pointing down.

"Hey." The greeting was gruff, and she had to turn around to see who it was. Daniel was alone and had his hands jammed in his pockets.

"Daniel." It was the safest thing she could think to say. "I promise I didn't speed getting here." The comeback fell flat, and she expected it to. She waited for Daniel to make his move.

"Iris said you talked to our daughter." The way he said it was a blatant act of possession. If there was a tree nearby he'd pee on it to mark his territory.

My kid, my wife, my life—stay back or I'll make you sorry. That was the message she got. "I did. She came to me and asked to talk about some things. I didn't go looking for her, if you're accusing me of something."

"I'm not, but I'm sure you'll want a relationship with her now. She's a good kid, but I don't want you putting things in her head that'll give us a hard time." He sat across from her and kept his hands in his pockets. It appeared uncomfortable and hopefully meant he wouldn't stay long.

"I didn't know you even had children until she walked up and introduced herself. Hell, I had no idea you and Iris had gotten married, and getting involved in your life is the last thing I'm thinking about." She'd give someone a thousand dollars for a decent drink, but she wasn't desperate enough to take another sip of this swill they'd served her. "If she calls me, I did promise I'd talk to her, but to give advice, nothing more."

"She probably told you I hate her," he said, and his body relaxed a bit. "I don't. It was a surprise when she was born, but I gave her my name and tried my best. Your shadow has been large, though."

"That's not the impression I got. It's been a long time, but I doubt the Iris I knew would've married you unless she loved you. That you have two kids means she hasn't given me much thought since I left." She pushed the plastic cup aside and tapped her foot. "I'm not here to take anything away from you that belongs fully to you. Understand?"

He finally pulled his hands free and produced a flask, then stood to get two new cups. "I'm not sure why they can't get anything decent." He poured two equal shares of amber liquor. "And thanks. You could've given me shit as payback."

"I'd like to think we've both matured a little. And for what it's worth, she is a good kid. You did a good job, and I think all teenagers are hardwired to hate their parents at some time or other. It's why I don't teach high school." She lifted her cup and tapped it against his. "And if you're dead set against me talking to her, I'll let her know that."

"And have her find some other reason to blame me for something? No, thank you. Just do me a favor."

She wondered if the guy from *The Twilight Zone* was going to appear and start to narrate what was happening because she didn't understand. "Sure, if I can."

"If she calls and is having a hard time, will you call me? I don't ever want her to think she's alone if things are tough."

"That's something I can do." She smiled when Iris walked up and put her arms around Daniel's neck and kissed the top of his head. "Why don't you dance with your wife? I think these other guys need an example of how it's done."

He seemed to think about it before he walked away, but he did stick out his hand. "Thanks, Jaxon."

"No problem." She waved them off and laughed as she saw some of the women run to the middle of the gym and start a line dance when the music cranked up again.

She couldn't be sure, but the moves looked like some they'd all mastered in high school. The way their male counterparts shook their heads and just stood around watching when the dancers invited them to join in hadn't changed at all in sixteen years. At least she hoped acne cream wasn't a big step in their daily hygiene routine now. The song ended, and the DJ started a slow song. It was one Margot loved, and it made her wish time would go faster, so she could get home.

Jax laughed a little harder when the men still couldn't be enticed to the floor. Then she saw what they were watching instead and couldn't blame them. If there was something she could do all day, every day, for the rest of her life, it was watch Margot Drake walk across a room. She hadn't expected her to be walking across this one, so she waited to see what Margot had in mind. At least now she knew why she wasn't answering her phone.

"It's not a prom dress, but I hope it'll do," Margot said. She laughed when Jax just smiled and nodded. "I see you wore a nice suit, Professor. Did you polish the boots?" Another nod and Margot put her hands on her hips as if waiting for her to make the next move.

"Margot?"

"Yes, Jaxon?"

"Would you dance with me?"

Daniel was the first one in his circle of friends to let his mouth hang open in shock when Margot took Jax's hand and followed her to the dance floor. Maybe there was a small part of herself that relished the reaction Margot usually got in a crowd of alpha males, who never seemed to understand why she wasn't interested in any of them. That Margot was going home with her made her want to puff her chest out a little, and she let herself laugh at the feeling.

"Can I admit that I missed you more than I can ever explain? I love that you're here." She put her arms around Margot, who felt wonderful when they started swaying to the music.

"I owe Judith a ton of favors for letting me come, but I missed you too. I can't spend another night alone, and it's good to hear you can't live without me." Margot ran her hands up her lapels and put them behind her neck.

"I'm glad you're here." She held Margot closer and was ready to leave when Margot kissed her neck right over her pulse point.

"You all right, baby?" Margot laughed and it gave her goose bumps.

"You do have ways of unraveling me, but I will be fine eventually. *Your fifteen-year reunion*, you said. *Think how much you can put to rest*, you said." She laughed when Margot rolled her eyes at her. "We live in California, and that's where we should've stayed. I keep trying to tell you that small towns in Louisiana are full of people who think the West Coast is one big cult full of wackos led by Barbra Streisand."

"Baby, you need to practice that deep breathing I keep trying to teach you." Margot pinched her lips closed and blew her a kiss. "I was talking more about Sean than your family or anything else."

"I'm kidding, and after I had some time to think about it, I'm okay, for the most part." She pulled back a little so she could see Margot's face. "I have you here, and that makes anything that was bothering me more than bearable."

After her talk with Iris that afternoon, all she'd wanted to do was talk to Margot. She'd needed the connection they had to center herself. "One of the things I learned about myself in the last few days is I need only one woman in my life." She kissed Margot's forehead and went back to speaking softly into her ear.

"That's good to know, but it doesn't answer my question."

"I had a lot thrown at me, but it doesn't really make a difference in the realm of what's important in my world. Just like two guys stomping around the forest with cutouts on their feet didn't make me stop believing in mythical creatures that live in the woods."

"You do have a way with your imagination, honey, but you suck at answering either yes or no."

"My brother got my old girlfriend pregnant, never told me, and I'm okay with that. If not completely *okay*-okay, I will be eventually. I'm not okay that he never took responsibility, but that isn't going to keep me from helping Sean." She pressed Margot closer and bent her head to kiss the top of her ear.

"I'm proud of you, and you can count on me to help you through all this."

"The most important thing to remember is that nothing is going to change anything when it comes to you and me. If it bothers you, then I'll find someone else for Sean to talk to. There are enough counselors out there, including Eugenia, that can help her make the right decisions when it comes to her college and life choices." She moved back so she could caress Margot's cheek, liking that she leaned into her touch. "And if you're wondering, I do have fantasies, darlin', but they all center around you."

Margot locked her hands behind Jax's neck and gazed up at her. "Roy was a good choice, but he wasn't her first choice. I watched Iris from the door after asking someone to point her out, and I'd say he still isn't her first choice. She might be married, but her eyes follow you around the room."

"It doesn't really matter what Iris's choices are. She was my first love, and I learned plenty from the experience. The most important lesson was what I wanted when I ever tried again." She placed a quick kiss on Margot's lips. "The most important person in my life is you. I love you, and you make me happy that I took the chance again."

"Then would you mind if I talked to Iris?" Margot winked at her and smiled. It was the type of smile that meant trouble.

"Sure, I'm sure she'd be thrilled to meet you. I'm curious as to why, though."

"Come on, honey. If Sean looks like you, it means she's perfected the making of little Jaxon Lavignes, and I might want access to the information in the near future."

That made her laugh, and Margot joined in. The song ended, and they headed back to the table, where they found Iris and Daniel waiting for them. "Margot, I'd like to introduce you to Iris and Daniel Gravois."

"It's nice to meet you. Jax tells me the decorations and planning were all you, so congratulations. The place looks great," Margot said, offering each of them her hand. "I haven't seen much of the town, but I'll have my big bear take care of that tomorrow." Margot put her arm around her waist and did her best to keep her voice light.

She'd been around Margot long enough to know when it was the actress doing her part to make the people around her feel at ease. It wasn't exactly a complete snow job, but Margot never opened up around people she didn't know. "The place isn't that big, but I'll be happy to play tour guide."

"How did you and Jaxon meet?" Daniel sounded like a police officer, and Margot smiled at the question.

"I took an English class with Dr. Lavigne in my senior year. I saw her in the student union working while downing a huge cup of coffee and nothing else. It took a moment for me to know she was the woman I'd not only marry, but would be ecstatically happy with for the rest of my life." Margot leaned in to her and kissed the side of her neck. "My father never got over it, but I was right."

"You were her student?" Daniel asked in a way that reminded her of Wilber.

"I sure was, and she gave me hell in the classroom," Margot said and laughed. "She also wouldn't go out with me until I graduated. Believe me, I tried everything to get her to change her mind, but she wouldn't bend."

"She's always been honorable," Iris said, and Daniel grimaced.

Jaxon noticed how hard Iris had pinched the top of his hand. "If you two will excuse us, I think they're playing our song," she said, taking Margot's hand.

"'When the Sun Goes Down' is our song?" Margot laughed when she walked her to the other side of the gym. "I'm not voting for that at our wedding."

"Did you want to stay over there and talk to Barney Fife and his bride?" She found another empty table and sat down, shaking her head when Margot sat in her lap.

"What I want is for you to introduce me to some of your classmates and then take me back to your grandmother's. She dropped me off, so I need a ride."

"I'll be happy to, and I'll teach you all about parking in a cane field."

She hadn't talked to that many people, but this trip had been worth every minute she'd spent in this town. One thing she hadn't realized before coming was that she'd had her own questions about her past, and the only way to get the answers meant having to face the people she'd tried to ignore. The not knowing had held her back from Margot, her life, and herself. She still didn't have everything she wanted, but the lightness of letting go made her want to embrace whatever came next.

CHAPTER SIXTEEN

As the night progressed—well, after Bert came over and gave her a big hug—more of Jaxon's old classmates felt comfortable coming up to Margot and asking for autographs and pictures. They shared a few more dances before she and Jaxon were ready to head back to the house. The evening wasn't as horrible as she'd expected it'd be, and she was looking forward to spending the night in Jax's arms.

After dropping Bert off, Jax kept a running commentary of the houses they were passing and who they belonged to. She asked questions, and Jax answered them without hesitation, a new and welcome change. She was enjoying the stories, and it seemed every family had a tale of the entertaining drunk, as well as touches of insanity that were more eccentricity than something ugly. Margot listened, enjoying the way Jaxon's hand felt holding hers as they drove down a road where the houses got farther and farther apart.

"Are you going to admit that you're glad you came?" She pulled on Jaxon's fingers when they turned onto a smaller road and she recognized it wasn't much longer to Birdie's. Jax's grandmother had picked her up at the airport and taken her home to change.

Jaxon stayed quiet until she turned onto her grandmother's driveway that led to the house. She put the car in park and cut the engine. All they could hear was the wind and the rustling of the cane that was blowing on both sides of them. Margot went willingly when Jaxon pulled her closer and kissed her like it was the first time in months. It was something she'd been wanting all night, but she also hadn't wanted to freak out the locals. As always, Jaxon holding her left her heart full of the sense of belonging.

"Can I think about that for a bit before I give you an answer?" Jax asked when they pulled apart.

"Are you still upset about all this?" She ran her fingers along the side of Jax's neck.

"I'm still trying to wrap my brain around all that's been thrown at me in the last couple of days. It was enough to make me punch-drunk." Jaxon kissed her again and smiled when Margot bit her lip before she could retreat to the driver's seat. "My new reality is both familiar and strange, but I'm looking forward to it."

"Honey, you know what I love about you?"

"My uncanny ability to remember and recite love poems on command?" Jaxon wiggled her eyebrows, and Margot started laughing.

"Besides that, lover." She pointed to the keys and made a circular motion with her finger. "Let's get going so we can finish this. You have much better ways to be spending time."

When they reached the house, she didn't let Jax stop anywhere but the bedroom. She'd already been there briefly when Birdie led her up after her flight, but now she knew this was Jaxon's room. Birdie had told her she'd moved all Jax's stuff from her parents' home when they'd turned their backs on her and had made it Jax's room in case she ever returned. Surrounded by Jaxon's history, she stopped and took a look around. This was one of the reasons she'd wanted to come with Jax in the first place. There was so much of who Jax still was wrapped up in all the ribbons and trophies that lined the shelves along with the books.

"You were saying," Jaxon said when Margot fell silent as she touched some of the books that seemed more handled than others.

"Do you remember when we met?"

She stepped closer and started unbuttoning Jax's shirt. With two undone, Margot slipped her hands in and ran her fingers lightly along her soft skin. She laughed along with Jaxon when she started squirming. That Jax was so ticklish was one of the things she found absolutely adorable about her.

"I remember it took quite a few dates before we got to this part," Jax said. More of the buttons popped open under Margot's agile fingers, and her belt came next.

"Not because I didn't work on you, honey. I set my sights on you from that first time I saw you, and I'm glad you gave in before I had to sic Daddy on you."

"Baby, if you want to get any farther than this, you might not want to mention Willy when we're getting naked."

"Ooh, you're afraid of Daddy?"

"I'm not afraid of your father." Jax took a step forward to keep her balance when her belt came off in one good pull. Margot stood with the belt in her hand holding it like a whip. "Maybe I'm a little afraid of him, but have you seen how many notches the man has in that gun?"

"Not as many as I have in mine, so you might want to cooperate." Margot stood there tapping the folded belt in the palm of her hand. "Now do you remember when we met?"

"Yes, baby, I do." Since her shirt was now unbuttoned all the way, Jaxon took it off and threw it on the end of the bed. "It's a time in my life I cherish because I got to learn so many new things about you. I'm not supposed to notice my students, but it was impossible not to notice you."

"That's what I'm talking about." Margot turned around and presented her back so Jaxon would unzip her. "I loved that you wanted to learn about and get to know me. That no matter what was going on in your life, it was something you went out of your way to do. It made me feel so special."

"I love you, so of course I went out of my way to do whatever it would take to make you happy." Jaxon kissed her shoulder after moving the material out of the way. "And you're the one special thing in my life. That's not something that's going to change."

Margot stepped out of her dress and placed it over Jaxon's shirt on the bed. In just her underwear she faced her and smiled at the desire in Jax's eyes. They had only been apart a few days, but she wanted nothing more than to press against all that delicious skin and reacquaint herself with this part of Jaxon that belonged to only her. As soon as she did, Jaxon kissed her like she wasn't interested in any more talk.

Her mother had always told her to wait for the person who spoke to you like a poet only you understood. Jax had done that from the very first day she'd met her even if she swore at the time she wasn't interested. The hours she'd spent in Jaxon's classroom were the best of her college career, and all the times that came after cemented in her mind the life they'd have together.

"That's what I remember too about that time. That part of you that never stops asking the why of everything. You do it because it's in your nature to want to know, and it's the reason I'm glad you came."

They were standing in the middle of the room, and Jaxon picked her up and carried her to the bed. Margot rolled on top and straddled Jax's hips. "What do you mean?" Jaxon asked.

"From our first date, there were certain things I expected." She threaded their fingers together and gazed down at Jax. "I wanted you to love me, want a life with me, and be happy with what we have."

"If I'm falling short in any area, you know you can tell me, right?" Jax sat up and kissed her. "I don't want you to think I don't care about your happiness like you do mine."

"That's not it at all. What I mean is that you've always been a caring soul. I wouldn't have fallen in love with you if you weren't. You might grumble about your students sometimes, but you always go beyond what you need to do to make sure they're successful." She let Jax's hands go so she could run her fingers through Jax's hair. "I love that about you, and it makes me dream about having a family with you."

"On top of having the best hair in America, you're a romantic at heart, my love."

Margot slapped Jax's shoulder and laughed. "You shit. I'm trying to be serious. I'm glad you came because it was time for you to meet Sean. She needs you, and she'll be in good hands. Do you think you could introduce me before we go?"

"I thought we were leaving tomorrow."

"Judith gave me until Tuesday morning, so you're stuck for another day. I also promised Birdie that we'd have breakfast with her and Eugenia in the morning, so they can tell me stories about you." She leaned in and bit Jax's shoulder. "Now do you think you can be quiet enough to make love to me?"

"I'm not the noisy one in this relationship," Jax said as she rolled them over. "Is this new?" Jax put a finger under the strap of the black silk bra she'd picked out the night before when she'd gone on a quick shopping trip.

"I got the set for your birthday. Do you like them?"

"My birthday isn't for three months." Jax lifted her up a little and snapped the bra open with one hand.

"Think of how good you've been this year, then." She laughed when it didn't take Jaxon long to get her completely naked. She stopped laughing when Jax put her hand between her legs and spread her sex open. "Can you tell I've been thinking about you for days?"

"What exactly were you thinking about?" Jax asked before licking her nipple to life.

"I'll be happy to tell you every nasty thought if you get busy with that hand." She sucked in a breath when Jax wet her finger and flicked it over her clit. The delicious contact made her lift her hips, wanting more. "Baby, if you make me wait, I'm going to torture you in ways… fuck," she said loudly when Jax followed the move and kept going.

"You want me, love?" Jax's voice was slow and full of lust. It was the way she loved her in the bedroom.

"Always, but it's not the time for slow." She held Jax's head when she sucked her nipple in and moved down her body. "That mouth is one of my favorite things about you."

Jax sucked in her clit and put her fingers in at the same time. It made her buck her hips and grab Jax's hair. The move seemed to give Jax a hint about what she wanted, and she pulled out and slammed her fingers back in. She had a death grip on Jaxon's head, but it didn't stop her from giving her what she wanted.

"Jesus," she said when Jax sucked harder. The fast pace was what she needed even if it meant the end would come way too soon. "That's so good." She put her feet on Jax's shoulders, knowing she couldn't hold out that much longer. "Yes…yes…ah, ah…yes." She had to pull Jax's head away from her sex after the orgasm made her supersensitive.

"If I haven't mentioned it, I missed you." Jaxon came up and kissed her forehead.

"Thank God I fell in love with a Southerner who knows the meaning of hospitality," she said, teasing. "Your welcome wagon is the true meaning of satisfaction, babe."

"Let's hope Birdie is a heavy sleeper, or we might have to stay at a hotel next time."

"Your grandmother wants you to have children for her to spoil, so I'm sure she's rooting for you." She put her arms around Jax's neck when she lay pressed up against her.

"I get you pregnant before I marry you, and I doubt I'd live to see Junior born," Jax said and laughed. That stopped when Margot kissed her, then bit her lip.

"You give Daddy a boy, and he'll forgive you anything."

"You give your dad a girl, and he'll be thrilled."

That Jaxon didn't balk at the idea made her wish she was pregnant already. It might be one way of getting her down the aisle. One step at a time, she reminded herself as she slid down Jax's body "You're right—it's not the time to talk about my father." She knelt between Jax's legs and smiled. "I believe you really did miss me."

She put her mouth on Jax before she had a chance to say anything else, and the grunt she got from flicking her tongue over Jax's hard clit made her want to laugh. If there was one thing Jax was not, it was talkative in bed. Sometimes, though, her silence said volumes.

"Son of a bitch," Jax said as her whole body tensed and then released as she threw her head back.

"Is that the first time you did this in here?" she asked. "And it's perfectly okay to lie to me right now if it's not." She moved back up into the circle of Jax's embrace.

"You're the first, love. Believe me, Birdie was tough when I was growing up, and it's nice that she kept all this stuff. I like knowing there's a place I can return to that's familiar if I ever do want to come here again."

"It's home, baby." She lay half on Jax and pointed to all the trophies. "She's proud of you and always has been."

"My home is with you. It's a little fancier than I would've imagined for myself, but I'm happy."

"It's okay to have two places to call home, and don't worry. I'm not letting you go anywhere. Now kiss me and go to sleep. You'll need to be well-rested to face all the teasing we'll be getting in the morning."

"Thanks for talking me into this. You were right, and while my parents haven't changed their minds, it's time to move on."

"Good. I don't want to share you with bad memories anymore."

She pressed her cheek to Jaxon's shoulder and relaxed against her, relieved that Jaxon was in a good headspace. When Bert had called her and given her a rundown about the old girlfriend, and her Jaxon-clone kid, she'd been worried. Well, not worried really, but a little jealous, if she was honest. It was irrational, but she loved Jaxon and wanted to think their life together had trumped anything that'd happened before and could come in the future.

She'd also feared that Jaxon would come back and figure it was where she belonged. That too was irrational, but the heart had a way of overriding the brain and making you stupid about things. All those insecurities had died the second she'd seen Jaxon's face when she'd walked into the room. She closed her eyes, sure about her place and that Jaxon would always be there. This spot was hers and hers alone.

❖

The next morning Jaxon got up and covered Margot before she sat on the window seat and looked out at the cane fields shrouded in fog. The crop still had a few months before the large harvesting machines would chop the cane for the mill that was about ten miles from here. In Jax's opinion, this time of year was when the land was the most beautiful. The cane was large enough to blow like those air gizmos they put in front of car dealerships and the like. The fields resembled a million arms in the air, saying *Hey, look over here.*

She remembered the last time she'd sat on this seat and looked out at the same scene. Her graduation from LSU would come after one more summer session, and she found nothing comforting in the scenery or anything in her life. Birdie was the only person who'd kept her from floating away on a wave of despair. Life had changed so much in that short period of time, and she was glad to have grown as a person and was lucky enough not only to have a job she loved, but to have found Margot.

The feel of Margot's arms around her neck made her smile, and she leaned back to make room for her on her lap. "Good morning," Margot said, her voice thick with sleep. "Why are you up so early?"

"The ghosts in this town won't let me sleep long."

Margot opened Jax's robe and wrapped the edges around her naked body. "If I asked nicely, would you tell me a story?"

"What would you like to know?" She kissed Margot's temple and rubbed her abdomen.

"Why would Roy agree to sleep with Iris if you said they didn't get along?"

She shrugged. "I'm not sure how to answer that one. Roy was never jealous of me, and he really didn't like Iris all that much. At least, that's what he told me. Back then I guess I was wrapped up in Iris and what was going on with me. If he had some hidden grudge or crush or whatever, he buried it deep enough that I never noticed."

"You need to talk to him, but you need to feed me first. Now, please tell me you have a bathroom around here somewhere. I'd like not to run into your grandmother before we take a shower."

"I'm sure Birdie's been up for hours waiting on us." She heard a car outside and saw Eugenia pulling in. "Thanks for asking, and for listening."

"There's plenty more I want to know, and you have to believe I want to hear all about little Jaxon Lavigne's formative years." Margot kissed her and whispered her love in her ear. "All I want is for you to stop blaming yourself for things that aren't your fault."

Jax smiled. "You know, I think I can finally do that. Thanks to you and Bert badgering me to come here."

"Come on and take a shower with me. After breakfast I want a tour." Margot stood up, and the sight of her made Jax want to go back to bed.

"Are you sure? I'm sure I can find some quiet place for us to have lunch." She reached up and placed her hands on Margot's hips. "Better yet, we can pack up after breakfast and drive to New Orleans. I'm sure Tully and Libby would love to see you."

"I don't think so. That does sound tempting, but I've already talked to Libby, and she knows as soon as I go on hiatus we'll be back." Margot backed out of her embrace and reached for the shirt Jax had worn the night before. "Let's get wet."

They showered and dressed and went down to the kitchen, and Jax's heart lightened as Eugenia smiled and opened her arms to Margot. "You're gorgeous," Eugenia said as she gave Margot a hug.

"I feel like I know you after all the stories Jax has told me—both of you." Margot kissed both women on the cheek, and her eyes were glassy with tears. "And thank you both for taking such good care of her. You raised an awesome human being."

"I'd like to think I had a little to do with that," a man's voice said from the doorway.

Jaxon turned around and lost her smile when she saw her father. It had been years since she'd laid eyes on him, and his hair was much whiter, but he still appeared fit. The sight of him made it feel as if there was a great weight holding her down in the chair, and she wanted to throw it off and run. The only thing that eased her discomfort was Margot putting her hands on her shoulders.

"I didn't think you'd claim you had anything to do with me." She purposefully didn't raise her voice and tried to bleed the emotion out of it.

"Are you going to introduce your friend?" Gene Lavigne looked like a man you'd follow into battle. He was imposing, but she remembered his patience as a father, teaching things that he felt were important for her and Roy to know.

"No. Why are you here, Dad?" She was too old to placate people simply because she was expected to. Respect had to be earned. That had been one of his most important lessons.

"I'm here because I was wrong. It's probably too late, but I'd like to think there might still be a chance."

Margot leaned down and kissed her cheek before she took Birdie's hand. "Do you want me to stay?"

"Go ahead. This won't take long." She smiled up at Margot and nodded. "Does Mom know you're here?" She put as much sarcasm as she could into the question. "I've seen her, and she said neither of you have changed your minds."

"I didn't think you'd be quick to forgive, and I don't blame you." He sat across from her and folded his hands on the table. It was the exact same pose he'd struck when he'd said nothing as her mother meted out punishment for some infraction or another. "Your grandmother reminds me constantly what an idiot I am. You are who you are, Jaxon, and I accept that."

"Stop." She put her hand up. "Please stop. The stuff you're saying…" She stopped and tried to find the best way to put it so as not to draw this out. "I waited a long time to hear you say this, but what you did, what you did is…" There were no words to finish that. "I waited until I didn't need your words any longer. And you accept me? That's the best you can do?"

"You're in love, Jaxon, and you'll eventually realize that you'll have to do things to make your partner happy. You might not agree, but to keep the peace you do it."

She had to laugh. "You led men in Special Forces, Dad. Your excuse is you were scared of Mom? That you let her chase me away to make her happy? That's more insulting than what you did."

"I wasn't scared. It was more like keeping my sanity. I'm sure your mother told you that we started divorce proceedings. Whatever years I have left I want to be filled with some semblance of happiness. It's been so long that I'm going to have to take some time to figure out what that is." Her father turned his head and stared out the window. "I come from a long line of farmers, and it's time for me to take my turn."

"Does Birdie even want you here?" She couldn't help but hurt him a little, though the news of the divorce was surprising.

"Your grandmother is a wise woman, and I should've listened to her no matter the subject. You're my daughter, Jaxon, and I'm proud of you. What you've accomplished, you've done on your own, which should make you proud of yourself." He made eye contact with her, and she was surprised by the tears on his face. The warrior he'd been all his life seldom showed this kind of emotion. "I don't deserve your forgiveness, but I'm asking for it anyway."

"It's not a question of forgiving. That I did a long time ago for my own peace of mind after Birdie told me to put that load down. My problem is *forgetting*." It was true. When her head couldn't find the answers that could rationally explain why, her heart could never really heal. She'd dealt with this by not dealing with it—putting it out of her mind as much as she could, eventually locking it away where she could insulate herself from the bleeding. But there he was, sitting across from her, tears running down his face, asking for forgiveness. The Band-Aid had been ripped off, and the wound was bleeding.

"I wasn't expecting a warm reunion, but maybe with time…?" He sounded hopeful.

"I'm not going to change who I am, Dad. Think about that before you go making promises you have no intention of keeping. Margot is my partner and eventually will be my wife, if she'll have me. I love her and the life we have. I don't live by a don't ask, don't tell set of rules." She saw her father's eyes lift before she felt Margot put her arms around her again and kiss the top of her head. "We're not roommates, and I'm never going to hide what she means to me."

"I realize that, and I wanted different for you." He put his hands up when she opened her mouth. "Not because I'm ashamed of you, Jaxon, but because I think life would've been easier for you."

"I wanted different *from* you. Understand that I live in a place where people don't stare when I hold Margot's hand, or think it's unnatural that I love her. It could be that way everywhere, but people like you and Mom have made that impossible. Hiding behind your patriotism and religion gives you the superior attitude that forgives how you treat people." She stood up and put her arm around Margot's waist.

"Take your half-assed apology and—"

"Honey." Margot squeezed her. "Give it time and stop talking. Mr. Lavigne, I'm Margot Drake, and I love your daughter. My father is retired military as well, and he sits this one in his study every week and gives her lectures on God knows what. She takes it with grace and patience because she loves me."

"I've made a mess of this, but I'm not condemning you, I swear it," her father said.

"The thing that most people think defines my father is the uniform he wore for most of his life, but he told me that while the uniform was important, it was becoming a father that made him the proudest." Margot gazed up at her and smiled.

"I am proud, and all I'm asking is for you two to think about it. Sixteen years of silence won't be undone in one apology or one day, but I want to be part of your life. Far too many years have been wasted, and I promise I won't let you down." Her father stood and wisely made no move toward them. "Actions sometimes have to be proven over and over before you believe them to be genuine. If you give me a chance, I give you my word—you won't be sorry."

Jax stared at him, unable to find the words, any words, to reply. Life had just been upended once again, and she had no idea how to react.

"Give us some time, Mr. Lavigne. I'm not judging you, and I'm not a psychologist, but what happened here is as hard to grasp as fog." Margot squeezed her side as she spoke. "Jax's only sin is that she's a lesbian. She didn't choose it to piss you off—it's as natural to her as her beautiful blue eyes. But allowing your wife to cheat you of all the amazing things Jax is because of her narrow-mindedness was pure cowardice, if I may say so. Think about all that, and maybe we'll try again. It was nice meeting you," Margot said politely as if she'd not just ripped into her father's character in the nicest way possible. "You ready, honey?"

Jax blinked and took a deep breath. "Come on, I promised you a tour." She took Margot's hand and walked out.

Standing up to the past was both maddening and satisfying. Sixteen years ago, she would've never had the guts to do it, but life had taught her that standing up for herself took courage. Maybe she'd have a relationship with her father, and perhaps she wouldn't, but she'd earned the right to decide for herself. They'd had power over her emotions for too long. Now she had that power back, and life would never be the same. It would be even better.

"You okay, my love?" Margot asked.

"I wasn't for a long time, but I think I am now. Thank you, and that was the nicest fuck-you I've ever heard. You're a poet, my love."

CHAPTER SEVENTEEN

The diner was mostly empty in the late afternoon. Jaxon had taken Margot for a ride and pointed out all the highlights of her hometown. That hadn't taken long, so they'd spent the rest of the time on the banks of the bayou at the back of Birdie's property. They'd avoided the subject of her father's visit, and for that Jaxon was grateful. It was a lot to process.

Birdie and Eugenia were cooking dinner, so they'd opted for the diner to split a burger as a late lunch, so they wouldn't be totally full. The young woman who came to their table seemed to be vibrating with what Jaxon assumed to be excitement when she stared at Margot. She was pretty sure this was Sean's girlfriend, but she hadn't gotten a good look at her the first time she'd been in here.

"Make sure you tell them to hold the onion and tomato on that, please," Margot said as she handed the menus back. "Are you okay?"

"Fine," the girl said in a voice pitched so high that Jaxon took her hand off her water glass in case it shattered.

"Are you Sean's girlfriend?" she asked, trying to break the spell Margot had cast over this kid.

"Yeah," the girl said, her eyes still on Margot.

"If you call her, I promise I'll take a picture of you and Ms. Drake."

The girl nodded. "I already did that," she said, taking a deep breath. "Are you two, like, together?"

"What's your name? And it's a total love connection," Margot said and winked. "But I hear you got the younger model. I'd like to meet Sean if she's coming by, and I'd also like that burger before I pass out."

"I'm Adeline, and I'll be right back."

Jaxon chuckled when the kid tripped on her feet and almost took a header into the kitchen. "I didn't realize you spoke teenager that well."

"Please, I graduated after taking your class. My vocabulary has gotten much better," Margot said, throwing a sugar packet at her.

Margot had asked to meet Sean, and this was the easiest way she could think to arrange it without involving Iris. "Do you think this is a good idea? Maybe I should've checked with Daniel and Iris first to make sure everyone is on the same page."

"One of the best dates you ever took me on was to see Shakespeare in the Park, the night they did *Romeo and Juliet*. That play stuck with me because the ending could've been so much better if only they'd had someone on their side." Margot got up and sat next to her in the booth. "I realize the play's a tragedy, before you start slipping into professor mode, but think of all the kids who find themselves in the same situation now, only it's Romeo and Romeo, or Juliet and Juliet. I don't want a kid who could grow up to be as awesome as you to fall through the cracks because they had no one to talk to."

"I love you more than life, Margot. I realize I don't say that often enough, but I do. I'm a lucky bastard that you love me back." She kissed the tip of Margot's nose and took her hand.

"I met your father this morning, babe. You're not the bastard in the family." Margot shook her head and laughed. "Sorry, that was mean, and the guy did apologize. It might've been the most awkward apology in the history of man, but A for effort." Margot pulled her down by the collar of her shirt and kissed her on the lips. "And I do love you."

"Hey," Sean said, standing by the table but looking like she wanted to run. "You want me to come back?"

"No, honey," Margot said. "Every so often I have to declare my undying love or break into song. Since I can't sing to save Jaxon's life, I stick to the sappy declarations." Margot kissed her again before pointing to the other side of the booth. "Can we buy you and Adeline a burger?"

"Thanks," Sean said, dropping into the booth like someone had tackled her.

"Thank you for coming. I should've gotten your number, and I thought this might be the best bet before we leave town." She watched Sean nod in a constant steady motion. Margot put her hand in Jaxon's pocket and retrieved her phone. "I talked to your parents and told them I'll be happy to help out when it comes to your future academic plans."

"You only want to talk to me about school?" Sean stopped nodding, and she appeared dejected.

"I'll be happy to talk to you about anything you want," she said, trying not to grimace at the pinch Margot was delivering to her leg. "You have my number, and if you put yours in there, I'll call you every so often—if you don't mind."

"That'd be great," Sean said, moving her fingers over the screen faster than seemed humanly possible. "Adeline told me not to sweat it, and she was right."

"I'd hang on to that one. She's smart and pretty. That's an awesome combination," Margot said as Adeline came out of the kitchen with a loaded tray. She delivered the food and sat next to Sean to eat. "So, what do you want to study after high school?" Margot asked before biting down on a fry.

"I want to be a teacher like Miss Eugenia and you," Sean said, pointing at Jax. "Adeline wants to be a nurse."

"Makes sense," Margot said and smiled up at her. "Must be in the genes, huh?"

That line made Sean's face light up as Margot as much as admitted she was the long-lost father figure, which was totally ridiculous, but Jax stayed quiet on that subject. She guided the conversation to scholarships and the other interests the girls had. After a few minutes she couldn't help but conclude what Iris had said was true. Sean was smart, driven, a lot like Jax, and a gift. Getting pregnant might not have been the wisest thing Iris ever did, but damn if her gamble hadn't evolved into an awesome person with a bright future.

They ate and talked some more before it was time to get back to her grandmother's for the night. If Margot was right, the afternoon was the first step in showing Sean the possibilities of what her life could be. The kid was already ahead of her in several ways. Adeline seemed like the kind of partner who wouldn't be afraid of fighting for what she wanted.

"Study hard, and the last two years of school won't be as long as you're thinking they're going to be," she said when they stepped outside. Margot and Adeline had hung back, talking and taking selfies. "Right now, it seems like the worst time of your life because you want to be with Adeline all the time, but do some stuff with your mom and dad. Those memories will be some that all of you will appreciate." She put her hand on the side of Sean's neck and smiled. "Remember one thing."

"What?" Sean said, her eyes wide.

"Daniel is your father, and he loves you just as much as your mother. Don't throw that away because of what's happened in the past. I think going forward will be a lot smoother as far as all that's concerned. Give the guy a chance, and cut your mother some slack." She squeezed before letting Sean go.

"What about you? What are you to me?" Sean stepped into her personal space and asked with the earnestness of a kitten.

She wasn't sure herself yet, so she answered as best she could. "I want to be your friend, and with time maybe we can have the kind of relationship that comes with being family. I had no idea you were waiting, so I'm sorry I didn't get here sooner." She held her arms out to her sides, and Sean lunged forward and wrapped her in a bear hug. "I'm a call away, and I care. Okay?"

"Thank you." Sean sounded like she was crying against Jax's shoulder. "You don't know it, but you help me make sense of me. Do you know what I mean?"

"I do, and I'll be right here if you ever need me." She hugged Sean and kissed her forehead. The thought of children didn't seem quite so scary now.

"I'll make sure to remind her," Margot said.

She let Sean go and turned to Margot. Sean stood on the other side of Margot when Nancy came out from the back and took some pictures. That Iris was with Nancy didn't surprise her, and it gave her a chance to say good-bye for now. "Thanks for all the work you did on the reunion. And thanks for allowing me to talk to Sean," she said when they moved away from the others.

"She's been waiting for you for a long time, even if she didn't know it. I'm glad you're happy, Jax, and I hope you know that a part of me will always love you." Iris took her hand and stepped closer. "I've missed you, and I wanted you to know I never betrayed you. Your relationship with Roy might not be as close as it once was, but he wouldn't have done that to you."

"It shouldn't matter, but it might've, a little. If it's too hard to admit, don't, but we both know Daniel isn't biologically her father."

"Does it really matter?" Iris asked. "And you're smart enough to know there's more than one way to conceive a baby. Being intimate with someone should be reserved for someone you love. Well, in my opinion, anyway. That's all the hints I'm giving."

"Thank you," she said, and the explanation did erase some of the hurt. "It shouldn't matter since it's your choice, but that does make me feel better. She's a good kid, and I'll be happy to help her when she needs it. Take care of yourself, Iris, and Sean has my number. There's a part of me that will always love you as well, but my heart belongs to Margot." She hugged her old friend and wiped her tears. "We both ended up where we needed to be."

"Thanks, Jax, and thank you for not turning away from her."

"She was a shock, but a good one."

The drive back to Eugenia's was quiet, and Margot looked at the picture she'd taken of Sean and Jaxon. The resemblance was uncanny, and she had to force herself to shut the phone down. She wouldn't mind staying a few more days, but tomorrow afternoon it was back to their lives.

"This is really something, huh?" It was the only thing she could think of to break the quiet.

"Would you mind one more stop before we head to Granny's?" Jax lifted her hand and kissed her palm.

"Sure." It was crazy, but she was jealous of Jax's old love and her kid who looked like the bastard Jax would've left behind. That was hard to compete with.

They passed the turnoff to Birdie's and went another two miles before Jax headed down a dirt road between the cane. It was close to sunset, and they drove another ten minutes before they came to a stand of ancient oaks next to a canal. The Spanish moss hanging from the trees and the slow-moving water were what she imagined this land must've looked like years before.

"What's this place?" She looked at Jax and smiled.

"I used to come out here to think, study, and write." Jax opened her door and motioned for her to stay put.

"Not make out?" she asked when Jax opened her door.

"You're going to be the first girl I kiss out here, unless you're mad at me for something." Jax helped her on with her coat since the temperature had dropped some. "When I was a kid, my dad built me a tree house in those trees, and I'd sit up there and watch the guys cut cane. They used different equipment back then, and I'd try to capture what the process was in words. Eventually Eugenia tore those essays to shreds and taught me to refine my writing."

"So this was your special place?" She could imagine a young Jax sitting in the branches dreaming big dreams.

"Before you this was the one spot I felt completely at ease. It's the one spot in the world I claimed as my own, and Birdie had this put out here." Jax walked her to the rock that sat almost at the center of the oak grove and pointed to the plaque bolted to the front: JAXON'S COVE. "This place fired my imagination when I was a kid."

"What did you dream about?" She put her arms around Jaxon's waist and rested her chin on her chest.

"I thought about all the adventures I'd have and the things in the world I'd see." Jaxon helped her sit on the rock and knelt in front of her. "I have seen and done plenty, but then I met you."

"You make it sound like that's a bad thing," she said combing Jax's hair back. The sky behind her was red and beautiful.

"Not at all. After I met you, I thought about all the dreams I had, and I knew I didn't have imagination enough to imagine you." Jaxon leaned in and kissed her. "I'd been limping along until you found me. You are the one thing in my life that's perfect."

"I'm far from perfect, love." She pulled Jaxon closer and kissed her again. The way Jaxon treated her had always made her feel special, and from the day she'd committed to only her, she'd never once felt like this. Seeing what Jaxon had left behind had made her realize that perhaps she might not be enough. It was silly, but Sean was real and hard to compete with.

"In the world there is but one perfect match for everyone. We weren't each other's first, but we are the only two people who match perfectly." Jaxon reached in her pocket. "There isn't a day that will come when I want to be anywhere but at your side."

"That's beautiful, honey. I do love the way you talk to me."

"We've built a good life, but the rest of it starts today. Sometimes you have to go back and find the parts of your history that hold special meaning. They lay the cornerstones of your future." Jax opened her fist, which held a jewelry box, and lifted the lid to reveal a beautiful ring. "When I decided to come back for all the ridiculousness of my reunion, Birdie decided to give me something. This is the ring my grandfather bought her, and she promised it to me when I found the right girl. She said it brought her the great fortune of happiness, and she wanted the same for us."

"It's beautiful," Margot whispered. And she meant it. The stone had to be at least two carats, and the square cut was gorgeous. Seeing it and Jaxon on her knees were doing strange things to her stomach and blink reflex. It didn't seem real, and she had to concentrate on breathing, so she wouldn't miss a moment of the one thing she'd really wanted. This was going to be her one and only proposal. Of that she was sure.

"You're beautiful, and you have the heart and soul to match. I promise I'll always love and take care of you. I'll always be faithful, and I'll always be there for you. Will you marry me?"

"Oh. My. God." She watched Jaxon take the ring and place it at the end of her finger. Jaxon's words made her start crying.

"Is that a yes?" Jaxon asked with a smile.

"Yes, yes, and yes." Jaxon slid the ring on, and she looked at her finger for a moment before she kissed Jaxon with all the passion she had in her. "I love you." She held her hand out and admired the ring again. "Daddy's going to be so happy."

"I'm sure he'll stand down after I get you down the aisle, but I doubt it." Jaxon kissed her again. "I called him while I was here, so I could ask you when I got home."

"Wait," she said, framing Jax's face with her hands. "You called my father?"

"Honey, do you honestly think I could've asked you without asking the general for his blessing first? It's archaic, I know, but your dad is an old-fashioned guy, and I respect that." Jaxon threaded their fingers together. "Don't be mad at him—the man loves you."

"I'm not mad, and you're incredibly sweet." She watched Jax stand and gladly went with her when she pulled her up.

"You're sure, right? All this stuff doesn't make you rethink us?" Jaxon held her and seemed to be looking into her eyes for the truth.

"Honestly, I was a little jealous." She held their fingers close together and laughed. "Iris is still pretty, and I can tell she's still in love with you. Maybe that's not the kind of love that makes you run away with the person, but she broke the rules and had, what she considers in her heart, your baby."

"The only way that could be true is if she'd told me. When I looked up and saw Sean, happiness wasn't my first reaction—trust me on that. Iris is my past, and you're the rest of my life. Sometimes you have to learn what love isn't before you know when it's real and lasting. That's you, and only you. There's no reason to be jealous."

"How about the rest of your family?"

Jaxon glanced at the water as if it held the best answer. "I'll have to think about that. Maybe it's not a dead subject, and maybe it is. Time is the only thing that'll decide that. The next move is theirs. I tried my best."

"You're such a poet, baby, and you're right. I'd rather celebrate us, and I'm sure Eugenia and Birdie will be more than happy to join us." She pulled Jax down to sit on the rock and sat on her lap. Jax took her phone for selfies, since she had the longer arms, and pressed their heads together with Margot's hand in the air to show off her ring and the red sky in the background. Margot studied the shot before sending it to her parents and making the call. "Hey, Daddy, she asked, and I said yes."

Jax laughed at the moan Wilber let out on speaker. "It's not too late to change your mind, baby. You could find a nice doctor to settle down with."

She couldn't be sure, but it sounded like a slap coming from the other end. "Don't listen to this old curmudgeon," Patty Sue said. "Tell me Jaxon was over-the-top romantic."

"She was, and she has wonderful taste in jewelry. And, Daddy, I already found a nice doctor to settle down with, and I'm keeping her."

"We're going to have so much fun planning, so hurry home." There was the sound of another slap when Patty Sue finished, and Wilber cleared his throat.

"Yes," he said. "So much fun. Jaxon, you there?"

"Yes, sir. I promise I haven't forgotten anything you said, and I'll take care of her forever."

"Good. Hurt her, and they'll never find your body."

"Love you guys," Margot said. "And stop threatening her before she dumps me." She hung up and looked at Jaxon. "I love you too. And thank you for asking me."

"That's nothing you need to thank me for. You had me from that first date, and the rest of my life is something I'm looking forward to."

"Me too, so let's go. The sooner I share you with other people, the sooner I get you all to myself."

❖

The next morning Jaxon got up early and walked to the back of the property to the dock that had been redone recently. There was another large stand of trees, and the one closest to the water had a tire swing she'd used to get to the middle of the bayou. Margot was still sleeping, and they were going to share one more breakfast with Birdie before heading to the airport.

She sat on the dock and breathed in the cool morning air, loving the way the steam was already dancing across the top of the water. She opened her journal, lightly caressing the pages. It was amazing how much life could change in a few days. One of the things she'd enjoyed was working on their high school yearbook. It had taught her plenty about writing, and it was the chance to record a little of their history. A slice that they could look back on, to remember who they were and how far they'd come. She still had all three of the books in her study at home but hadn't opened them from the day she'd put them on the shelf. She stared at the water, letting her mind wander, before she began to write.

History is a collection of experiences that teach, sometimes with pain and at times with love. I tried hiding from those lessons, but if there is one thing I've discovered, it's that burying pain only makes it fester.

I finally found the courage to go back to where I came from and threw open the doors on the parts of my heart that housed all my secrets and fears and found that time had cleaned out the wounds in my absence. The years had let my captives free, let in the light, and swept away the pain I have a tendency to hold on to. I'd convinced myself there was no other choice but to embrace the choices I'd made and the mistakes those choices brought.

Margot has shown me that cleansing your soul of the feelings that weigh you down makes moments like proposing that much sweeter. It took walking away from all I knew to find my own idea of paradise, and that's protected me from the landmines of my past. And now I've found peace, which makes any road easier to travel. Having a foundation here helped me find not only the treasures I'd forgotten to take with me, but allowed me to discover the ones that waited for me to uncover.

Time teaches us many things. The most important is you have no choice but to make peace with change. Our high school yearbook was titled *Calumet*, which means peace pipe. A strange title then, but one I appreciate in a different way now.

Given the chance, Time waits patiently by the fire with a smile, a calumet in one hand. Time whispered that it wasn't my enemy and happily showed me never to hide from it. It knows I am my own harshest critic, and most likely to forgive a stranger before giving myself the same consideration. And so I can sit with time, letting the smoke from the peace pipe wash over me, flood my soul, and leave me ready to make the most of my time going forward.

I know now that some friendships are worth missing, and my sense of loss over them was justified. But most importantly I've found home isn't where I grew up or the place I put my keys down at the end of the day. That can only be found in the rhythm of the heart that beats next to mine now that I've allowed Margot in. Margot is my home, and Sean is my permission to think of the future's possibilities. I look forward to embracing both.

She closed the book and capped her pen, taking one last long look at the water. If she could talk Margot into it, perhaps they'd come back a few times a year with Bert and drag Tully's family along, so she could visit her grandmother. The relationship they had was important to her, and Birdie wouldn't be here forever.

"Still writing stuff down, I see," Roy said, surprising her.

"Some days are more interesting than others. Lately it's been epic." Roy was the last chapter of this fucked-up episode of *This Is Your Life*. "Imagine my surprise when I got a load of all the gifts you left me, especially one."

"I knew you'd be pissed, and I should've told you." He sat next to her and let his hands hang between his knees. "I really should've told you."

"Yes, you should've. Was the reason you didn't because you're an asshole?" Her question made him grimace. "What I don't get is why you didn't help her after the fact. It sounds like she married Daniel to save face. If you helped her with that, why not go all the way?" Her brother was an honorable guy, she'd thought that all her life, and Sean was the one dent in that picture.

"I offered—don't think otherwise if she didn't mention it. But it wasn't me she wanted, and she made that clear. There was no denying how you felt for Iris back then, and I admired you for standing up to Mom." He laughed at what seemed to be a private joke. "She threw you out and said she didn't want anything to do with you, but believe me, she hasn't stopped talking about it from that afternoon. It might've died down, but then you go and fall in love with someone who puts you front and center at the grocery store checkout."

"Yes, I know. She told me how embarrassing it is. If I wrote all this down and published it, there's no way anyone would believe that it's a true story. It's kind of fucked-up, now that I've had more time to process it." With maturity came understanding, that was true, but sometimes life came with instructions in Russian with Rorschach tests for the pictorial explanations.

"Think of it this way," Roy said, reaching over and squeezing her forearm. "Mom did fuck up, and Dad was right there with her."

"I got that part, brother."

He laughed at her sarcasm. "That's not what I want you to think about. You were special enough for someone to have created a life that so much resembles you. There's no way I'd ever step on Daniel's toes, but Iris has shared as much of Sean with me as she could through the years. I've been the silent uncle Sean knows nothing about, but her creation had nothing to do with me and everything to do with you. She's a wonder to me because it was like watching you grow up all over again. Even without your influence, which I think she's needed, she's you in every way."

"Thank you for saying that, but I am shocked at your part in this." She shook her head when he started to say something. "Not for the reasons you think. I mean, I thought you never cared for Iris."

"Her explanation was enough to convince me. I think she wanted you to come back and share the experience with her. She had some idea that if she told you she was pregnant with our family line, you'd come back and help her raise the kid. My excuse is that I'm only two years older than you, so I also wasn't thinking of the long-term ramifications. I guess I was kind of hoping you'd come back too."

"Long-term ramifications? That's the best you can come up with?"

"I have no idea why she never told you, and why she married Daniel instead. She must have her reasons, I guess. Anyway, I didn't sleep with her. All she asked me for is what she needed to make a baby. She was so earnest when she begged me that we worked out how to get it done, thanks to Google. We didn't even know if it would work. Trust me, she's my biological daughter, but I wasn't in the room when she was conceived." He appeared embarrassed, and the whole thing sounded so progressive.

"Are you serious?" Now what Iris had said about not betraying her made sense.

"It was Miss April who turned me on that night, not Iris. I'm not an asshole, and I'm so sorry you found out the way you did. I'm glad it's out in the open." He smiled, but it didn't reach his eyes. "If you're going to lump me in with Dad, at least give me the chance to apologize until you believe how truly sorry I am."

"I'm sure you know he came by, but you also know what it was like. I'm not a heartless bitch who can't forgive, but I'm not quite there yet."

"I know, and so does he. You have to realize, though, what it's been like. Mom has been spreading misery all these years, and he tuned her out when he could and went along when he couldn't." Roy sighed like he was carrying a weight that was dragging him down. "Both of us should've cut and run a lot sooner than this, but the guilt kept us tethered way too long."

"She's my mother too, and I get that. I'm not denying the relationship, and I'd like to think that if she needed me, both her and

Dad, I wouldn't turn my back on them." She'd like to believe that, and Margot would not so gently nudge her in the right direction if she was wrong. "All I've done was try to forget and give her what she wanted." "I know that, Jax. The last person who had any blame in this is you. I've told you that more than once, and I hope you believe me. I'm also sorry I've been ducking your calls. There was a little part of me that figured you were aiming your proverbial shotgun and were ready to unload."

She ran her fingers over her notebook and thought about what she'd written. It was time for peace. "We're okay—don't worry about it. Fighting over dumb high school decisions isn't worth the energy it takes. A few days ago it might've been iffy, but I got engaged, and I'm too happy to be pissed at anyone at the moment." She smiled and he stood to hug her.

"Congratulations, and Granny told me last night she's a keeper." He sat back down and sighed again. "Look, now that you're not mad, I should tell you something else."

"What? Iris's son is yours too, only he didn't inherit the dark hair and blue eyes?"

"Good Lord, no. Once was more than enough. After I started practicing and making money, I thought about what I'd done. My part in all this, I mean." He tapped his fingers together, and she recognized the nervous tic he'd had all his life. "I respected what Iris wanted and, more importantly, didn't want from me. There was no way I'd have married her, but I didn't want to neglect what I thought was my responsibility."

"Sounds like she didn't want you to have any."

"I still did it, and I have to live with it, so I set money aside for Sean. Granted, I doubt her parents will let me give it to her, but Eugenia thought of a way. When she graduates, she'll receive the Picard Scholarship for academic and sports excellence. It should be enough, even if she has UCLA in mind."

Picard was Granny's maiden name, so Roy had kept it in the family. Sean was, after all, Birdie's great-grandchild. "The hardest part of this was thinking you were an asshole," she said and laughed. "It's good to know I was right, and you aren't. I think it's a fantastic idea." They both laughed at that, and she turned when she heard Margot talking on the phone as she headed toward them. "Hey, love."

"Hey," Margot said when she hung up. "That was Judith. Britt has the flu and won't be at work for the next two weeks." The way Margot smiled made her laugh. "What? I wish him well."

"I'm sure you do, baby, but come over here and meet my brother." Roy surprised her by hugging Margot and kissing her cheek. "Thank you for loving my sister," he said, and Margot nodded. "Anything you need, feel free to ask."

"Anything?" Margot asked as she sat on the arm of Jax's chair. "Have a seat, Roy."

"Did you need something?" he asked. He glanced at Jax briefly, but she shrugged.

"I need you to take a short vacation…Actually, you can stay as long as you want, but I need you to give us the same gift you gave Iris. You do good work. Obviously, you know, in a more science-based way than the horny teenager used." Margot's request made Roy blush so deeply that she feared his face would carry a permanent tint.

"I can do that, and I'd love to."

"Great, and you're welcome in our home even if it's not for that. I'd love to sit with you and Birdie and listen to stories about this one. I owe you my thanks as well. You never turned your back on her, and it's been too long since you've visited, so don't wait any longer to rectify that."

"I promise, and I expect an invitation to the wedding. That ring looks good on you."

They talked for another few minutes before it was time for them to go. Roy, Birdie, and Eugenia walked them to the car and promised to see them soon. She'd opened Margot's door when another car drove up, and her father hesitated before stepping out. He was holding a small box and headed to Margot.

"I thought you might like these," he said, handing it over.

Jaxon recognized the old photo albums as well as her baby book. "Thank you, Mr. Lavigne."

"It's my way of saying that there might be some more memories we can put in there, but no pressure." He took the box from her and placed it on the back seat. "And please, call me Gene."

"Thank you, Dad," Jax said but couldn't force herself to hug him.

"The day you were born was the second happiest day of my life. The first was when Roy was born, and I loved you both the same. Becoming a father took precedence over everything else in my life," he said, glancing at Margot. "Your dad's right about that." He turned back to her, and Birdie put her arm around his waist. "It hadn't been long after we lost Dad when you were born, and I wanted to honor my new love with the name of the greatest man I've ever known."

"You don't have to do this," she said, and Birdie glared at her.

"I do. You're the best legacy he could've hoped for, Jaxon. If he was still alive, he would've kicked my ass until I bled for what I've done to you. That I've tarnished who he was as a father and all that he taught me shames me deeply." He cried again and let the tears fall unacknowledged. "I love you, and I want you to try to remember the father I once was in those pictures. I'd like to be that guy again."

If Margot pinched her one more time, she was going to go home with a slew of bruises. "I'm not running off because I don't want that, Dad, but we really need to get going. How about you call me, and we'll start finding some middle ground?"

"Thank you." He lunged forward and wrapped his arms around both of them.

It was amazing. He still smelled the same, and he still felt like a warm blanket when he put his arms around her. The memories came like traitorous bastards until her eyes watered. She'd missed him, and the embrace made her realize how much. "Thank you for trying. It means a lot."

"Until next time, then," he said, wiping his face.

"Until then." She started the car and drove away, watching them in the rearview mirror. She allowed herself to ponder the things she'd write down later.

Yes, time taught valuable lessons, and one of them was that forgiveness had to be felt as well as given. The past wasn't a scary place any longer, and she was glad not to look back at it in horror. She realized now that if given the chance to do it again, she wouldn't change any decision she'd made. Doing that would mean Margot wouldn't be sitting next to her, ready to get on with what was in store for them.

"You okay, my love?" Margot asked.

"I am. Right now, I have every single thing I need and want. Actually, there's one thing I'm missing." She looked at Margot and smiled.

"I'm not having sex with you in the car in broad daylight, so forget it," Margot teased.

"Not that, I'm talking about a ring right here." She pointed to the ring finger of her left hand.

"Ah, don't worry, Dr. Lavigne. I'm rectifying that before Daddy sends you running into the night. I love you and I can't wait to marry you."

"Let's go home."

EPILOGUE

Two years later

"Remember, people, midterm assignments are due on Friday. That means if you haven't read the book, I'd suggest you crack the thing open instead of whatever mindless activity you had planned." A groan followed Jaxon's statement, making her laugh. "And I suggest you actually pay attention to what you're reading. This paper's worth a little less than half your grade, so if you mess up, it'll be hard to recover." There was less groaning this time, and she guessed it was the people who hadn't done a damn thing. "Now I'm going to be nice and let you go fifteen minutes early, so you can get to work. Good luck, and try to show me the English language isn't as dead as the eight-track tape."

Jax walked out, surrounded by students asking her about the book she'd asked them to read. It was like they were looking for pointers to put in their essays. Her experience in the classroom made her realize students didn't change much through the years, but every so often one of them surprised her. They came to class, paid attention, and didn't ask her to do their thinking for them. They just did the assignments and turned them in early, like the essay sitting on her desk, which she'd already graded.

The name of the student didn't surprise her, since the kid was as punctual as she was earnest. She'd found herself running her finger down her freshman class roster at the beginning of the semester to the Gs after Sean and Adeline had spent a couple of weeks with them before the fall semester. She and Margot had shown them around town, and she'd given them the tour of campus before their dorm room was ready.

The softball coach had sent her and Margot a basket of flowers for the great find they'd come back with from a little town in Louisiana, a great athlete the coach figured would elevate their program substantially. With her softball scholarship and the scholarship Roy had funded, Sean, as well as Adeline, would be fine.

The relationship she and Sean had started at the café and cultivated through numerous phone calls had grown into a friendship they both treasured. Sean had turned to her when Iris had finally told her the full story, and Sean finally learned about Roy. The initial anger was something Jax could understand, but with her help, Sean finally understood her mother's choices.

Sean had not only forgiven Iris, but the truth had also given her a newfound respect for Daniel. In Sean's eyes he was an honorable man who'd given her a good life even if in Iris's mind Sean belonged to Jax. The other bonus was Roy was finally able to fulfill his role as Uncle Roy and often visited Sean and Adeline with Birdie. The whole new side to her family had made Sean happy, and Daniel and Iris had also taken it well.

Once they'd graduated, Sean and Adeline were both anxious to leave home, but the first couple of months away had been tough. Their bravado had withered some in the face of homesickness, but she and Margot had done their best to combat it by inviting them over for dinner and for swims on the weekends.

When the crowd around Jax thinned, she found Margot with her arms crossed, leaning against her car, talking to Sean. Whatever she said sent Sean off with a smile before Jax made it over to them. Margot was running her thumb along the bottom of the rings on her left hand as if trying to convince herself they really had gotten married.

"Hey, pretty lady. You're early." Margot had driven her to work because of a rare day off, and now she was here to pick her up.

"Daddy called and asked us over for dinner, so I came before I had to interrupt the faculty meeting."

"Wait," she said, squinting. "Wilber called and invited us?" She pointed between them. Wilber loved her, and his gruffness now was more teasing than serious.

"Yes, he did, and he made it clear it was for both of us." Margot reached for her hand and pulled her closer.

"What's the occasion?"

"Nothing special, but he did say he wanted to talk to you." Margot put her arms on Jax's shoulders and kissed her chin when she put her bag in her new Yukon.

"Talk to me alone in his study?"

"I believe so, since he didn't invite me. He did ask if we'd stop at the grocery on the way over and pick up a few things."

"Pick up what?" Wilber still invited her into the study every week, but they mostly talked about sports and books after his prerequisite threats to keep treating Margot right.

"I believe diapers, formula, and cigars were the top things on the list."

Jax laughed so hard she had to lean against Margot to keep from doubling over. Wilber, as always, got his point across in the most Wilber way possible. At least this time there'd be no milk and talk about buying the cow.

The passage of time was the subject of the book she was writing thanks to Margot's encouragement. The last few years had been memorable, and she was glad her father had been right. There'd been plenty of other memories to add to the pictures he'd given Margot. He, Roy, Birdie, and Eugenia had come to the wedding and were genuinely happy for them. Her mother had decided not to bend on her feelings, and she was okay with that. The family she had was enough.

"Granny and your dad confirmed they'll be here at the end of next week, and he said he's looking forward to meeting up with Daddy."

"With those two together, I'm sure they'll buy me a nose ring you can lead me around with." She opened the door for Margot and kissed her when she was seated. Now that they both knew the paparazzi photos of them in this position bothered her mother, the invasion of privacy didn't seem so bad. A little petty never hurt anything.

"I already have one of those, thank you." Margot laughed, and Jax started for her in-laws. "I also invited Adeline and Sean over tomorrow for movie night. The studio gave me a preview copy, so you all can tell me the unvarnished truth."

"Are you kidding me? Baby, you still have the most popular hair in America. There's no way your adoring fans aren't going to love you." Margot had gotten the lead role in a romantic comedy but was still doing the show.

"Enough from the peanut gallery."

It took them another thirty minutes to get to Margot's parents', and as usual Wilber was waiting outside. He went to Margot's door and pulled her into the bear hug Jax had seen for years and smiled when he finally put her down and glanced her way. "Well?"

"I didn't stop for diapers, but I did buy you something the other day that I think you'll enjoy," she said to him as she handed him a gift-wrapped box. "Wait to open that until we're inside. The study can wait for a few minutes."

Patty Sue was checking something in the oven, and from the aroma of the kitchen it was either carrot or spice cake. After years of lemon, she'd decided to add some variety into their dessert lives. Whatever it was, Margot went a sickly shade of green.

"Oh my God, it's about damned time," Patty Sue screamed as Margot ran for the bathroom.

"What in the hell is going on?" Wilber demanded as Patty Sue ran after Margot.

"Open the box, though this wasn't exactly the plan for breaking the news," she said, pointing to the seemingly forgotten item in his hand.

It was a box of cigars with a note on top. *Congratulations, Grandpa!* The writing was Margot's, and she almost left the room when Wilber started crying. Granted, it was the same reaction she'd had when the doctor had told them they'd finally succeeded in getting pregnant, but it was a strange thing to see tears on Wilber's face.

"Really?" he asked.

"Really, and you might want to open a few windows and the back doors to air out this room. Either that or we have to go out to eat. Grilled cheese seems to do the trick." She hugged him, and he surprised her by giving her a Margot hug. "I'll be right back."

Margot was brushing her teeth when she got to the bathroom, and Patty Sue seemed to be vibrating she was so excited. "I'm so happy for you both," Patty Sue said.

"Thank you, and we'll be right out." She rewet the towel at the back of Margot's neck and wiped her brow. "Are you okay?"

"This kid had better be cute," Margot said when she spit the toothpaste out. "And did you have Daddy air out the kitchen?"

"Their mother is beautiful, so of course they'll be cute, and yes.

I'm sorry you're still having trouble with this. The six weeks are up, so calm down in there," she said to Margot's stomach.

"No need to apologize. Morning sickness my ass, though. But I guess it's not so bad. I'm getting the other thing in life I've always wanted." Margot rested her head on her shoulder and sighed.

"What's that, my love?" She kissed Margot's forehead and held her.

"A little Jaxon Lavigne of my very own. I'm thrilled, even if you can't see it when I'm hanging my head in the toilet." Margot laughed and whatever had triggered the nausea seemed to have passed. "I love you, and seven months is going by at a snail's pace."

"I love you too, and I think your father is as happy as we are. I can't wait either, and I'm going to enjoy every single minute."

"You'll be too busy to do anything but have fun," Margot said as she led them back to the kitchen.

"What do you mean?"

"You have another three years to get me pregnant two more times. After all, you have to have something to brag about at your twenty-year class reunion," Margot said and winked at her.

"That'll be something, but I'm married to the most beautiful woman I know, and there's that hair thing. No one I went to high school with can top that."

Margot laughed with her, and she let her go so her father could hug her again. He was a lot gentler this time, and she smiled at the sight. She felt incredibly light, and it stemmed not only from Margot and all their blessings, but from letting go of all those things that had held her back for so long. That had been one of the things time had taught her.

Given enough of it, she'd allowed herself to face what had happened and admit with conviction that she'd survived it. She was who she was because of all that and so much more, and she deserved to be happy. There was Margot, a new baby, and hope for the future. It was the simple truth. Happiness was a choice, and all you had to do was accept it.

And she had.

About the Author

Ali Vali is the author of the long-running Cain Casey "Devil" series, the newest being *The Devil Incarnate*, and the Genesis Clan "Forces" series, as well as numerous standalone romances including three Lambda Literary Award finalists, *Calling the Dead*, *Love Match*, and *One More Chance*.

Originally from Cuba, Ali has retained much of her family's traditions and language and uses them frequently in her stories. Having her father read her stories and poetry before bed every night as a child infused her with a love of reading, which she carries till today. Ali currently lives outside New Orleans, where she enjoys cheering LSU and trying new restaurants.

Books Available From Bold Strokes Books

Calumet by Ali Vali. Jaxon Lavigne and Iris Long had a forbidden small-town romance that didn't last, and the consequences of that love will be uncovered fifteen years later at their high school reunion. (978-1-63555-900-2)

Her Countess to Cherish by Jane Walsh. London Society's material girl realizes there is more to life than diamonds when she falls in love with a non-binary bluestocking. (978-1-63555-902-6)

Hot Days, Heated Nights by Renee Roman. When Cole and Lee meet, instant attraction quickly flares into uncontrollable passion, but their connection might be short-lived as Lee's identity is tied to her life in the city. (978-1-63555-888-3)

Never Be the Same by MA Binfield. Casey meets Olivia, and sparks fly in this opposites-attract romance that proves love can be found in the unlikeliest places. (978-1-63555-938-5)

Quiet Village by Eden Darry. Something not quite human is stalking Collie and her niece, and she'll be forced to work with undercover reporter Emily Lassiter if they want to get out of Hyam alive. (978-1-63555-898-2)

Shaken or Stirred by Georgia Beers. Bar owner Julia Martini and home health aide Savannah McNally attempt to weather the storms brought on by a mysterious blogger trashing the bar, family feuds they knew nothing about, and way too much advice from way too many relatives. (978-1-63555-928-6)

The Fiend in the Fog by Jess Faraday. Can four people on different trajectories work together to save the vulnerable residents of East London from the terrifying fiend in the fog before it's too late? (978-1-63555-514-1)

The Marriage Masquerade by Toni Logan. A no-strings-attached marriage scheme to inherit a Maui B&B uncovers unexpected attractions and a dark family secret. (978-1-63555-914-9)

Flight SQA016 by Amanda Radley. Fastidious airline passenger Olivia Lewis is used to things being a certain way. When her routine is changed by a new, attractive member of the staff, sparks fly. (978-1-63679-045-9)

Home Is Where The Heart Is by Jenny Frame. Can Archie make the countryside her home and give Ash the fairytale romance she desires? Or will the countryside and small village life all be too much for her? (978-1-63555-922-4)

Moving Forward by PJ Trebelhorn. The last person Shelby Ryan expects to be attracted to is Iris Calhoun, the sister of the man who killed her wife four years and three thousand miles ago. (978-1-63555-953-8)

Poison Pen by Jean Copeland. Debut author Kendra Blake is finally living her best life until a nasty book review and exposed secrets threaten her promising new romance with aspiring journalist Alison Chatterley. (978-1-63555-849-4)

Seasons for Change by KC Richardson. Love, laughter, and trust develop for Shawn and Morgan throughout the changing seasons of Lake Tahoe. (978-1-63555-882-1)

Summer Lovin' by Julie Cannon. Three different women, three exotic locations, one unforgettable summer. What do you think will happen? (978-1-63555-920-0)

Unbridled by D. Jackson Leigh. A visit to a local stable turns into more than riding lessons between a novel writer and an equestrian with a taste for power play. (978-1-63555-847-0)

VIP by Jackie D. In a town where relationships are forged and shattered by perception, sometimes even love can't change who you really are. (978-1-63555-908-8)

Yearning by Gun Brooke. The sleepy town of Dennamore has an irresistible pull on those who've moved away. The mystery Darian Benson and Samantha Pike uncover will change them forever, but the love they find along the way just might be the key to saving themselves. (978-1-63555-757-2)